SOUNDLESS

razOr
bill

Penguin.com
Razorbill, an Imprint of Penguin Random House

Copyright © 2015 Penguin Random House LLC

ISBN: 978-1-59514-763-9

Printed in the United States of America

1 3 5 7 9 10 8 6 4 2

Interior design by Lindsey Andrews
Chapter ornaments © Shutterstock images

SOUNDLESS

RICHELLE
MEAD

razor
bill

An Imprint of Penguin Random House

In memory of my father, who lost his sight but never his vision.

CHAPTER 1

MY SISTER IS IN TROUBLE, and I have only minutes to help her.

She doesn't see it. She's having difficulty seeing a lot of things lately, and that's the problem.

Your brushstrokes are off, I sign to her. *The lines are crooked, and you've misjudged some of the hues.*

Zhang Jing steps back from her canvas. Surprise lights her features for only a moment before despair sets in. This isn't the first time these mistakes have happened. A nagging instinct tells me it won't be the last. I make a small gesture, urging her to hand me her brush and paints. She hesitates and glances around the workroom to make sure none of our peers is watching. They're all deeply engrossed in their own canvases, spurred on by the knowledge that our masters will arrive at any moment to evaluate our work. Their sense of urgency is nearly palpable. I beckon again, more insistently this time, and Zhang Jing yields her tools, stepping away to let me work.

Quick as lightning, I begin going over her canvas, repairing her imperfections. I smooth out the unsteady brushstrokes, thicken lines that are too thin, and use sand to blot out places where the ink fell too heavily. This calligraphy consumes me, just as art always does. I lose track of the world around me and don't even really notice what her work says. It's only when I finish and step back to check my progress that I take in the news she was recording.

Death. Starvation. Blindness.

Another grim day in our village.

I can't focus on that right now, not with our masters about to walk in. *Thank you, Fei,* Zhang Jing signs to me before taking her tools back. I give a quick nod and then hurry over to my own canvas across the room, just as a rumbling in the floor signifies the entrance of the elders. I take a deep breath, grateful that I have once again saved Zhang Jing from getting into trouble. With that relief comes a terrible knowledge that I can no longer deny: My sister's sight is fading. Our village came to terms with silence when our ancestors lost their hearing generations ago for unknown reasons, but being plunged into darkness? That's a fate that scares us all.

I must push those thoughts from my mind and put on a calm face as my master comes strolling down the rows of canvas. There are six elders in the village, and each one oversees at least two apprentices. In most cases, each elder knows who his or her replacement will be—but with the way accidents and sickness happen around here, training a backup is a necessary precaution.

Some apprentices are still competing to be their elder's replacement, but I have no worries about my position.

Elder Chen comes to me now, and I bow low. His dark eyes, sharp and alert despite his advanced years, look past me to the painting. He wears light blue like the rest of us, but the robe he has on over his pants is longer than the apprentices'. It nearly reaches his ankles and is trimmed in purple silk thread. I always study that embroidery while he's doing his inspections, and I never grow tired of it. There's very little color in our daily lives, and that silk thread is one bright, precious spot. Fabric of any kind is a luxury here, where my people struggle daily simply to get food. Studying Elder Chen's purple thread now, I think of the old stories about kings and nobles who dressed in silk from head to toe. The image dazzles me for a moment, transporting me beyond this workroom until I blink and reluctantly return my focus back to my work.

Elder Chen is very still as he takes in my illustration, his expression unreadable. Whereas Zhang Jing painted dreary news today, my task was to depict our latest food shipment, which included a rare surprise of radishes. At last, he unclasps his hands from in front of him. *You captured the imperfections of the radishes' skin*, he signs. *Not many others would have noticed such detail.*

From him, that is high praise. *Thank you, master*, I say before bowing again.

He moves on to examine the work of his other apprentice, a girl named Jin Luan. She shoots a look of envy in my direction before also bowing low to our master. There's never been any question who his favorite student is, and I know it must frustrate her to feel that no matter what she does, she never grasps that top spot. I am one of the best artists in our group, and we all know it. I make no apologies for my success, especially since I've given up so much to achieve it.

I look to the far side of the room, where Elder Lian is examining Zhang Jing's calligraphy. Elder Lian's face is as unreadable as my master's as she takes in every detail of my sister's canvas. I find I'm holding my breath, far more nervous than I was for my own inspection. Beside her, Zhang Jing is pale, and I know my sister and I are both braced for the same thing: Elder Lian calling us out for deceiving them about Zhang Jing's sight. Elder Lian lingers much longer than Elder Chen did, but at long last, she gives a cursory nod of acceptance and strolls on to her next apprentice. Zhang Jing sags in relief.

We have tricked them again, but I can't feel bad about that either. Not when Zhang Jing's future is at stake. If the elders discover her vision is failing, she will almost certainly lose her apprenticeship and be sent to the mines. The very thought makes my chest tighten. In our village, there are really only three jobs: artist, miner, and supplier. Our parents were miners. They died young.

When all the inspections are finished, it is time for our morning announcements. Elder Lian is giving them today, and she steps up on a platform in the room to allow her hands to be visible to all who are gathered.

Your work is satisfactory, she begins. It's the usual acknowledgment, and we all bow. When we are looking up again, she continues. *Never forget how important what we do here is. You are part of an ancient and exalted tradition. Soon we will go out into the village and begin our daily observations. I know things are hard right now. But remember that it is not our place to interfere with them.*

She pauses, her gaze traveling around the room to each of us as we nod in acknowledgment at a concept that has been driven into us with as much intensity as our art. Interference leads to distraction, interrupting both the natural order of the village's life as well as accurate record keeping. We must be impartial observers. Painting the daily news has been a tradition in our village ever since our people lost their hearing centuries ago. I'm told that before then, news was shouted by a town crier or simply passed orally from person to person. But I don't even really know what "shouting" is.

We observe, and we record, Elder Lian reiterates. *It is the sacred duty we have performed for centuries, and to deviate from it does a disservice both to our tasks and to the village. Our people need these records to know what is happening around them. And our descendants need our records so they can understand the way things have always been. Go to breakfast now, and then be a credit to our teachings.*

We bow again and then shuffle out of the workroom, heading toward the dining hall. Our school is called the Peacock Court. It's a name our ancestors brought with them from fairer, faraway parts of Beiguo beyond this mountain, meant to acknowledge the beauty we create within the school's walls. Every day, we paint the news of our village for our people to read. Even if we are only recording the most basic of information—like a shipment of radishes—our work must still be immaculate and worthy of preservation. Today's record will soon be put on display in our village's heart, but first we have this small break.

Zhang Jing and I sit down cross-legged on the floor at a low table to wait for our meal. Servants come by and carefully measure out millet porridge, making sure each apprentice gets an equal amount. We have the same thing for breakfast each day, and while it chases the hunger away, it doesn't exactly leave me feeling full either. But it's more than the miners and suppliers get, so we must be grateful.

Zhang Jing pauses in her breakfast. *It will not happen again*, she signs to me. *I mean it.*

Hush, I say. It's a topic she can't even hint at in this place. And despite her bold words, there's a fear in her face that tells me she doesn't believe them anyway. Reports of blindness have been growing in our village for reasons that are just as mysterious as the deafness that fell upon our ancestors. Usually only miners go blind, which makes Zhang Jing's current plight that much more mysterious.

A flurry of activity in my periphery startles me out of my thoughts. I look up and see that the other apprentices have also stopped eating, their gazes turned toward a door that leads from this dining room to the kitchen. A cluster of servants stands there, more than I normally see at once. Usually mindful of the differences in rank, they stay out of our way.

A woman I recognize as the head cook has emerged from the door, a boy scurrying in front of her. *Cook* is an extravagant term for her job, since there's so little food and not much to be done with it. She also oversees running the Peacock Court's servants. I flinch when she strikes the boy with a blow so hard that he falls to the floor. I've seen him around, usually doing the meanest of cleaning tasks. A frantically signed conversation is taking place between them.

—think you wouldn't get caught? the cook demands. *What were you thinking, taking more than your share?*

It wasn't for me! the boy tells her. *It was for my sister's family. They're hungry.*

We're all hungry, the cook snaps back. *That's no excuse for stealing.*

I give a sharp intake of breath as I realize what has happened. Food theft is one of the greatest crimes we have around here. The fact that it would occur among our servants, who are generally fed better than other villagers, is particularly shocking. The boy manages to get to his feet and bravely face the cook's wrath.

They're a mining family, and they've been sick, the boy says. *The miners already get less food than we do, and they had their rations cut while not working. I was trying to make things fair.*

The hard set of the cook's face tells us she is unmoved. *Well, now you can join them in the mines. We have no place here for thieves. I want you gone before we clear the breakfast dishes.*

The boy falters at this, desperation filling his features. *Please. Don't send me to work with them. I'm sorry. I'll give up my rations to make up for what I took. It won't ever happen again.*

I know it won't happen again, the cook replies pointedly. She gives a curt nod to two of the burlier servants, and they each take one of the boy's arms, hauling him out of the dining room. He tries to free himself and protest but can't fight against both of them. The cook watches impassively while the rest of us gape. When he's out of sight, she and the other servants not working our breakfast service disappear back into the kitchen. Zhang Jing and I exchange glances, too shocked for words. In his moment of weakness, that servant has just made his life significantly more difficult—and dangerous.

When we finish breakfast and head to the workroom, the theft is all anyone can talk about. *Can you believe it?* someone asks me. *How dare he give our food to a miner!*

The speaker's name is Sheng. Like me, he is one of the top artists at the Peacock Court. Unlike me, he is descended from a family of artists and elders. I think he forgets sometimes that Zhang Jing and I are the first in our family to achieve this rank.

It is certainly a terrible thing, I respond neutrally. I don't dare express my true feelings: that I have doubts about whether the food distribution is fair. I learned long ago that to keep my position in the Peacock Court, I must give up all sympathies to the miners and simply view them as our village's workforce. Nothing more.

He deserves a worse punishment than dismissal, Sheng says ominously. Along with his skill in art, Sheng has the kind of brash confidence that makes people follow him, so I'm not surprised to see a few others walking near us nod in agreement. He lifts his head proudly at their regard, showing off fine, high cheekbones. Most of the girls around here would also agree he's the most attractive boy in the school, but he's never had much of an effect on me.

I hope that changes soon, as we are expected to marry someday.

Boldly, knowing I'm probably making a mistake, I ask, *You don't think the circumstances played a role in his actions? Wanting to help his sick family?*

That's no excuse, Sheng states. *Everyone earns what they deserve around here—no more, no less. That's balance. If you can't fulfill your duty, you shouldn't expect to be fed for it. Don't you agree?*

My heart aches at his words. I can't help but give a quick glance at Zhang Jing, walking on my other side, before turning back to Sheng. *Yes*, I say bleakly. *Yes, of course, I agree.*

We apprentices begin gathering up our canvases to take them out for the other villagers to view. Some are still wet and require extra caution. As we step outside, the sun is well above the horizon, promising a warm and clear day to come. It shines on the green leaves of the trees among our village. Their branches create a canopy that shades much of the walkway to the village's center. I watch the patterns the light creates on the ground when it's filtered through the trees. I've often thought about painting that dappled light, if only I had the opportunity. But I never do.

I'd love to paint the mountains too. We are surrounded by them, and our village sits on top of one of the highest. It creates breathtaking views but also a number of difficulties for us. This peak is surrounded on three sides by steep cliffs. Our ancestors migrated here centuries ago along a pass on the mountain's opposite side that was flanked by fertile valleys perfect for growing food. Around the time hearing disappeared, severe avalanches blocked the pass, filling it up with boulders and stones far taller than any man. It trapped our people up here and cut us off from growing crops anymore.

That was when our people worked out an arrangement with a township at the mountain's base. Each day, most of our villagers work in the mines up here, hauling out loads of precious metals. Our suppliers send those metals to the township along a zip line that runs down the mountain. In return for the metal, the township sends us shipments of food since we can't produce our own. The arrangement was working well until some of our miners began losing their sight and could no longer work. When the metals going down slowed, so did the food coming back up.

As my group moves closer to the center of the village, I see miners getting ready for the day's work, dressed in their dull clothing with lines of weariness etched on their faces. Even children help out in the mines. They walk beside their parents and, in some cases, grandparents.

In the village's heart, we find those who have lost their sight. Unable to see or hear, they have become beggars, huddled together and waiting for the day's handouts. They sit immobile with their bowls, deprived of the ability to communicate, only able to wait for the feel of vibrations in the ground to let them know that people are approaching and that they might receive some kind of sustenance. I watch as a supplier comes by and puts half a bun in each beggar's bowl. I remember reading about those buns in the record when they arrived a couple of days ago. They were already subpar then, most of them showing mold. But we can't afford to throw away any food. That half bun is all the beggars will get until nightfall unless someone is kind enough to share from their own rations. The scene makes my stomach turn, and I avert my gaze from them as we walk toward the central stage where workers are already removing yesterday's record.

A flash of bright color catches my eye, and I see a blue rock thrush land on the branch of a tree near the clearing. Much like Elder Chen's silk trim, that brilliance draws me in. As I'm admiring the sheen of the bird's azure feathers, he opens his mouth for a few seconds and then looks around expectantly. Not long after that, a duller female flies in and lands near him. I stare in wonder, trying to understand what just took place. How did he draw her to him? What could he have done that conveyed so much, even though she hadn't seen him? I know from reading that something happened when he opened his mouth, that he "sang" to her and somehow brought her, even though she wasn't nearby.

A nudge at my shoulder tells me it's time to stop daydreaming.

Our group has reached the dais in the village's center, and most of the villagers have gathered to see our work. We climb the steps to the platform and hang our paintings. We've done this many times, and everyone knows their roles. What was a series of illustrations and calligraphy in the workshop now fits together as one coherent mural, presenting a thorough depiction of all that happened in the village yesterday to those gathered below. When I've hung my radishes, I shuffle back down with the other apprentices and watch the faces of the rest of the crowd as they read the record. I see furrowed brows and dark glances as they take in the latest reports of blindness and hunger. The radishes are no consolation. The art might be perfect, but it's lost on my people in its bearing of such dreary news.

Some of them make the sign against evil, a gesture meant to chase away bad luck. It seems ineffectual to me, but the miners are extremely superstitious. They believe lost spirits roam the village at midnight, that the mist surrounding our mountain is the breath of the gods. One of their most popular stories is that our ancestors lost their hearing when magical creatures called pixius went into a deep slumber and wanted silence on the mountain. I grew up believing those tales too, but my education in the Peacock Court has given me a more practical view of the world.

Slowly, the miners and suppliers turn from the record and begin the treks to their jobs. Elder Chen signs to us apprentices: *Go to your posts. Remember, observe. Don't interfere.*

I start to follow the others, and then I catch sight of Elder Lian taking the steps back up to the dais where the record is displayed. She seems to be examining the work all over again, painstakingly studying each character. Such scrutiny isn't part of the normal routine. The other apprentices have left, but I can't move, not until I know what she's doing.

She stands there a little longer, and when she finally turns away, her gaze meets mine. A moment later, her eyes fall on something behind me. I turn around and see Zhang Jing is standing there, hands clenched together nervously. Elder Lian descends the stairs. *Go to your posts*, she signs. The silk thread that edges her robe is red, and it flashes in the light as she walks past.

Swallowing, I take Zhang Jing's elbow and steer her away from the village's center, away from the blind beggars. Most of them are old and former miners, I remind myself. She isn't like them. She isn't like them at all. I squeeze her hand as we walk.

She will get better, I tell myself. *I will not let her become one of them.*

I repeat the words over and over in my mind as we move past the beggars, but saying them to myself can't erase the image of those cavernous faces and blank, hopeless stares.

CHAPTER 2

WE SOON NEAR A SMALL PATH branching from the main track through the village, and I nod at it. Zhang Jing nods back, turning toward the fork.

Before we get very far, a group emerges unexpectedly from a nearby wooded area. It is Sheng with two boys dressed in suppliers' attire. They're dragging someone between them, and I recognize the servant from our school, the one who was caught stealing. New bruises and welts accompany the one the cook gave him, and from the gleeful look on the faces of the others, they have more planned. I can understand their outrage at what he did, but the enjoyment they take in doling out such pain sickens me. Zhang Jing cringes back in fear, not wanting to get involved in any altercation. I know I should do the same, but I can't. I step forward, ready to speak my mind.

Before I can, I am knocked to the side by yet another person rushing past. He wears the dull clothes of a miner and strides right up to Sheng and the others, blocking their way. When I realize who this newcomer is, my breath catches, and I feel as though the very ground beneath my feet has shifted, knocking me off-balance.

It is Li Wei.

What do you think you're doing? he demands.

Sheng regards him with a sneer. *Teaching him a lesson.*

Look at him, Li Wei says. *He's learned his lesson. He can barely stand anymore.*

That's not good enough, one of Sheng's supplier friends says. *Are you saying he should be let off easy? You think it's okay for him to steal food?*

No, Li Wei replies. *But I think he's been punished enough. Between your "lesson" and losing his job at the school, he's more than paid for the crime of trying to help his family. All you're doing is hurting his ability to help us in the mines. We can't afford that right now. It's time to let him go.*

We'll say *when it's time to let him go,* Sheng says.

Li Wei takes a menacing step forward. *Then say it.*

Sheng and the suppliers hesitate. Although the numbers are in their favor, Li Wei is unquestionably one of the biggest and strongest in our village. Muscles gained from long hours of grueling work in the mines cover his arms, and he towers over them by nearly a head. He stands straight and tall, his tough body braced and ready for a fight. He doesn't fear three-to-one odds. He wouldn't fear ten-to-one odds.

After several tense moments, Sheng gives a shrug and smirks as though this is all one big joke. *We have work to do,* he says far too casually. *He deserves worse, but I don't have time for it. Let's go.*

The supplier holding the servant releases him, and Sheng and the others begin sauntering away. Seeing me, Sheng asks, *Are you coming?*

We're going a different way today, I say, nodding toward the path.

Suit yourself, he replies.

When they are gone, Li Wei reaches out a helping hand to the servant, whose face is filled with terror. The boy backs up and then scurries away, fear having given him a burst of energy, despite his pain. Li Wei watches him go and then turns in our direction, looking surprised to see us still there. He bows in deference to our higher station, having noticed our blue robes, and then stiffens slightly when he looks up and sees my face.

It's the only outward indication of his surprise. Everything else about him is perfectly respectful and proper. *Forgive me, apprentices*, he says. *I was in such a hurry to help, I'm afraid I jostled you earlier. I hope you aren't injured.*

Although he is addressing both of us, his eyes are locked on me. His gaze is so piercing, I feel as though it will knock me over. Or maybe that's just the earlier dizziness I felt from being near him. Regardless, standing there before him, I find myself unable to move or speak.

Zhang Jing, unaware I am reeling, smiles gently. *It's okay. We're fine.*

I'm glad, he says. He starts to turn from us and then pauses, his expression both curious and hesitant. *I hope you don't think I was wrong to help that boy.*

It was very kind of you, Zhang Jing says politely.

Although she has answered for us, Li Wei's gaze lingers on me as though he hopes I will add something. But I can't. It's been too long since I've seen him, and this sudden, unexpected confrontation has caught me unprepared. After several awkward moments, Li Wei nods.

Well, then. I hope you both have a good day, he says before walking away from us.

Zhang Jing and I continue on our path, and my heart rate slowly returns to normal. *You didn't say much back there,* she remarks. *Do you disapprove? Do you think he should have let Sheng and his friends take their revenge?*

I don't answer right away. Zhang Jing is a year older than me, and we have been nearly inseparable our entire lives, sharing everything. But there is one secret I have kept from her. When I was six, I climbed an old rotting shed our mother had warned us about many times. The roof collapsed while I was on it, trapping me below with no one in sight. I was stuck there for two hours, frightened and certain I would be there forever.

And then he appeared.

Li Wei was only eight but had just begun working full-time in the mines. When he came to me that day, he was returning from his shift covered in fine, golden dust. As he held out his hand to help me, the late afternoon sunlight caught him just right, making him shine and glitter. Even back then, the striking and beautiful always moved my heart, and I was spellbound as he helped me out of the rubble. His easy smile and sense of humor soon helped me overcome my shyness, beginning a friendship that would span almost ten years and eventually become so much more. . . .

Fei? asks Zhang Jing, truly puzzled now. *Are you okay?*

I push my memories aside, shaking off the dazzling image of that golden boy. *Fine,* I lie. *I just don't like to see that kind of violence.*

Me neither, she agrees.

We divert to a path that is much narrower than the village's main thoroughfare but sees enough foot traffic to be well-worn and packed down. It takes us along one of the cliff's sides, giving us spectacular views of the peaks surrounding us. It's early enough in the morning that mist still hangs in the air, obscuring the depths below.

Zhang Jing and I come to a halt when we reach the cypress tree. It looks greener and fuller than the last time I saw it, now that summer has fully arrived. I feel a pang in my heart for not having been here more recently. The venerable cypress clings doggedly to its rocky perch, its branches spreading wide and high into the sky. *See how it stands proudly, even in such inhospitable conditions?* our father used to say. *This is how we must always be—strong and resilient, no matter what's around us.* Our family used to go on evening walks together, and this path past the tree was one of our favorites. When our parents died, Zhang Jing and I had their ashes spread here.

She and I stand together now, saying nothing, simply gazing out at the vista before us and enjoying a faint breeze that plays among the needled branches of the tree. In my periphery, I notice her squinting, even here. As much as it hurts, I feel compelled to finally say something. Stepping forward, I turn so that she can better see my hands.

How long has it been going on?

She knows immediately what I'm referring to and answers with a weary face. *I don't know. A while. Months. It wasn't that bad at first—just occasional hazy spells. Now those spells are more frequent and more intense. On some days, I can still see perfectly. On other days, things are so blurred and distorted I can't make any sense of them.*

It will get better, I tell her staunchly.

She shakes her sadly. *What if it doesn't? What if it's only a matter of time before I'm like the others? Before everything goes dark?* Tears glitter in her eyes, and she obstinately blinks them back. *I should tell our masters and give up the apprenticeship now. It's the honorable thing to do.*

No! I tell her. *You can't.*

They'll eventually find out, she insists. *Can you imagine the disgrace then, when they throw me out on the streets?*

No, I repeat, even though a secret, scared part of me fears she is right. *Don't say anything. I'll keep covering for you, and we'll find a way to fix this.*

How? The smile she gives me is sweet but also full of sorrow. *Some things are beyond even you, Fei.*

I look away, fearing my own eyes will fill with tears at the frustration I feel over my sister's fate.

Come on, she says. *We don't want to be late.*

We continue on our way, walking along the cliffside path, and my heart is heavy. I won't admit it to her, but this might indeed be beyond me. I might dream incredible things and have the skills to paint any vision into reality, but even I can't restore sight itself. It's a humbling and depressing thought, one that so consumes me that I don't even notice the crowd of people until we practically walk into them.

This path that traces the village's edge goes past the station where the suppliers receive shipments from the township below. It looks as though the first shipment of the day has arrived up the zip line and is about to be distributed. While that's often a cause for excitement, I rarely see it draw this many people, which makes me think something unusual is happening. Amid the sea of dull brown clothing, I spy a spot of blue and recognize another artist apprentice, Min. This is her observation post.

I tug her sleeve, drawing her attention to me. *What's happening?*

They sent a letter to the keeper a few days ago, telling him we need more food, that we cannot survive with the recent cuts, she explains. *His response has just arrived with this shipment.*

My breath catches. The line keeper. Communication with him is rare. He's the one our existence depends on, the one who decides what supplies come up the line to us from the township. Without him, we have nothing. Hope surges in me as I join the others to learn the news. The keeper is a great and powerful man. Surely he'll help us.

I watch with the others as the lead supplier unrolls the letter that came up with the food. The letter was tied with a tiny green ribbon that he clutches as he reads, and for a moment, I'm transfixed by it. I shift my gaze back to the man's face as his eyes scan the letter. I can tell from his expression that the news isn't going to be good. A flurry of emotions plays over him, both sad and angry. At last, he gives the letter to an assistant and then stands on a crate so that we can all see his hands as he addresses the crowd.

The keeper says: "You receive less food because you send less metal. If you want more food, send more metal. That is balance. That is honor. That is harmony in the universe."

The lead supplier pauses, but there is a tension in the way he stands, the way he holds his hands up, that tells us there is more to the message. After several seconds, he continues sharing the rest of the letter, though it's obviously with reluctance: "What you have suggested is an insult to the generosity we have shown you these long years. As punishment, rations will be reduced for the next week. Perhaps then you will better understand balance."

I feel my jaw drop, and chaos breaks out. Shock and outrage fill everyone's faces, and hands sign so fast that I can only catch snippets of conversation:

Reduced? We can't survive on what we have—

How can we get more metals? Our miners are going blind and—

It's not our fault we can't mine as much! Why should we be punished for—

I can't follow much more than that. The crowd turns on

the lead supplier with angry faces, striding right up to where he stands on his makeshift perch.

This is unacceptable! one woman signs furiously. *We won't tolerate it!*

The lead supplier regards them wearily. There's an air of resignation around him. He doesn't like the way things have turned out either, but how is he supposed to change them? *What do you suggest we do?* he retorts. When no immediate response comes, he adds, *Everyone needs to get back to work. That's the only way we're going to survive. It's like he says: If we want more food, we need more metal. Standing around and complaining won't accomplish that.*

This enrages one of the men standing near the podium. He wears a miner's dirty clothes. *I'll go down there!* he insists, face flushed red. *I'll make the keeper give us food.*

Others in the crowd, caught up in the heat of the moment, nod in agreement. The lead supplier, however, remains calm in the face of rising hostility. *How?* he asks. *How will you go down there? On the line?* He pauses to make a great show of studying the other man from head to toe. Everyone knows the zip line can only hold about thirty kilos. *It will fray and snap under your weight, and then we will have nothing. Your son might be able to make the trip. Perhaps you could send him to negotiate. He's, what, eight years old now?* That earns a glare from the miner, who's very protective of his young son, but the supplier remains unfazed. *Well, if you don't want to risk yourself or your loved ones in the basket, you could always just climb down instead.*

The lead supplier takes a rock the size of his hand and throws it off the edge, hurling it toward a bend in the cliff. We all watch as it hits the mountainside and is momentarily followed by a small avalanche of other stones, some of which are significantly larger than the original rock. They kick up dust as they fall down to depths we cannot see. The unstable nature of the cliffside is well-known throughout the village and has been documented in records for years. Some of our ancestors who could hear would attempt the climb, supposedly because their hearing aided them in knowing when avalanches were coming. But even they were wary about the cliffs.

Of course, then you face the risk of being crushed by falling rocks before you even get the chance to express yourself to the keeper. Anyone still want to go down there? asks the lead supplier, looking around. Unsurprisingly, no one responds. *Return to your work. Get more metals so that we can restore the balance, as the line keeper said.*

Slowly, the crowd disperses and everyone goes off to their assigned tasks, including Zhang Jing and me. As we walk, I think about what was said about balance and how we have no choice but to do what the keeper asks. We're at his mercy—his and the line's. Is that truly balance? Or is it extortion?

Zhang Jing and I arrive at the mines, and it is there we finally part ways. She waves farewell before disappearing into the darkness of the cavernous entrance, and I watch her go with a pang. This has been her post for a while now—going deep within the mines to observe the workers at their daily labors. Even though she stays well away from any situation that might be dangerous, I still worry about her. Accidents happen, even with the best of intentions. I'd switch places with her if I could, but the elders would never allow it.

I was recently assigned a post just outside the mine. With increased accidents and discontent over the food situation, the elders wanted another set of eyes to observe. My job is to keep track of the miners' morale and any incidents that happen, as well as note the amount of metal being unearthed. My last post was in the center of the village, and this is usually a calm one by comparison.

I perch on an old tree stump off to the side of the entrance. It's comfortable and gives me a good view of both the mine and the forested trail Zhang Jing and I took earlier. Near the trail, I notice a cluster of pink-veined white mountain orchids that are finally blooming. They're cup-shaped and make a pretty spot of color among the mostly green and brown foliage surrounding the trail. Flowers rarely bloom up here, and I pass much of my day studying and memorizing the orchids, going over ways I'd depict them if only given the luxury to do so. Sometimes I dream up even more fantastical visions to paint, like fields and fields of orchids stretching out into a carpet of pink.

A blur of movement near the mine's entrance draws my attention back to the real world. For a moment, I wonder if I've truly lost track of time and if the miners are coming out for lunch. That's when my assignment is busiest. But no—it's not quite midday yet, and only two men emerge from the entrance, one young and one old. Neither of them notices me, sitting out of the way on my stump.

One of them is Li Wei, and I'm astonished to encounter him twice in one day. Our lives have taken such different directions that I rarely see him anymore. The older man with him is his father, Bao. He shows the signs of having worked in the mine his entire life: a strength of body and character that's let him survive all these years but that's also taken its toll. He doesn't stand as straight as he once did, and there's an exhaustion in him that's almost palpable, despite the resolute look in his dark eyes.

Studying the two together, I can see how Li Wei serves as a reminder of what Bao must have looked like in his youth. Li Wei still shows all the strength and none of the wear. His black hair is pulled into the same neat topknot the other miners have, though a few strands have escaped and now cling to his face, which is damp with perspiration. Fine gold dust from the mine glitters across his skin and clothing, almost as it did on that day long ago in my childhood. The light plays over him now, and I feel an ache in my chest.

Bao turns his head, revealing an oozing red gash on his forehead. Once Li Wei has made sure his father can stand, he begins cleaning the wound with some supplies he removes from a small cloth bag. Li Wei's hands are quick and efficient, a contrast to his towering strength and size. But his touch is delicate as he helps his father, and soon the older man's head injury is clean and bandaged.

You can't let this keep happening, Li Wei tells him when he's finished. *You could've been killed.*

I wasn't, Bao signs back obstinately. *Everything's fine.*

Li Wei points to his father's forehead. *Everything's not* fine!

If I hadn't intervened at the last minute, this would've been a lot worse. You can't work in the mines anymore.

Bao remains defiant. *I can and I will! I see well enough to do my work. That's all that matters.*

It's not just about your work. Li Wei looks as though he's trying very hard to remain calm, but there's an obvious panic behind his eyes. *It's not even just about your life. It's about the lives of others. You endanger them by staying down there. Let go of your pride and retire.*

Pride is the only thing I have left, says Bao. *It's the only thing any of us have. They're taking everything else away from us. You heard the news about the food. With rations decreased, they need me more than ever down there. That's where I'll be—doing my duty. Not sitting around the village's center with the other beggars. It is not your place to dictate your father's actions, boy.*

Li Wei gives a reluctant bow, but it's clear that it's out of respect, not agreement. With that, Bao turns around and returns to the mine, leaving his son staring.

I hold my breath. Their conversation could have been a mirror to the one I had earlier with Zhang Jing. Bao is yet another villager going blind.

Once his father is out of sight, Li Wei punches a scraggly tree growing near the mine's entrance. I've seen him make impulsive gestures like this since childhood. They're born out of passion, when his emotions run high, and they're usually harmless. Except, when his hand makes contact with the tree, blood spurts out, and he jumps back in surprise. Recalling how notices are sometimes hung on the tree, I realize he's struck one of the old nails. Without thinking twice, I'm on my feet, retrieving the supply bag he brought out for his father.

What are you doing? Li Wei signs, even with blood dripping off his hand. The surprise on his face tells me he didn't know I was nearby.

Stop talking, I scold. *Stay still.*

To my astonishment, he complies and stops moving so that I can help him. The cut is on his right hand, which could be catastrophic for a miner. As I clean it, though, I can see it's actually pretty shallow. It reminds me of the paper cuts I sometimes get back at the Peacock Court, cuts that are barely skin deep but still manage to put out a lot of blood. But there's something a little bit more sinister about an old nail, and even after I've poured water on the cut and wiped away most of the blood, I worry about infection. I hurry over to the stump and return with a small belt pouch, searching through tiny packets of pigment. When I find the one I want—yellow—I sprinkle a little of the powder on his cut before wrapping a clean cloth bandage around it. Once the bandage is secure, I examine his hand one more time, turning it over in my own. His fingers start to entwine with mine, and I abruptly pull back.

What was that? Li Wei asks when I tuck the packet back into my pouch.

It's pigment for a special type of paint. We make the color from a root that also has medicinal properties. I saw my master use it once on another wound. It will prevent infection. I don't tell him how valuable the pigment is and that I'm not even supposed to be bringing it out with me on my observations. It'll be a while before our masters do inventory, and I hope I'll have some reason for explaining why I'm low.

Won't you get in trouble for interfering? Li Wei asks. *With a miner?*

His words startle me. Everything happened so fast that I didn't even really have a chance to think about what I was doing. I just broke our primary commandment, interfering when we're only supposed to be observing. I'd be in serious trouble if my master or any of the others found out.

If I get in trouble, so be it, I say at last. *I make my own decisions.*

That's not what I remember. A moment later, he realizes how mean that was. *I'm sorry.* His hands waver again before he asks: *I suppose you'll have to tell them about my father? That he's going blind?*

Li Wei is right. Technically, as part of my duty, I should report back everything I observed—including their discussion. I can tell that as much as it pains him, Li Wei secretly wants me to report on his father. It will take the burden of responsibility away and finally get Bao removed from the mines and the danger there. I think about the old man's words, about holding on to his pride. And then I think about Zhang Jing and her own fears of being found out. Slowly, I shake my head.

No, I won't tell. I hesitate before continuing on. *And you shouldn't be so hard on him. He's just trying to do what he's always done. It's noble.*

Li Wei stares at me incredulously. *Noble? He's going to get himself killed!*

He's providing for others, I insist.

Providing? he asks, still outraged. *We slave away, putting our lives at risk and our own dreams aside so that we can feed everyone else. We have the entire village's hopes and fears resting on our shoulders. If we don't work, they starve. That's not providing. That's certainly not noble. That's being given no choice. That's being trapped. You've been with the artists so long, you've forgotten what it's like for the rest of us.*

That's not fair, I say, feeling my own anger rise. *You know the job we do is vital to the village's survival. And of course I know what it's like for the miners! That's the whole point of my job: observing everyone.*

Observing is not the same as experiencing. Li Wei gestures angrily to my stump. *You sit there and judge others from a safe distance every day. You assume because you watch us, you understand us. But you don't. If you did, you never would have—*

He can't finish, so I do. *Bettered myself? Accepted a position that raised my sister and me out of that hovel and gave us a place of honor and comfort? One that allowed me to actually use my talents? What is so wrong with wanting to improve my life?*

He doesn't speak for several moments. Then: *Did it, Fei? Did it improve your life?*

I think back to lazy summer days, lying in the grass with him, our hands linked as we talked about the future. I only ran errands for the artists back then. It wasn't until I was offered an official apprenticeship that my status in the village changed, raising me up from a miner's family to Elder Chen's successor. My parents had just died, and Zhang Jing and I were living in a small, ramshackle place, given the barest of rations while waiting for the results of the testing we'd undergone at the Peacock Court in order to be accepted. The elders so coveted my talents that they took Zhang Jing on as well, though her skills were less than mine. That move gave me everything I could ever have wanted, with one exception: Artists only marry other artists.

Did it improve your life? Li Wei asks again.

In most ways, I say at last, hating the pain I see flash through his eyes. *But what could we do? You know I had to take the opportunity. And with it came sacrifices. That's life, Li Wei. That's the way it's always been.*

Maybe it's time things change, he shoots back. He stalks away from me just as other miners begin emerging from the main entrance for lunch. I watch him until the crowd swallows him, wondering what exactly he meant should change. The system that traps Bao and others in the mines? Or the one that has kept Li Wei and me apart? After a moment, I realize that they are one and the same.

As the miners settle down in various clusters, eating and talking, I flit about them as unobtrusively as possible, trying to watch conversations and gather all the information I can—and trying not to think about what Li Wei said. A busy time like this one is when our observing-without-interfering mandate is most important.

When I return to my stump, I do a double take when I discover that someone has taken a knife to its surface. What was previously simply flat and weathered has now been carved up with a chrysanthemum design—a really remarkable one. Carving is not a trade cultivated very much at my school, but my artistic eye can't help but notice the skill and detail that has gone into every single petal of this king of flowers—a flower I've only ever seen in books. These chrysanthemums are beautiful, and the fact that they've been created in such a short time makes them even more amazing.

I sigh, knowing where they came from. Throughout our youth, whenever we had a dispute, Li Wei and I would apologize to each other by exchanging gifts. Mine would be in the form of drawings, crudely done with whatever natural supplies I could find. His would always be carvings. There was only one time the exchange didn't happen, the day I told him I was accepting the apprentice position and would never be able to marry him. We argued then, and after the fact, I painted chrysanthemums outside his door as a peace offering. Nothing ever came in return.

I touch these carved ones now, amazed at how his skill has progressed in the last two years. Bittersweet memories cling to me, and then, reluctantly, I let go of them and continue my observation.

CHAPTER 3

BOTH LI WEI AND HIS FATHER are on my mind that night when Zhang Jing and I return to the school. Seeing her reminds me of Bao and how both of them are trying so desperately to hide their blindness from the rest of the village. How many others are like that? How many other villagers are making a slow descent into darkness?

When we begin our evening work on the record of the day's events, I have difficulty staying focused. My mind keeps wandering, making it difficult to paint the scenes I need to. Elder Chen notices as he strolls by.

Are you daydreaming again, Fei? he asks, not unkindly. *Imagining beautiful colors and wonders that you'd rather be painting?*

Yes, I lie, not willing to tell him what's truly on my mind. *I'm sorry, master. There is no excuse.*

A mind like yours, one capable of appreciating and imagining beautiful things, is not a detriment, not by any means, he says. *But unfortunately, it is not necessarily called for here. This is the fate we have been given.*

I bow in acknowledgment. *I will not go to bed until this piece is flawless.*

The other girls are all asleep when I finally return to our dorm room. Once in bed, I realize I never got a chance to go over and check Zhang Jing's work. By the time I finished with mine, I was so tired I probably wouldn't have been much help anyway. We still have more work to do on the record in the morning, and I make a mental note to check her portion of it then. Sleep consumes me quickly, but I don't find peace.

I dream I am walking in a field of pink orchids, just like I imagined earlier. They transform into chrysanthemums, and the richness of their petals is intoxicating, making me run my fingers through them. Soon I find myself walking out of the flower field and onto the path that runs by the cliff's edge. It takes me to the supply line, where the crowd gathered this morning. They are here again, waiting for some important news. Only this time it's me who stands on the crate, forced to deliver a terrible message to my fellow villagers. My hands move quickly as I sign the news, and I barely process what it is I'm telling them, only that it signifies a bleak future of worse conditions and no hope. When I finish, I find the courage to look out at the faces of the crowd, and I gasp at what I see.

All of them gaze up at me with blank eyes, their irises gone white. And even though their faces are lifted in my direction, it's clear none of them can see me. Everyone around me is blind.

Only I have been left with all my senses. Despair fills the villagers' features, and they all open their mouths at the same time.

What happens next is like nothing I've ever experienced before, a sensation that's almost like a vibration and yet something more. It seems to reach a part of my brain I didn't even know existed. I have no words for it, no way to articulate this experience. The villagers open their mouths wider, and the sensation grows more intense, pulsing in my ears. My head begins to ache. Then, as one, they all shut their mouths. The sensation abruptly stops, and all is still. I feel a pull in my chest, as though I am reaching out to someone or something far away.

And then my own vision goes black.

Panic fills me until I realize I've simply awakened and am looking around the girls' bedroom of the dormitory. I sit up in bed, gasping, peering around me and waiting for my eyes to adjust to the darkness. Faint moonlight trickles in from behind the window blinds, and eventually I can see well enough to make out my surroundings. Zhang Jing sleeps peacefully in the bed beside mine, and beyond her, the other girls are asleep as well.

But something is different. Something strange tugs at the edges of my senses as I search and take in the darkened room. I'm experiencing it again—that same sensation from the dream, that thing that's almost like a vibration but not. Only it's much less intense. It doesn't make my head hurt, and it's fleeting, coming and going. As I look down at Zhang Jing, I notice that the sensation I'm perceiving seems to be timed with her breathing. I study her for a while, watching and trying to understand what I'm experiencing.

I have no answers, only the nagging thought that I must be overtired. Finally, I snuggle back into bed and pull the covers over my head to block out the moonlight. The sensation diminishes. On impulse, I take my pillow and put it over my head, covering my ears, and the sensation fades so much that I'm finally able to ignore it enough to fall asleep. This time, I have no dreams.

Morning comes, and we are awakened in the usual way: by a servant standing in the hall, turning a crank connected to a device that makes our headboards shake. But something is different today. Accompanying the usual vibration is more of that strange sensation, which I find shocking. It's still with me. What I perceive now, as my bed frame taps against the wall, has a different quality to it. This is sharp and short compared to the long, drawn-out phenomenon created when the crowd opened their mouths. I kneel down, studying the shaking frame, trying to understand how it's creating this other effect. Zhang Jing taps my arm, and I jump in surprise.

What are you doing? she signs.

What is that? I ask, gesturing to the bed. She looks at me, puzzled, and I notice the servants have stopped turning the crank. Gingerly, I shake the frame so that it hits the wall. To my surprise, I recreate the effect to a lesser extent and immediately look to Zhang Jing for explanation. *What is that?* I repeat.

What is what? she asks, completely baffled.

I strike the wall with more force from the bed, making the effect more intense. But Zhang Jing doesn't seem to notice. She only looks more and more confused.

You don't notice it? I ask.

She frowns. *Is the bed broken?*

The other girls have dressed, and some are already on their way to breakfast. Zhang Jing and I hurry to follow suit, carefully checking each other over to make sure our robes are straight and hair is pinned in place. We have the same fine, black hair, and it often escapes its pins. She can tell I'm still troubled and asks me if I'm okay as we walk to the dining room, but all I can do is shake my head by way of answer. Part of it is because I have no way to explain what I'm feeling. And the other part is that I very quickly become too overwhelmed to talk anymore.

Everywhere we go, everything we do that morning, the foreign sensations follow me. They are caused by all sorts of things and come in all different forms. Two china cups hitting each other. The sliding of the door when the servants come through. Porridge splashing into bowls. Feet hitting the floor. People coughing. At first, I'm curious about what new sensation will come next, riveted as I watch cause and effect happening all around me. But soon my head is hurting again, and I'm lost in a sea of stimuli. I can't process it all, and for once, I can barely eat. Only the conditioned knowledge of the importance of food drives me to finish my porridge.

When we go to the workroom, there are fewer sensations hitting me, but they're still present as we all finish up yesterday's record. Even my calligraphy brush touching canvas creates an effect, just barely perceptible. As I'm finishing up, a much more intense, more jarring sensation occurs—one that sets my teeth on edge and causes me to look up in alarm. I quickly find its source: Another apprentice has dropped a ceramic pot of paint, making a terrible mess of both paint and shattered pieces. I'm the only one in the room, aside from those working immediately beside him, whose attention is drawn to the accident.

Increasingly agitated, I remember how covering my ears with the pillow last night reduced the stimuli. I put my hands over my ears now, and to my amazement, things mercifully fade once more. Even though the reprieve is welcome, my heart races as the implications slam into me. What I'm perceiving when two objects hit each other, the way my ears respond . . . it's almost like the way the old writings describe . . .

. . . sound.

I immediately shake my head for even considering such a ridiculous thought. It's ludicrous and impossible. Growing wings would be only slightly more farfetched.

You are unwell? Elder Chen's hands sign in front of me.

I realize my hands are still pressed to my ears, and I quickly lower them. *It's just a headache*, I lie. *It's nothing.*

His sharp eyes take me in for a few moments and then turn to my work. Even I can see the imperfections. My mortification increases when he takes up the brush himself and repairs some of my sloppiness. When he finishes, he tells me, *Stay back today and rest.*

I feel my eyes widen in astonishment. We've been taught that doing one's duty is crucial. Only the direst of illnesses should keep us in bed. The miners, whose work keeps us alive, never get days off.

Elder Chen smiles. *You are clearly not yourself today. It's written all over you. You are one of the most talented artists I have seen in a long time. I'd rather lose one day of labor than risk a long-term ailment. They will make you tea in the kitchen to help with your headache. Spend the duration of the day in rest and study.*

There's nothing to do but bow at the great act of generosity he is showing me. I'm embarrassed at being singled out but even more relieved not to have to face the blur of village activity.

Thank you, master, I tell him.

Who knows? he asks. *Perhaps I will take a walk and keep watch at your post. If not, we still have your sister on watch over there, so that part of the mines won't go unobserved.*

My sister! At his words, a jolt of panic hits me. Master Chen's presence tells me the other elders must be here as well. I didn't have a chance to check Zhang Jing's work last night and promised myself I'd do it this morning. I look across the room, and Elder Lian is strolling around, making her way to Zhang Jing's canvas. Desperately, I search for some sort of distraction, something that will slow Elder Lian and allow me to save Zhang Jing like I always do. Maybe someone will faint from exhaustion. Maybe a servant will burst in with news of another food theft.

But none of that happens. Elder Lian comes to a stop beside my sister, and I am frozen where I stand, unable to help her. It is an unusual and terrifying role for me to be in. Zhang Jing appears calm, but I can see the fear in her eyes. I think she, like me, is ready for Elder Lian to turn on her in rage, to call her—and me—out for the deception we've been furthering. But that doesn't happen either. Elder Lian sizes up my sister's work for long, agonizing moments before finally moving on. I nearly fall over in my relief.

Things proceed as usual, and soon the apprentices are carrying the canvases to the village center. They move too quickly for me to get a good look at Zhang Jing's portion, and I pray it was a good day for her. I wave goodbye to her and then heed Elder Chen's instructions to go to the kitchen for tea. It's rare for the elders or apprentices to set foot in there, and the servants scurry and bow to me as I wait. The clothing they wear is stained with grease and smoke, only a little better than what the miners wear. One of the cooks sets an iron kettle down heavily on the counter, and the resulting effect makes me wince and grit my teeth.

At last, an older servant deferentially brings me a cup of medicinal tea. Although she is too intimidated to make much in the way of eye contact, she nonetheless explains that I should drink the tea and go to bed. If my headache isn't gone in six hours, I can return for more. I thank her and take the tea away, but I don't go to my room to rest.

Instead, I head toward the school's library, carefully sipping the tea as I walk. I haven't been able to shake my earlier suspicions about sound, despite every reasonable part of me knowing it's impossible. I decide this may be the only chance I have to figure out what's happening to me, short of asking a person for help. And I know better than to do that. If I described what's been happening to me, I'd be labeled insane.

I finish the tea as I enter the library. Immediately, I seek out the oldest section. It contains writings from when our people could still hear. I've skimmed them before, and there is one author in particular I'm seeking. Her words meant little to me in the past, but now they are perhaps my only hope.

The writer's name was Feng Jie, and she was one of the last of our people to lose her hearing. Three of her scrolls are in the library, and I settle down with them, pleased that my headache has abated. I begin reading the first one:

I wish I was writing some great wisdom, some understanding of why this great tragedy is happening to us. But there is none.

I pause, contemplating her words. Throughout my life, the loss of our people's hearing has always been referred to as a tragedy, but I've never really seen it that way. I haven't really thought much about it at all since it's hard to miss something you've never known.

Feng Jie continues: *Those wiser than me have long sought answers for why hearing is disappearing, and their ponderings have come to nothing. I don't expect to achieve what they could not. Instead, it is my intent here to record a memory of sound, for I fear what will happen to future generations if they have no knowledge of it. Already, children born today have no understanding when those few of us who still hear try to explain it. With each passing day, my hearing declines more and more. Sounds become fainter and fainter, softer and softer. Soon what is simply quiet will become silent.*

And so I want to describe sound to those who don't have it, so that the words will not be lost and so that those who will never hear have as close an understanding as they can. And perhaps someday, if sound returns, this will guide those who might have forgotten the words of sound.

Riveted, I feel my breath catch. This was why I sought out this scroll, what I remembered from my long-ago browsing. At the time, it had seemed fanciful, the idea of sound returning. But now . . .

Feng Jie's writings go on to detail a list of sounds. Reading them is like trying to understand another language. I can't even follow some of the words she uses to define other words.

When a small bell rings, the sound is high and sweet, clear and often staccato. It is a tinkling, almost like the babbling of a brook. When a large bell rings, the sound is deep and ponderous. It echoes in the soul, causing vibrations you can feel in your entire body.

A whistle is the sound made when you blow air between pursed lips. It is high-pitched and often continuous, unless you start and stop the airflow to create some tune. Whistling is also a primary component in birdsong, and their range far surpasses ours.

My mind struggles to hold on to all these new terms and assign them meaning. *Ring. High. Staccato. Tinkling. Babbling. Deep. Echoes. Whistle. Pitch. Tune. Song.*

All three of her scrolls are written this way, and I absorb as many new concepts as I can. I think back to what I already observed in this short morning. My bed frame was *knocking* against the wall. Zhang Jing's breathing was *quiet*. The dish *crashed loudly* in the workroom. And the iron pot on the counter . . . was that a *clang*? Or a *bang*? What's the difference?

As the afternoon wears on, my head is starting to hurt again—and it has nothing to do with sound but rather with the overload of knowledge from the scrolls, which I have now gone through several times in the hopes of memorizing them. Some of the concepts are so hard to understand that memorization is useless. Still, there is comfort in the terminology. It's a way to reconcile this unknown sense with the ones I do know.

Something startles me from my study—*a sound*, I tell myself, trying to use the terminology correctly. It seems neither particularly loud nor quiet, and I wonder if *medium* is a correct term for volume. Feng Jie didn't mention it.

The sound came from the library door opening, and I look up to see Elder Chen entering. I quickly put the scroll away and get to my feet so that I can bow to him. He told me to spend the day in study, but I'm nervous he'll ask what it is I've been researching.

You're feeling better? he asks.

Yes, master, I say. *Thank you for this day of rest.*

He looks amused, and a soft sound comes from his throat, making me wonder which of Feng Jie's words apply. *Laugh? Chuckle? Giggle?*

You didn't rest much, from what I hear, he replies. *The servants say you've spent most of the day in here. Even when you have a day off, you still work.*

There was pleasure in it, master, I say, hoping to hide my purpose. *Not all of it was serious reading.*

I used to spend much of my free time here too when I was your age. He pulls out a scroll, seemingly at random, and opens it, revealing images of fanciful creatures. He admires it a moment before returning it to its place. *Those are the things I would read over and over—I was always off on an adventure with some fantastic beast. Dragons, pixius, phoenixes.*

Something he has said stirs a memory, and I ask carefully, *Isn't there a story about pixius and our ancestors losing their hearing?*

I'm not really interested in imaginary creatures, but my hope is that Elder Chen might say something about sound that could be of use to me. Still smiling at me, he nods.

Yes, just a story. One my mother used to tell me. Legend says the pixius used to roam our village long ago. Then they decided to rest and took away all the sounds on our mountain so that they could sleep in peace.

It's a silly reason for losing our hearing, but no more outlandish than most. All sorts of stories abound about why hearing went away, many having to do with divine retribution. I hope Elder Chen will say more about sound disappearing, but as his thoughts turn inward, I can see he's more caught up in the pixius than sound.

I always wanted to paint pixius, he remarks. *Like winged lions. Can you even imagine? My master would chastise me for having my head in the clouds.*

Seeing my surprise at that admission, he laughs again. *Yes, you aren't the only one who daydreams. You remind me of myself at your age.* He pauses, and that humor fades from his features. *That's why I want you to come with me.*

He turns, and I follow quickly, my heart rate picking up. Has he found out about what's happened to me? Has someone reported me? The thought is terrifying as I follow him back through the school. A part of me almost welcomes the chance to unburden this secret. Because while Feng Jie's writings were full of information about hearing, there was no mention of how or why it might come back after being gone for generations. To my knowledge, no one has ever written about such a thing—because it's never happened.

Elder Chen brings me to a small room usually reserved exclusively for the elders. There, inside, I see Zhang Jing standing before Elder Lian, with the other elders seated beyond them. One look at my sister tells me this isn't about me at all.

Elder Lian is surprised by our presence. *What is Fei doing here?*

I thought it appropriate she be present, Elder Chen responds.

This has nothing to do with her, Elder Lian insists.

I am the only family she has, I quickly interject, even though I know it's impertinent. *If she is in trouble, I need to know.*

A gleam of triumph shows in Elder Lian's eyes. *You've known she has been going blind for some time, haven't you?*

I make no response.

There is no place for blindness among the artists, Elder Lian declares, looking back at Zhang Jing. *You've lost your apprenticeship. You must gather your things and leave.*

Zhang Jing cannot speak. In fact, she goes so pale I'm afraid she'll pass out. My instinct is to comfort her, but instead I take a bold step toward Elder Lian. *She's not blind yet!* I notice some of the other elders are holding up pieces of canvas: samples of Zhang Jing's past work. *Look at those. She still has skill. A blind person couldn't do that.*

They're imprecise, Elder Lian argues. *Flawed. We know you've been covering for her. We need perfection in the record, and that requires a perfect set of eyes.*

She might get better, I protest. Elder Lian snickers in disbelief. I do not like the sound. It is harsh and ugly.

No one's sight gets better, Elder Lian says. *We all know that. Be grateful her vision is good enough to let her join the miners. At least that way she will be able to contribute. It's better than begging.*

An image of the beggars in the village's center comes back to me, and I can practically see Zhang Jing among them. It makes me feel sick. But Zhang Jing joining the miners isn't much better. I think about Li Wei and his father, how dangerous it is to be in the mines with limited vision. I think about how even then, the rations miners receive are smaller than what we get here. It was what drove the servant to steal for his family.

Don't send her away, I say suddenly, addressing all the elders. *There's an opening among the servants, right? After yesterday's theft? Let Zhang Jing take it. Please. Her vision is more than adequate to perform those kinds of duties.*

I don't know if that's true or not. I've never thought much about what the servants do. I haven't had to. But it has to be a better fate than mining or begging.

The shock that meets me in Zhang Jing's eyes suggests she disagrees, but I make a small gesture, urging her not to protest as the others deliberate.

The elders exchange glances, and it is Elder Chen who finally speaks. *It's true that we lost one of the cleaners yesterday. Zhang Jing needs a place, and a place has opened up. It is a fortunate thing. Balance, yes?*

Elder Lian looks skeptical for a moment and then shrugs. *I will allow it.* Behind her hard exterior, I catch a glimpse of regret in her eyes. Maybe her initial decision to kick Zhang Jing out wasn't born of cruelty so much as necessity. Elder Lian pities what's happened to my sister, and somehow that makes all this even worse.

The full impact of what I've just brought about hits me. My sister, a servant? Not just any servant—a cleaner? We've spent so much time as artist apprentices that I've come to take this lifestyle for granted. It's demanding, but there is a prestige to it. There's a pride in knowing our craft is what keeps the village orderly, that hundreds of years from now, our descendants will look upon what we've created and learn from it. Our art will endure when the rest of us are gone. Others rightly treat us with deference, just as the servants in the kitchen did earlier. I suddenly imagine Zhang Jing groveling as they did, bowing and avoiding eye contact with the other artists. Worse, I imagine her scrubbing the floor or doing some other demeaning task.

I see despair in Zhang Jing's face, but she is nonetheless quick to give the proper response. She bows three times to Elder

Chen. *Thank you, master. It is a great honor. I will fulfill my new duties with as much dignity as I fulfilled my previous ones.*

My heart sinks. Honor? There is no honor in this, but at least I will be able to sleep easy knowing my sister has a roof over her and food to eat. Elder Chen dismisses us with a small gesture, and after more bowing, we retreat to the hallway and head back to the girls' dormitory.

Don't worry, I tell Zhang Jing. *Once your vision comes back, they will reinstate you in your apprenticeship.*

She comes to a halt and shakes her head sadly. *Fei, we both know that's not going to happen. I must accept this miserable fate now.*

Miserable? But you were grateful back there.

Of course, she says. *I had to be for the sake of your honor after you pleaded for me. But I would have rather walked away with my dignity and gone to the mines than slink around in the shadows of my former position.* As though making her point, a servant comes by pushing a broom, sweeping up dirt tracked in from the apprentices. The noise made by the broom's bristles is interesting, but my grief and outrage are too great to give it much thought. I can understand Zhang Jing's disappointment, but how could she prefer to be out on the streets? *This is a good place for you,* I insist. *You'll be safe here. Fed. Protected.*

I suppose that's something, says Zhang Jing. *At least this way I won't have to lie anymore, and I'll be able to do tasks around here for a long time, even if my vision gets worse. Then I really will have to find another place.*

Don't say that, I protest, unable to handle the thought. *Everything will be okay as long as we're together.*

I hope so, she tells me, just before pulling me into a hug.

When we get back to our room, we find another servant waiting for us. *I'm here to show you to your new quarters,* she explains to Zhang Jing. *You will sleep with the servants now.*

Zhang Jing's earlier calm turns to embarrassment, and her face reddens. The other girls stop and gawk at this news, and it's all I can do not to shake my fists or kick something in my rage. I hadn't expected this when I made my plea. Zhang Jing's demotion was bad enough, and now she's also being taken from me. Who will look after her without me by her side? Ever since our parents died, we've been inseparable. How can I go on without her, especially in this new and terrifying time? How am I supposed to contend with this plague of sounds that's bombarding me if I don't have her to rely on?

Zhang Jing holds her head up, mustering every last bit of pride she has as she gathers her few possessions and ignores the covert conversations that are flashing around the room as our peers take in this new development. I want to tell them this is only temporary. . . but I can say and do nothing as the servant escorts her out. Zhang Jing gives me one last sweet smile before she steps out the door, and for the first time in my life, I feel truly alone.

CHAPTER 4

THAT NIGHT, I DREAM I am in a house with chrysanthe-mums carved on its walls, just like my stump. It's beautiful and elaborate but completely impractical. As I admire this fanciful house, I am again unable to shake the feeling that something is beckoning me. It's as though there's a line running out of my chest, pulling me to someone else. It's strange, but at least the dream is quiet, giving me a welcome reprieve from the onslaught of noises that has tormented me all day.

A new set of sounds rouses me from sleep, a succession of short ones that occur simultaneously, over and over, with great frequency. I sit up in my bed, trying to determine what this new source might be. The early morning light coming in through the window is sluggish, and gray skies outside give me my answer. It is the sound of rain hitting the building.

My stomach is in knots as I go about my morning duties. I want to see Zhang Jing, but am afraid to as well. Her absence pains me like a wound that cannot heal, yet I'm afraid to see her in this new role she's taken on. Whatever they've assigned her to do, however, it doesn't involve crossing my path. I paint and go to breakfast with the others, and then we make the usual journey to the town's center and our observation posts.

The rain stops by the time I reach the mine's entrance, which is a small blessing. It's still damp and miserable, and my heart aches for my sister as I sit on my stump and touch the carved chrysanthemums, thinking back to last night's dream. My head hurts too, as I've had to contend with a barrage of new sounds all morning. I went to the library seeking information on what might bring hearing back, but now I wonder if there's a way to make it go away again. I can't see why our ancestors thought hearing was such a great thing, why they mourned its loss so much. It's jarring and distracting, making it impossible to focus on anything else. What value could all this extra stimulus add to life?

And even more confusing, why is this happening to me? The old stories say that people began to lose hearing in groups. If that sense is coming back to us, wouldn't it happen to multiple people at a time? Before bed last night, I made sure to check the record in the workroom and even ask some of the other apprentices if anything unusual had happened yesterday or if they'd noted any strange stories. I'd played it off as curiosity about missing my observation, but secretly I'd hoped that maybe others were experiencing what I was and that I could talk about it and get some understanding.

I still don't know what to do. Should I tell the elders? Will they think I'm crazy? There are times I wonder if maybe I am.

It's true that what I'm experiencing falls in line with what we know about sound and hearing, but maybe I'm just *imagining* I'm experiencing those things? Is it possible that some old story has lodged itself in the back of my mind and is now manifesting itself this way? That actually seems like a more plausible explanation than suddenly becoming the only miraculous recipient of hearing.

My dark spiral of worries pauses when I hear what I've come to recognize as the sound of feet and people moving. I look up, trying to determine its location, and realize it's coming from the mine's entrance. I get to my own feet and hurry over in time to see a group of workers emerging, carrying something—no, someone—between them. I back up to give them room and watch in horror as they lay Bao out on the ground. Someone signals for water, but another man shakes his head and signs, *It's too late.* Bao's eyes are closed, and there's blood on his temple—new blood, different from yesterday's wound. He isn't moving.

Sorrow wells up in me, but I push through it, knowing I have a job to do. I tap one of the workers and ask, *What happened?*

Recognizing me and my status, she bows before answering. *A section of wall had become unstable. The foreman put a placard up with a warning to keep us away from that area, but Bao didn't see it.*

Someone pushes his way through the crowd, and I feel my breath catch when I see Li Wei. He pauses to wipe sweat from his brow and peers around avidly, his dark eyes sharp and concerned. When he spies his father, Li Wei hurries over and kneels down by the old man. Whereas yesterday Li Wei was fiery and indignant, today he is all tenderness and compassion. I feel myself choke up as I watch him gently touch Bao's face, hoping for a response. An overwhelming urge to run over and comfort Li Wei sweeps me, but I stay where I am. Resignation soon fills his features as he realizes what the rest of us already have: Bao is gone. That resignation turns to a mix of rage and grief. Li Wei clenches his fists and opens his mouth.

A sound comes out like none I have heard so far. Really, I've heard little in the way of human sounds. There is no need for us to make them. We stopped communicating with our mouths and voices ages ago. But the instinct is still there, especially in times of high emotion. I've felt the vibrations myself when I've sobbed, when I've let out little cries of sorrow, though of course I had no idea what they sounded like.

I do now, and it sends chills through me as I listen to Li Wei. A section of Feng Jie's words comes back to me:

A scream is a sound we make that is born of intense feeling. A scream of fear, of being startled, is often high-pitched. It may be short or prolonged. A scream may also accompany delight or amusement, though often that is more of a squeal. And a scream of sorrow or rage . . . well, that is an entirely different thing. That comes from a darker place, from the depths of our souls, and when we scream in those times, because we are sad or angry, there is a terrible knowledge that accompanies it, that we are giving voice to our emotions, to what is simply too big for our hearts to contain.

And as Li Wei cries out, I know Feng Jie is right. It is his heart I am hearing, a way of expressing what he feels over his father's loss that is both primal and far more eloquent than any words can convey. It is terrible and beautiful, and it comes from his soul and reaches something within mine. It is the sound my own heart made when my parents died, only I didn't know it until now.

Li Wei attempts to pull himself together and peers at those gathered around. *This shouldn't have happened!* he tells the crowd. *He shouldn't have been working down there, with his vision failing. Many of you knew it was. The foreman knew. But everyone pretended not to notice. How many more of you are like that? How many more of you are hiding your failing vision so that you can keep working?*

No one answers that question, but one man at last bravely says, *We have to work, or we can't eat.*

Only because you allow it to be that way! Li Wei protests. *You further the system by continuing to be a part of it! So long as you keep sending metals down the mountain without question, nothing will ever change.*

A woman responds, *As long as we send metals down the mountain, my children continue to have dinner. If there is no food, they will starve. I will work my fingers to the bone to stop that from happening.* Several other miners nod in agreement.

But there must be another way, Li Wei tells them. *At the very least, if you are losing your sight, don't go back to work. Don't go down there to risk your lives and the lives of others.*

Don't end up like him. Tears brim in his eyes as he clutches his father's sleeve.

The other miners shuffle uncomfortably, but no one takes up his rally. One man finally claps Li Wei on the shoulder in sympathy and then simply says, *We must get back to work. The priest has been sent for to tend to your father. I'm sorry for your loss.*

Others make similar gestures of condolence and then trudge back to the mine's entrance. Not long after that, the village priest's acolytes come and deferentially cover Bao's body before lifting it and taking it away for preparation. They tell Li Wei he will be able to view the body at sunset, and the funeral will follow. Li Wei makes no response as they take his father away.

Soon we are left alone. Li Wei slams his fists against the muddy ground and lets out another cry of frustration. Again, I am awed, overwhelmed by the strength and emotion conveyed in the human voice. For the first time since this phenomenon started happening to me, I begin to understand the power it could have and why our ancestors mourned its loss. Every sound around me—the renewed pattering of rain, the wind in the leaves—all of it suddenly has a new meaning. I can see how these sounds don't interfere with the world so much as enhance it. The scope and potential are huge. It's like having a new color to paint with.

Li Wei gets to his feet and notices that I am still here. His dark eyes lock with mine. There is a remarkable contrast in the emotion playing over his face and the imposing figure he makes with his height and build. Sorrow radiates off him, and I know I should say something, offer condolences, at the very least. But I'm still stunned, still awestruck by the effect his cry of grief had on me. His voice was the first human one I have ever heard outside of that first dream, and its impact was staggering. I can only stand there.

Li Wei snorts in disgust and storms away. His abrupt departure snaps me from my daze. I realize I must have come across as rude and cold, and I instantly feel terrible. Abandoning my observation post is a serious offense, but I can't stand to let him go off like that, not when he thinks I was indifferent to his father's death. I hesitate only a moment before leaving the mine and running after Li Wei. When I reach him on the path near the cliff's edge, I tap him on the shoulder, and he spins around with a ferocity that makes me take a few steps back.

What do you want? he asks. I know the anger he wears is an attempt to hide his heartache.

Li Wei, I'm sorry about your father. I'm so sorry, I say. *I know how you feel.*

He scoffs. *I sincerely doubt that.*

You know I do, I chastise. *You remember when I lost my parents.*

Yes. Legitimate compassion flashes in his eyes, but soon that outrage returns. *They died in the fever, just as my mother did. But that was different. None of them could've stopped that. Not like with my father. He had no business working when his vision was failing! It was agony watching him go into that mine day after day. It was a death trap. I knew it would only be a matter of time, but he refused to stop working and become a beggar.*

I understand that too, I tell him. *Zhang Jing . . . she is going blind.* I pause, hit with the full impact of finally admitting this to someone. *Our masters found out, and she can no longer be an apprentice. We had to take other action, make a big decision in order to save her from being a beggar.*

Li Wei is very still now, regarding me with new interest. *What did you do?*

I take a deep breath, still having my own difficulties resigning myself to Zhang Jing's fate. *She is going to become a household servant at the Peacock Court.*

He stares at me in confusion and then throws up his arms in disbelief. *That is your big decision? To move her to a comfortable, safe job, where she'll be well fed and face no risks? You actually deliberated about that and think you have* anything *in common with me or the other miners?*

I know his harsh words are born from grief, and I try to respond calmly. *I'm saying I know what it's like to be scared for your loved one in that way. To have your life turned upside down. You aren't the only one going through this.* That earlier urge returns, the one that makes me want to go over and put my arms around him, comforting him as I would have years ago. But I can't, not when others might see. Not when so much distance has built up between us.

He's still upset but works to calm himself. *Your life has changed, but I wouldn't say it's been turned upside down—not yet,* he says. *And that's what no one seems to realize, Fei. Everyone knows things are bad, but everyone thinks if we just go forward like we always have, it will all be okay. Instead, we're just moving toward darkness and ruin. Can't you see that?*

I start to reply, but then a sound I've never heard before catches my attention. It's incredible, and I want desperately to hear it again. Unable to help myself, I immediately turn my head toward its source, and I see a flash of blue. It's a thrush, just like the one I spotted the other day. It's perched on the branch of a tree, and it opens its mouth, producing that exquisite sound . . . a song? I long for the bird to sing again, but it takes flight and disappears out of sight.

I stare after it, awestruck, and then quickly turn back to Li Wei in embarrassment. He stares at me, understandably confused, and then shakes his head. *Clearly, this isn't a discussion you care about.*

No, wait. I do care, I say. But he's already turned from me. I reach out to grab his arm, and as my fingertips touch his bare skin, he tenses and glances back at me. Something of my heart must be in my eyes, because his expression softens. My hand still rests on his arm, and I am dizzyingly aware that there are only a few scant inches between us. I'm also suddenly reminded that no matter how often we held hands or dreamed of the future, we've never actually kissed. There'd always been a spark between us, one we were both hesitant to acknowledge until the day we realized we were being torn apart.

I quickly snatch my hand away and take a step back, hoping my thoughts aren't obvious. *What is your plan then?* I ask him. *What do you think we should do to save ourselves from darkness and ruin?*

He studies me intently for a few more moments, and I'm breathless as that gaze wraps around me. *We start by ending this line system*, he says at last. *It's what's enslaving us, what has put us in this miserable situation.*

I can't hide my shock, and for a moment our history is forgotten. *And how would we end the line system?*

Li Wei points over the cliff's edge. *By going to the line keeper. By getting to the bottom of everything. Either he is a reasonable man who will understand our plight, or he's a tyrant who must be overthrown.*

He isn't the first person I've met who wants to go talk to the line keeper, but as I stare into Li Wei's eyes, I realize he might be the first person I've met who's truly serious about doing it. And the thought of that suddenly terrifies me. I may have willingly walked away from him when I joined the apprentices, but at least I knew he was still alive and safe in our village—not attempting some impossibly dangerous stunt.

How would you do that? I demand. *By climbing down?*

Yes, he says, crossing his arms defiantly.

That's suicide! The climb is too dangerous by hand. No one has done that in centuries! Not since our ancestors stopped being able to hear the falling rocks—

I cut myself off, my hands dropping to my side. The implications of what I've just stated hit me like a slap to the face, sending me reeling. For my entire life, my village has accepted that no one can climb down the mountain. It's too dangerous, both because of the unstable nature of the cliff face and the difficulties of not being able to hear the rocks. Others have stated this fact over and over. I've even said it myself, parroting it as an unfortunate truth. And yet . . . here I stand, suddenly realizing it's not the truth anymore. Someone *can* hear the rocks now. Me. But what does that even mean? And is it enough to truly make a difference?

Li Wei, not knowing what I'm thinking, assumes I'm simply too afraid and too shocked at his proposition in general.

And that's why nothing changes, he states imperiously. *Everyone clings to the way things have always been. And those ways are killing us. If we're going to die one way or another, then I'll face my death trying to make a difference—trying to save myself and others. Just getting by one more day isn't good enough anymore. There must be more to life, more to hope for.*

I don't answer, and again he reads that as disapproval and fear. I'm normally so quick with a response, but too much has happened this past couple of days. Even if I could trust Li Wei enough to explain how I'm feeling, I don't know if I really would be able to articulate it correctly. It's all so strange and new, so I continue standing there, stunned.

A group of miners appears on the trail, and Li Wei stiffens before giving me a formal bow for their benefit. *Thank you for your condolences, apprentice,* he states properly, and then he turns away and leaves me.

CHAPTER 5

THE REST OF THE DAY, I move around like someone in a dream. I do all the correct things. I return to my post until the miners' shift ends, then take my notes back to the school so that I can paint the record. To any outward observer, I look the same as ever. But on the inside, everything about me has changed. My whole world has changed, and I don't know how to come to terms with it.

My sister is no longer at my side. Until this day, it's never truly struck me how much I took her presence for granted. Everything I do feels incomplete now. At dinner, another student sits beside me in Zhang Jing's usual spot. In our room, her bed remains empty and stripped of all its covers. But it's in the workroom where I feel her loss the most keenly. As I dutifully paint my portion of the record, I find myself constantly looking to the spot where she used to work. Each time I see it vacant, the pain hits me all over again.

It's a mercy when the elders come in and tell us we are

excused early from our evening work—until I realize it's so that we may attend Bao's funeral if we wish. I'm torn on whether to go. I respected Bao immensely, but the mystery of my new condition weighs on me. Some students choose to continue working. I leave my work, wanting to get away from this room, with its memories. My hope is to sneak back to the library and try to figure out why these sounds are assaulting me—and no one else. I checked the record again, and so far I remain the only person experiencing this phenomenon.

But when I get to the hallway with the others who have chosen to leave, I spot Zhang Jing, sweeping up the dirt in the hallway. It's the first time I've seen her in her new role, and my heart nearly stops. She wears the dull uniform of a servant, and her face is deferentially lowered as the others pass by her. I tense, waiting to see if anyone will say anything or comment on her new station—but no one says a thing. Really, it's as if no one sees her at all. In some ways, that's worse than if someone had made a derogatory comment. She has become invisible to everyone else. Beyond that—she's become nothing to them.

I stop in front of her when the others have gone, and she quickly signs to me, *Please don't, Fei. You'll only make things worse.*

I flinch at the insinuation, that it's me who's brought her to this position. *You're safe*, I tell her. *That's what matters. I just wanted you to be okay.*

She stares off for a moment and sighs heavily before answering. *I will be okay today. Tomorrow and the next day as well.*

Beyond that? Who can say? But there's no point worrying that far ahead. I'll just focus on getting by one day at a time and hope that my vision lasts a little longer.

Another apprentice comes down the hall just then. He nods politely to me and then does a double take, recognizing Zhang Jing. He gapes for a moment, seeing her in the servant's outfit, then looks embarrassed to be caught staring. He quickly averts his eyes and hurries past. Glancing over at Zhang Jing, I see the mortification in her face.

You should go before anyone else sees you, she says. *Don't call any more attention to either of us. Your position still brings great prestige to our family.*

I'm sorry, I tell her, feeling tears spring to my eyes. *I didn't mean for this to happen.*

None of us meant for any of this to happen, she says simply. *We must make the best of a bad situation. And I know you did the best you could.*

She takes her broom and continues working her way down the hall, leaving me feeling terrible. Did I do the best I could? Was there something else I could have done to help her? Her words bring back what Li Wei said to me before he stormed off: *Just getting by one more day isn't good enough anymore. There must be more to life, more to hope for.*

A lump forms in my throat as the full impact of what he meant hits me. Zhang Jing has resigned herself to nothing more than hoping for short-term survival, hoping the blindness will stay away one day more, prolonging the time until she joins the beggars. It is a terrible, dreary existence. It's no kind of existence at all.

As she disappears around a corner, I suddenly find myself walking toward the nearest door. My plans for the library are forgotten, and instead I join the others going down to the heart of the village for Bao's sunset funeral. I'm not sure what it is that draws me. At first, I think that Zhang Jing's plight has driven home the tragedy of what happened to Bao. But when I reach the edge of the crowd gathered for the ceremony, I understand what has really drawn me here.

Li Wei.

For the first time in a while, that dazzling childhood memory doesn't immediately come to mind as I stare at him. That inescapable attraction and the emotional fallout from joining the artists still burns within me, but it too is momentarily subdued. What pulls me to him now is his sense of loss and his rage at the situation our people are locked into. It resonates with the pain I feel over Zhang Jing, and although I don't know if he'll want to talk to me, I know have to try.

He stands near the front of the crowd, his back straight and tall and his face proud and almost haughty. As usual, though, it's his eyes that betray his otherwise tough exterior. I see the emotion brimming in them, and my own heart aches in answer. I know him well enough to understand that he's using every ounce of self-control to remain calm in front of the others. I wish I could run forward and clasp his hands, let him know it's okay to grieve and show how he feels.

He wears a white shirt, undoubtedly borrowed from a community source. In the old days, it was written, every villager would come out in white for a funeral. When trade down the mountain became restricted, however, our clothing supply diminished. Now only the immediate family is granted white, from a closely guarded communal supply. Even though the color has sad connotations, I'm moved by how striking Li Wei looks when he's cleaned up and in something other than those muddy work clothes. It's not something I've seen very much. He looks almost regal once the dirt is washed away, like someone who could lead and command attention, rather than toil away in a dark mine.

The priest bows before the memorial altar, which has already been set with the sacred lamp, two candles, and five cups. His assistants bring forward incense, which he adds to the altar and lights with great ceremony. Soon the scent of sandalwood wafts to where I stand. The priest goes through the familiar signs and dances, and although I watch respectfully, my mind wanders. With the blindness has come an increase in funerals, and we are all too familiar with this ceremony.

I focus again on Li Wei, thinking about his words and his conviction. Did he mean what he said? Is he really going to attempt to leave and go down the mountain? Perhaps he was only speaking in anger . . . yet, as I study him closely, something tells me what he said wasn't an impulse. I wouldn't be surprised if he's been planning his journey for a long time. He simply needed a strong enough reason to spur him on; his father's death provided it.

My thoughts are suddenly, jarringly interrupted by a noise

that nearly makes me jump out of my own skin. It's a sign of both my internal struggles and my ability to adapt that in only a couple of days, I've learned to tune out many background noises. Noises that initially overwhelmed me. Now, in this short time, I find myself ignoring many common sounds and focusing on those that either directly affect me or are particularly noticeable.

This one sets my teeth on edge, and I search for its source. In the priest's direction, one of his assistants has just struck a ceremonial gong. My eyes widen as I realize that monstrous noise was caused by a gesture I'd seen countless times at funerals and other rituals. I never realized that noise was the end result. I look around, desperate to see if anyone else reacted. But they're all respectfully watching the priest—well, everyone except the older woman standing next to me who noticed when I flinched.

Do you know why they hit the gong? I ask.

The woman bows in acknowledgment to my station and then answers: *It is to scare evil spirits who might delay the deceased's journey.* She pauses. *That is what my grandmother told me, at least. I don't know why hitting it scares them. Perhaps it is magical.*

I thank her and turn back to the ceremony. Despite the grim circumstances, I almost want to smile. I'm not sure I believe in that kind of superstition, but I certainly understand how our ancestors thought the gong could frighten away evil spirits! All this time, I'd had no idea of its true purpose. No one did. For generations, the priests have just continued using the gong out of habit, long after anyone could hear it anymore. I wonder how many other things like this were lost to us when sound disappeared.

And why, I ask myself for the hundredth time, am I the only one who has had this sense restored?

When the funeral ends, Li Wei is surrounded by those wishing to offer condolences. A number of them are girls our age, and while they look legitimately sorry for his loss, part of me questions their motives. I can't be the only one who goes weak-kneed around him, and I really don't know how he's spent his free time since I joined the artists. It'd be reasonable for him to turn his attentions to someone else. The thought troubles me more than it should, considering how Sheng and I were matched. When the last of Li Wei's sympathizers leaves, I follow him as he walks alone from the village's center. I pass a cluster of beggars as I do, their sad plight bringing Zhang Jing to mind. My resolve strengthens, and I tap Li Wei's shoulder when he heads down a path that leads to a group of small houses. He turns, looking surprised to see me—and possibly a little exasperated, considering how we last left things.

What do you want? he asks. His harsh response is almost enough to make me flinch.

Mustering my courage, I bow and give the proper condolences offered in these situations. *I am very sorry for the loss of your father. May his spirit live in immortality.*

Thank you, Li Wei responds, but he is clearly suspicious that there is more to come.

I make sure no one else is around before dropping the formalities: *Are you still planning on leaving?*

His face hardens. *Yes. Why? Are you going to tell someone? Try to get them to stop me?*

No. He regards me expectantly, and I take a deep breath, summoning my strength. *I . . . I want to come with you.*

The words fly from my hands before I can stop them. The idea has been brewing in the back of my mind all evening, but until I said it, I hadn't consciously realized that's what I was going to do. Zhang Jing's plight has made me realize that things will never change . . . unless someone makes them change.

Li Wei stares incredulously at me and then lets out a laugh with a harsh edge to it.

You? Pampered, prized apprentice? You aren't that bold little girl anymore. Stop wasting my time. I have things to do. He shakes his head and starts to walk away, but I catch his sleeve. Remembering the effect touching him had on me last time, I'm careful to promptly let go and keep a respectful distance.

What bold little girl? I ask, puzzled.

He hesitates. *The one who climbed the rotten shed even though she knew it was dangerous. Just to prove she could. I thought you were so brave back then. Brave and bold and beautiful. I always believed that over the years until . . . well, you've changed.*

My heart lurches at all the misunderstandings that have arisen between us. *I haven't,* I say. *Look, I thought about what you said, about how it isn't enough to just keep getting by day after day as we are. I saw my sister . . . and she's exactly like that. Not happy with her life but convinced there's nothing more. I can't let her go on like that, with nothing else to hope for. I want to help you. I want to talk to the keeper too and see if there's a way to change things.*

It all comes out in a jumble, not nearly as eloquent as I'd hoped. Li Wei studies me for several long moments. The earlier rain clouds have passed. With the sun down and the moon still rising, torches light the paths around the village, casting flickering light and shadows, but I can see well enough to know he's trying to decide if I'm speaking the truth. Unless I'm mistaken, I even see a flash of hope in his eyes, as though he too wonders if there might be a way to repair our past.

At last, he shakes his head again. *No. It's too dangerous, Fei. You wouldn't be able to handle it. I'm already going to have my work cut out for me keeping myself alive. I can't allow myself to worry about you the whole time.*

I won't be a burden! I insist. *I can help you.*

Now he looks amused. *How? Will you win the line keeper over by drawing him a picture?*

I sigh in irritation. *Clap your hands*, I tell him.

He stares in understandable confusion. I gesture impatiently, and with a shrug, he claps three times. The sounds are short and loud.

Now do it again, I say, just before turning around. I wait and hear nothing. After several seconds pass, I look back and glare. *You didn't clap.*

He looks a little surprised but shrugs. *What's the point?*

Just do it, I insist. I turn my back to him, and this time he claps. I face him once more. *You just clapped three times.*

His face is understandably puzzled at this exercise, but he doesn't yet seem to grasp that anything unusual is happening. *So? That's what I did before.*

Then clap a different number of times, and I'll tell you the amount. Seeing his baffled look, I add, *Do it.*

He claps four times, and I tell him the number. Then two. Then seven. The last time, he doesn't clap at all, and when I turn around, his eyes are impossibly wide.

You didn't clap that time, I say.

How are you doing this? he asks.

I steel myself, working up the courage to state what I can barely believe myself. *I can hear the sounds—they're caused when you clap. I don't understand it, but somehow my hearing has returned. I hear this. I hear all sorts of things.*

The idea is so ludicrous, so beyond our everyday experience, that Li Wei can't even try to take it seriously. He looks at me like we're children again, caught up in a game. *It's some kind of trick. Come on, Fei. Tell me how you're really doing it.*

It's not a trick! I tell him. *It's been going on for almost two days, and I don't understand it. That's why I was so distracted earlier when your father died. Li Wei . . . you're the first person I've told. You must believe me.*

He scrutinizes me intently. *It's impossible,* he says, though his expression isn't so certain. *Hearing is gone for us.*

Not for me, I say.

Why just you then?

I wish I knew. . . . You can't even begin to imagine what this has been like. The burden of carrying this secret is catching up with me, and I think Li Wei is beginning to realize this. His expression softens, filling with an affection I haven't seen in him in a long time. Out of habit, he reaches for me, wanting to comfort me like he might have in our childhood.

I nearly let him, but the importance of what's at stake enables me to push aside my own desires. Stepping back, I try to look tough. *Look,* I say, *believe me or not, but the point is, I can help you on this trip. Maybe I can communicate with the line keeper. I can certainly help in other ways.* I pick up a small stone on the path's side and hand it to Li Wei. *Throw it at one of these trees.* I turn around again and wait. After a pause, I hear a sharp sound off to my left. When I face him again, I point in that direction. *There. You threw it over there.*

It's impossible, he repeats. But I can see in his face that, despite whatever reason is telling him otherwise, he's daring to believe my story. *How? How did this happen? Fei, you must have some idea!*

I don't, I say. *I really don't. But it seems to be here to stay, and as long as I've got it, it can be helpful. If I can hear where you just threw the stone, I'll be able to hear when stones are falling on the climb down.*

His breath catches as understanding hits him, and for the first time in our acquaintance, he is at a loss for words. At last, he lifts his hands to speak. *Perhaps . . . perhaps you might be useful on this trip after all.*

CHAPTER 6

WHEN I RETURN TO THE dormitory later that night, I'm certain that everyone will notice my nervousness and excitement, but much like my hearing, the storm of emotions churning inside is apparent only to me. The other apprentices who went to the funeral have returned, and everyone is preparing for bed. I'm certain if Zhang Jing had still been in my room, she would have noticed something was amiss. But my sister is on the other side of the school, with the servants.

I change for bed and slip under the covers dutifully, just like all the other girls in my room. Darkness descends, lit only by peeps of moonlight shining through the edges of the blinds. Soon my roommates fall into sleep, and the room is filled with the soft sounds of what I've come to recognize as breathing. Sometimes I find that sound oddly soothing, but tonight I'm too anxious to give it much thought. I have hours to wait until I can spring into action, and my mind is spinning with all the things that can go wrong on the journey I'm about to embark upon with Li Wei.

It took some time for us to come up with a plan. Neither of us was sure if anyone would try to stop us when we left. It isn't that climbing down is forbidden; it's just that no one has ever really attempted to do it. Both of us are valued for different reasons: I am valued for my artistic skill set, and he is valued because of the village's burning need to mine more metals. It's possible others might prevent us from leaving simply to keep us in the workforce. Leaving under cover of darkness will be our best chance of escape.

That will make our descent even more dangerous, but the moon is full and bright tonight. We will get our start by its light and be far enough down by sunrise that no one can stop us. Around that time, most villagers will still be getting up and preparing for the day, walking to the center to read the record. My absence will be noticed before Li Wei's, but it seems unlikely the masters will guess where I've gone.

The hours drag by as I lie in bed, analyzing our plan and how I'm going to proceed. I know rest will help me, but I can't risk sleeping and missing when I need to get up. I track the moon's position outside, and at last the time comes for me to begin. I slip out of my bed and out of the room, heading toward the servants' wing of the school. My eyes dart everywhere, looking for signs of activity, but I soon realize my ears will serve me better. I hear footsteps and spot a servant on night watch heading toward me from an adjacent hall. I duck into a doorway, crouching in the shadows, until he passes. He stifles a yawn as he goes by, never guessing anyone else is up and about.

I'm not familiar with the servants' wing. We have more rooms in the Peacock Court than we have need for, and it takes me a few tries to find the laundry room. I strip off my nightgown and change into a clean set of apprentice clothes intended for a boy. They're the same blue I usually wear, but instead of a girl's long skirt, they have pants paired with a wrap top. Wearing them feels a little strange at first, but I know they'll be infinitely more practical than my skirt for climbing. The laundry room also has a small knapsack that I take, adding a spare change of clothes for myself.

I next make my way to the kitchen. It too has a servant on watch, and I recognize her as the intimidating head cook. She sits in a chair near the back door, sewing by the light of a small lamp to keep herself awake. I'm not sure if her presence is a result of the recent theft or a precaution always taken. All I know is that if she catches me, my rank won't save me from her wrath. At the moment, her focus is on her sewing, and she's angled in such a position as to allow me some freedom of movement out of her sight.

She doesn't see me slipping in through the door that leads to the rest of the school, and I creep around the kitchen, watching her carefully and listening for any signs of movement. Several times, she shifts position and forces me to duck or seek other cover. I find a table where lunches for the coming day have been prepared and neatly laid out. It's the kind of food meant to be packed and stored easily, ideal for the journey I'm about to undertake.

And yet my fingers hesitate as I reach for it. Stealing food is a grave crime. Everyone is hungry, and I hate the thought of depriving someone else. I find small comfort in knowing that one of the ration bags I take would have been my own lunch tomorrow. Li Wei and I don't know what we'll find at the bottom. Maybe when we get there, we'll find a land of plenty. Or maybe the township sends us small amounts simply because they too are starving. After much deliberation, I take three more packs, giving Li Wei and me two meals each. We will have to fend for ourselves once these run out.

A long, drawn-out sound catches my attention, and I duck into the shadows, searching for the source of the noise. It is one of the doors from the servants' wing being opened. The servant I saw in the hall earlier enters the kitchen, heading over toward the chef. They have a conversation I can see only part of, but it appears to be a status check, verifying all is well. While they are speaking, I seize the opportunity to dart out of the kitchen.

I'm about to take the hall that leads to a side exit when I notice another corridor. In searching for the laundry room and the kitchen, I encountered most of the areas that the servants work in, which makes me think this must be their living quarters. I need to be on my way, but I just can't bring myself to leave without seeing Zhang Jing one last time. In a moment, I've made my choice, and I turn down the hall, carefully peeking in each room. Many doors make that same long noise the kitchen door did, and I'm grateful no one else can hear it. If I ever get a chance to read Feng Jie's book again, I intend to learn what the name for that sound is.

At last, I find where the servant women sleep. The space is

smaller than my bedroom but with more beds crammed into it. Zhang Jing is sleeping at the end of the room, her bed up against the wall. I lean over her, feeling my heart ache as I take in the features of her beloved face. With a pang, I suddenly wonder if I'll ever see her again. Li Wei and I have no idea what we'll find at the bottom. We don't even know if we'll reach the bottom. What will happen if I die? Who will take care of Zhang Jing then— especially if her sight goes?

The fear is almost enough to make me change my mind about the journey. Then I remind myself that while there are risks, there's also the chance that I might be able to change everything—not just for Zhang Jing but for others in my village. Whatever it is we find—more food, answers about the blindness—it has the possibility of improving the world of those we know and love. Li Wei is making this journey regardless, and he needs every asset he can get. I am one of those assets.

I smooth Zhang Jing's hair from her face, my touch as light as a feather. She shifts slightly but continues sleeping peacefully, her cheek on her pillow and hand underneath it, just as she has slept since childhood. I look around the room. Along with a bowl of water on a table, there are some scraps of paper and a pot of ink resting on a shelf. I go to it, and in the moonlight I write a brief note: *I will be back with help. Trust me.*

I take the scrap of paper and tuck it under Zhang Jing's pillow, near her hand. She will feel it when she awakens and hopefully have faith in what I'm doing. I have no doubt my disappearance will eventually be linked to the theft of the food, and I hate the thought of her believing the worst of me—especially after she told me how my position brings prestige to our family. Knowing I'm risking throwing that all away, I place a gentle kiss on her forehead.

I give my sister one last fond look and make my way out of her room. The patrolling servant is back on his rounds, but I dodge him, winding through the corridors until I reach a side door. Although I don't expect there to be many people out this time of night, this door is less exposed than the main one, allowing a more discreet exit. Keeping to the shadows, I follow paths and trails until I reach the spot on the outskirts of our village that Li Wei and I had both agreed on: the place where our ancestors used to mount climbs from, farther up the trail from where the supply line is. And it is where I find Li Wei waiting.

You're late, he signs to me in the moonlight. *I thought maybe you'd changed your mind. Or feared the restless spirits that come out at night.*

I stopped believing in them when I stopped believing in pixius, I respond haughtily. *I had to say goodbye to Zhang Jing.*

Shock fills his face. *You told her?*

No, no. I just checked on her—while she was asleep. No one knows. I pat my knapsack. *And I found food, just as I promised. Did you get the things you need?*

He gestures to a pile of equipment near his feet. Some of it, like the ropes, look like gear I'd find among the miners. Other items—metal rings, spikes, and hammer-like tools—are beyond me.

Some of this is from the mines, he confirms. *The rest is from the magistrate's supply shed. It has been stored there for centuries, but I was able to find pieces still in good shape.* His face darkens. *I had to steal all of it.*

I know, I tell him. *I had to steal the food too.*

He shakes off his dismay and forces a smile. *None of that will matter when we return with new supplies, right?*

Right, I say, trying to smile back. I don't bother pointing out what he already knows: that there's no guarantee we'll make it back, let alone with any bounty. *Do you know how to use this stuff?*

Much of it works like what we've used in the mines, he tells me. *I've read up on what I don't know and made some inquiries in the past.* He glances up at the sky, where the full moon is descending in the west, still bright. In the east, however, I see a faint purpling of the sky as the sun readies itself for the day. *Ready to go?*

Ready as I'll ever be, I reply.

He gives me a quick primer on the basics of the equipment and then shocks me when he uses some of the rope to tie us together. He grins when he sees my astonishment.

Nervous about being so close to me? he asks, giving the rope a slight tug.

I cross my arms, refusing to be baited by that dangerous question—even if there is truth to it. But whatever my feelings for him, I must focus on the larger picture: Zhang Jing and our village's future.

Don't get any ideas, I warn.

A small smile tugs at his lips. *And what kind of ideas would those be, apprentice?*

You know what kind of ideas. Just because we're going on this journey, it doesn't mean anything has changed. I meant what I said two years ago: My life has taken a different course. We can't be together. I cross my arms imperiously, hoping I am convincing and that I'm not letting on that his nearness makes my pulse quicken.

He scrutinizes me, trying to determine if I'm telling the truth. *Very well,* he says. *If that's the way you feel, far be it from me to interfere.* He gives the rope around my waist a test tug. *There. It's an older rope, but it should hold. I can't risk you slipping and falling,* he explains. *This way, I can help you.*

Or go down with me, I point out.

Then don't fall, he advises.

The ropes and rings become a confusing web to me, but Li Wei understands them and how they'll work to keep us safe. He secures our climbing ropes at the top of the cliff and hands me a pair of miner's gloves. Although we are loosely tied to each other, we each have our own rope to rappel down with, and I grip mine with a tightness born out of fear as much as necessity. Li Wei makes the first leap, launching himself over the edge. A pit opens up in my stomach as I watch him drop, but then the rope goes taut in his grip, and his feet land on the mountain's stony face, securing his position. Stable and safe, he glances up at me nonchalantly, as though what he just did was perfectly ordinary. Easy, even. I'm sure I look terrified, but there is no coddling from Li Wei. The challenge in his gaze spurs me on, and before I have a chance to second-guess myself, I leap over the edge as well.

I do exactly as he did, hopping only a short distance down, but that first leap feels a hundred miles long. The air rushes past me, and for a few terrifying seconds, I feel as though I'm floating, with nothing to save me. Then my feet strike the mountain's side with a teeth-rattling jolt. The rope above me holds true, and I squeeze it tightly, grateful for its security . . . yet fully aware that its security is a tenuous thing. One snap, one slip, and there would be nothing to save me from the drop.

Li Wei nods at me in approval, and with that, our journey begins.

I've climbed and played on ropes before, especially when I was younger. I have the strength to do it, but it's been a long time. My hands, more used to the delicate work of painting and drawing, are unaccustomed to this type of labor and soon begin to hurt from the exertion. I refuse to let Li Wei see my pain, however, and keep pace with him as we descend the rocky mountain face in the moonlight.

We've only been going a few minutes when I hear rocks crashing and realize holding the rope requires both hands. I can't signal to Li Wei that we've triggered our first avalanche. Panicked, I twist my hips in a way that tugs our adjoining rope. He looks over at me, and I jerk my head to my opposite side. Understanding, he quickly drops and swings off in the other direction, making room for me to take his spot just as a tumble of rocks falls near my original position.

When they are gone and all is quiet, I stay frozen where I am, feet planted on the cliff and hands clinging tightly to the rope.

My heart is racing frantically at the close call, and despair starts to hit me as I squeeze my eyes shut. The journey has barely started, and we've already faced a rockslide. How can we possibly make it to the bottom?

A tug at the joining rope makes me open my eyes. I look over at Li Wei, and his face is strong and calm as he meets my gaze. Although he can't speak, the conviction in his expression tells me what he would say: *We can do this. I need you. You are still that brave girl who climbed the shed.*

I take a deep breath and try to force calm. He does need me. Zhang Jing needs me too. After several more tense seconds, I give a short nod to let him know I'm ready to keep going. He smiles encouragingly—one of those rare, wonderful smiles that transforms his whole face—and we continue with our descent.

It is slow, painstaking work. We have to be careful of every move we make, and more rocks follow those initial ones. Some are avoidable. In some cases, we find it's best just to freeze and cling to the side, waiting for the rocks to pass. We work out a system of tugs with our adjoining ropes and head gestures to help us determine what to do.

When we take our first true break, I'm unsure how much time has passed. But the moon has gone, and sunrise is now lighting our way. We come across a relatively flat piece of rock jutting out and leading to a shallow cave. Li Wei tests the rock ledge and deems it safe for us to sit on and rest as he gathers up excess line and prepares for the remainder of the climb. I exhale and stretch my legs, surprised at how tense my muscles have grown.

The top of the mountain, where we started, looks impossibly far away. Glancing down, though, the bottom is farther still, hidden in mist. For a moment, I am dizzy as I contemplate my position here, suspended between heaven and earth. Li Wei's hands move in my periphery.

Don't do that, he says.

Do what?

He gestures around. *That. Looking up and down. It will overwhelm you.*

You talk like a seasoned climber, I tease. *Like you do this all the time.*

I've done similar things in the mines—nothing on this scale. After a moment, he gives me a grudging smile. *You're doing well.*

Better than you expected? I ask.

He looks me over, his gaze lingering a bit longer than it needs to. *No. I knew you could do it.*

I nod in acknowledgment and glance around, trying to do as he says and not focus on the top or bottom of the climb. Here, on this small perch, I'm struck by how still everything is. Back in the village during the day, there was always an abundance of sound. Here, there is very little, and I enjoy the small respite. Is this silence? No, I decide, thinking back to the writings I read. Silence is no sound—the way I lived before. This is merely quiet, because some noises still come through to me. The sound of my feet shifting on the rock. Faint wind blowing past us.

What is it like? Li Wei asks, his face solemn once more. *Being able to hear?*

I shake my head. *It's too hard to explain.*

Why? he asks.

Even describing it . . . well, it uses words you wouldn't understand. It's like another language.

Then use words I do know, he suggests.

I think long and hard before answering. *Imagine if everything you saw, your entire life, was always a shade of gray. Then one day you blink, and suddenly you see the world as it is with all its colors. Blue, red, yellow. How would you react? How would you handle literally not having the words to describe what you're experiencing?*

Some things don't need words, he says after a moment, and I wonder if he's still talking about sound.

Everything needs a word, I insist. *We need to know how to describe the world. Otherwise we'd fall into ignorance.*

Spoken like someone who spends her days organizing and cataloging everything. Sometimes it's enough to just feel. You don't have to label and articulate all that's around you.

I roll my eyes. *Spoken like a barbarian.*

He laughs at that, and there's a warmth in it that makes me smile. We split one of the lunch packs and then begin climbing down once more. There are a few more close calls as small stones skitter down the cliff. I'm able to warn him with tugs of the rope, but our system is cumbersome and delayed. A couple of times, when he clears his throat or coughs, my attention is immediately drawn to him by those sounds. It gives me new appreciation for how our ancestors used to communicate with their mouths:

speech. The concept was always foreign to me when I read about it, but now I see how much simpler it would be if there was a sound I could make to warn Li Wei of the next avalanche.

Morning gives way to noon, and we see a huge plateau jutting out of the mountain, promising another break. Beyond it, I can actually make out the ground at the mountain's base. Hope surges in me that we might pull this off after all. Then I hear the sound signaling another avalanche. I look up, and it is not a small scattering of stones like we've encountered before. Large boulders are tumbling down toward us. They create vibrations in the cliff face that even Li Wei can sense, though he doesn't immediately ascertain the direction.

I have no time to tug and point. Clinging to my rope, I push off with my feet and swing toward him, knocking him off the cliff face. He loses his footing but keeps hold of the rope. For a terrifying moment, we are both swinging in the air, with only our grip on the ropes to keep us from falling. A cascade of rocks begins tumbling beside us, far too close. The sound created is soft at first, almost like an exhalation of breath, but soon grows into a roar as the stones increase in number. One of them strikes my head, and I wince. The instinct to shield myself with my hands is overwhelming, but letting go means certain death. Both of us scramble for footholds, trying to move out of the way of the growing rock fall.

Li Wei swings hard and almost manages to land on another small outcropping, but the added weight of being tied to me throws him off. A second attempt also fails. He tries yet again, harder this time, and is at last able to land on the edge. With his footing secure, he scuttles back and tugs me toward him with the adjoining rope. My feet make contact with the ledge, and he pulls me forward into his arms, leaving us cowering against the mountain as a full-on avalanche of boulders cascades beside us. The falling rocks keep triggering more avalanches, and it is spectacular and terrifying to watch.

When it finally ends, we are both shaking, shocked by how close we came to being caught in the full force of it. I let him hold me a few moments longer before reluctantly breaking the embrace. He gestures to my cheek.

You're bleeding, he says.

I vaguely recall the rock that hit me and am now aware of a stinging sensation. I lightly touch the side of my face with my fingertips and see blood when I remove them. I dab again and see less blood. *It's nothing*, I say. *It's already stopping*.

Here, let me clean it. He pulls his sleeve over his hand and reaches for me. I shrink back.

What are you doing? I ask.

Wiping up the blood, he says.

Not with that filthy shirt! I retort. *And I told you, I'm fine. No need to stain your shirt even more.*

I'm a barbarian, remember? His grin fades as concern returns to his features. *Perhaps we should rest longer.*

For me? I ask indignantly. I get to my feet and hope I'm not still shaking. *There's nothing wrong with me. I'm not some delicate flower. I'm ready to go now.*

Fei, it's okay if we take a break, he says. *There's no need to let your pride get the best of you. Again.*

Again? I ask, unable to ignore the barb. I gesture imperiously to the rope. *Just fix it so that we can keep going.*

He gives me a mock bow. *Yes, apprentice.*

Tension fills the air between us as he readjusts our line to set us on a new trajectory down. My hands hurt badly, even with the gloves, but fear and pride compel me to keep my grip through the discomfort. We continue rappelling down, and though we are still cautious, both of us move a little more quickly. That last avalanche was too close a call, and we're eager to make it to the plateau I'd noticed earlier and finally get a real rest. Closer and closer it gets, and despite Li Wei's warnings, I find myself sneaking peeks down. I don't know what I was expecting in the lands near the mountain's bottom, but the terrain below us looks similar to what we left behind on the mountain's top, filled with green, dense forest. The only difference is that from this height, it is all in miniature, almost as though we're looking down at an incredibly lifelike map.

When we are level with some of the trees growing on the plateau, I hear another boulder above us—in Li Wei's direction. I tug the joining rope and nod. He scurries to get out of the way, but in his haste, his grip on the rope slips.

He loses his foothold, and all I can do is gasp as he starts to fall. The rope around me snaps tight, pulled taut around my torso by his added weight, cutting off my ability to get air. I jerk forward, struggling to keep my grip firmly on the rope.

Gravity wants to take me down with him, and the rope begins to slip through my fingers.

I fight for breath, watching the terror on Li Wei's face as he is suspended in the air, hanging only by the rope connecting him to me. Panicked, he kicks wildly, reaching out with his hands and feet to make contact with something—anything. He is too far from his original rope or the cliff face to truly touch them, and his frantic flailing only makes it more difficult for me to cling to my rope. It's slipping through my hands, bit by bit. Soon I will be at its end, and there will be nothing to stop us both from falling to our deaths.

Gritting my teeth, I squeeze my fingers tightly around the rope, refusing to give another inch. More wild maneuvering from Li Wei throws me off balance, causing me to lose my foothold on the cliff. I cling to the rope for dear life now, but I can see it is a losing battle. Li Wei's weight is too great, his pull on the adjoining line too strong. Pain sears my stomach as the rope digs into me, stretched as taut as it can possibly get. My hands slip again down the rope, and I struggle to draw breath until—

—in seconds, it's all gone.

The pressure is gone. There is no more pull, no impossible weight for me to fight against. I can breathe again.

Because the rope has snapped, and Li Wei is falling.

There is nothing to save him, and I can only watch in horror as he falls the rest of the way down, his eyes wide with terror. I hear my second human scream in as many days. This time, it's my own.

CHAPTER 7

THE SCREAM DIES FROM MY LIPS, and for a heartbeat, I hang there, stunned at what has just happened. I take in the awful sight of Li Wei's body lying inert on the plateau below. A million things go through my mind, all that I should have said to him . . . and never did. A moment later, I spur myself to action. Moving quickly—maybe too quickly—I rappel the rest of the way down, knowing I'm being reckless but too anxious to get to his side. A few rocks skitter after me but nothing else significant. When I hit the ground, I run over to his side, afraid of what I will find.

He can't be dead, he can't be dead, I keep telling myself.
He can't be.

The first thing I see is that he is breathing, and I nearly collapse in relief. I gently tilt his face toward mine, and his eyes flutter open. He looks a bit addled, but his pupils are normal size, and it's clear he recognizes me. My heart nearly bursts. He starts to lift his hands to speak, but I shake my head.

Don't, I sign to him. *We need to assess the extent of your injuries.*

Carefully, I help him sit up. I make him test the functionality of each limb, and amazingly, nothing appears to be broken. There is some tenderness in the foot he landed on, but he's still able to put weight on it. Rather than falling straight down, he slid a fair amount of the way on the rocky wall. It saved him from the brunt of the impact but tore up his exposed skin and his clothes. If he'd come down at a different angle or if we'd been just a little higher in elevation, I know this story wouldn't have had a happy ending. As it is, it's clear Li Wei is still in a lot of pain, though, as usual, he's trying to appear tough.

An outcropping of rock provides a protective roof, and I decide this area will be our camp. Although the afternoon skies are clear, there's a psychological safety to being under some cover—especially if any more rocks come falling. I leave Li Wei resting there and venture out into some of the scraggly trees nearby in search of wood, so that we can make a fire when night comes. I have to break a few larger limbs in half, but for the most part, there is an ample supply of fallen branches. When I have an armful of firewood, I decide to search for a water source to refill our canteens.

I haven't gone very far when I hear the snapping of a branch behind me. I spin around in alarm, relaxing when I see Li Wei. Surprised, he asks, *How did you know I was here?*

I heard you, I tell him, briefly setting my firewood down. *What are you doing here? You're supposed to be resting.*

I'm no delicate flower, he teases. I raise an eyebrow at that, and he explains, more seriously, *I was worried. You were gone awhile.*

I wanted to find some water.

Our supply will last a little longer, he says. *Wait until I can come look with you.*

I nearly snap back that he's coddling me again, but after his near-death experience, I find it difficult to chastise him. It's still hard for me to shake the pall cast by those terrifying moments, when I saw his body lying motionless on the rocks below. Looking him over now, I see that his concern isn't because he thinks I'm incapable but simply because he cares about me. That realization stirs up the already conflicting emotions within me, and I avert my eyes.

Okay, I say. *Let's go back to camp.*

Back by the shelter of the cliff, we each eat one of the lunch packs and try not to think about how little food there is left. The terrain on this plateau seems as inhospitable to growing food as our own village, so it's unlikely we're going to find anything in the wild. We'll just have to wait until we get to the bottom of the mountain. Surely the township must have a reliable way of sustaining its food supply.

This is good, Li Wei says, gesturing to the food in front of him. *Almost worth going on this crazy climb and getting myself killed.*

You shouldn't joke about that, I say. But it's hard not to smile. *You know . . . that's why I climbed the shed that day. For food.*

He tilts his head curiously. *What do you mean?*

His gaze holds mine, and I try not to blush as I explain. *There was this story going around about how there was a stash of food being hidden on the roof. I think it was just something the older kids made up to tease us, but I believed it. Zhang Jing was sick at the time, and I thought she'd feel better if she had more to eat. So I climbed up to see if the story was true.*

And you found out that the only true thing was that the shed really was in bad shape, he finishes. I nod, expecting him to laugh at me. But he only asks, *Why didn't you ever tell me this before? I always thought you did it for the thrill of it.*

I know, I say. *And I've always known. . . . I've always known you thought I was brave because of it, even back then. I guess I liked you thinking of me that way. I was afraid of you knowing the truth.*

That you did it to help your sister? You don't think that's brave too?

It doesn't sound as exciting, I say. *Certainly not when you're six.*

You care about her a lot, he remarks.

I lift my head so I can squarely meet his eyes. *You know I do.*

That's why you're here. And why you joined the artists—to give her a better life.

It's more than that, I tell him. *Painting is part of me. It's more than a job. It gives me meaning and makes me feel complete.*

I can see he doesn't understand, and I don't blame him. Mining is the only vocation he's ever had available to him, and there's no love in it. As he said before, it's obligation. If he doesn't mine, others starve.

He stifles a yawn, and I urge him to sleep while I keep watch. He doesn't argue and stretches out on his side of the fire, soon falling asleep with ease. I watch him for a long time, studying the lines of his face and noting how strands of dark hair have come loose from their bindings. They rest gently on his cheek, and I have an overwhelming desire to brush them aside.

No good can come of that, so I try to distract myself by taking in the other sights and sounds around me. The observer in me is still doing her job, still wanting to make note of every detail so that I can paint them into the record. Already I can imagine how I'd depict what's happened to us so far, which scenes I'd draw and how I'd annotate with calligraphy. My fingers itch for paint and brush, but there's nothing but rock and barren trees. Looking down at my hands—bloodied and scraped from the rope, even with gloves on—I wonder if I'd be able to do much even if I had the right tools.

When Li Wei wakes, he claims to be feeling better, but we both agree to spend the night here. He says it'll be better for us to go when the light returns, but I'm still worried about his foot and ankle. The climb is treacherous enough without injury. He assures me he'll be fine and encourages me to sleep while he takes a turn at keeping watch.

I'm exhausted but have difficulties falling asleep. I didn't think much about our situation when he was sleeping, but now I'm overwhelmed with the realization of how taboo it is for us to be out here alone together. It has nothing to do with rank either, though that simply increases the forbidden nature of it all. Elder Lian has lectured us many times on proper behavior between boys and girls, darkly warning of how "dangerous feelings" can arise. I'm not that worried about any feelings arising, though. They're already here, no matter how I try to suppress them.

At last, I shift so that my back is to him, giving me a faint sense of privacy. Despite the uncomfortable ground, I finally fall asleep. Strange dreams fill my sleep, more puzzling than frightening. I keep hearing that noise that startled me so much that first night, when hearing returned to me, the sound I recognize now as many voices crying out. It's paired with that sense of someone trying to reach me, but I'm still unable to determine who or why.

When I wake, the sun is setting. Li Wei has started a fire, and to my surprise, I see he has a knife out and is carving a piece of wood. A memory of the chrysanthemums he made for me returns, and I scoot over to watch him work. Beside him is a pile of small, round discs. I pick one up and smile when I see the character for *soldier* carved on it.

You're making a xiangqi *set?* Sifting through the discs, I recognize other pieces from the game: general, advisor, and elephant.

Li Wei shrugs and sets his work down. *I needed something to do. Maybe you can draw us a board, apprentice.*

I set the pieces down and begin smoothing out the dirt in a flat area near the fire. I use a narrow, pointed branch as a stylus, and even with my injured hands, I find I can still draw a steady line. There is comfort in this kind of work, something familiar in an otherwise strange place. I draw all the lines with as much diligence as I would in painting the daily record. When I finish, I discover Li Wei watching me work. He seems embarrassed when I notice.

You really are good at that, he says. It is almost grudging.

Drawing in the dirt?

You know what I mean. Those lines are perfect. I can't draw anything that straight.

I couldn't do that, I say, nodding to the neat rows of game pieces he's crafted. *You've improved over the years.*

It's just a hobby, he says modestly. His face darkens a little. *Something my father and I used to do to pass the time when we weren't working.*

You have a lot of skill, I say honestly. *You should do something with it. . . .*

I trail off, unable to finish the thought. There is no real need for artistic woodworking in our village. All construction is simply done with brute labor. The focus is on practicality, not aesthetics. My skills with brush and pen are coveted by the elders, but the record has no need for a carver. The sculptures that have survived in our village come from a different era. I think back to what I told Li Wei earlier, about how painting gives me meaning. I wonder if he'd feel the same way if he could make woodworking his vocation.

I'm of more use to our village hacking metals from the earth than coaxing beautiful things from wood, he says, guessing my thoughts.

I know, I reply. *And it's a shame.*

A lull falls between us, marked only by the shifting of wood in the fire. I've made and watched countless fires burn throughout my life but never had any idea of the sounds they made. They're fascinating, and I long to know the words to describe them. Li Wei gestures at the chess pieces. *Shall we play before all the light is gone?*

We don't have a lot of time for recreation at the Peacock Court, just occasional holidays. Xiangqi boards are rare. Like carvings and sculpture, no one has the time or means to make them anymore. Li Wei beats me in our first game, and I insist upon a second—which I also lose.

I sign to my defeated army in exasperation: *What are you doing to me? You lost us the game!*

A sound draws my attention, and I look up sharply to see that Li Wei is laughing. Just as his cry of mourning conveyed grief so perfectly, his laughter is full of a joy that soon makes me start laughing too.

My little general, he says. Although he is teasing, there is something warm in his eyes that suddenly makes me acutely aware of how close we've drawn to each other. It was out of necessity, needing to be near the light as we played, but our arms practically touch as we lean over the board. Our fingertips are only a few inches away from each other. A rush of heat goes through me, and it has nothing to do with the fire.

We should get some more rest, I say, pulling away. *I'll take the first watch.*

I'm pretty sure I can see a flush in his cheeks. He nods in agreement and soon curls up and sleeps. Once again, I have to fight the urge to watch him and find other things to distract myself. We switch halfway through the night, and I fall asleep easily, with no dreams this time.

When morning comes, I wake to find Li Wei gone. Panic hits me, and then I hear footfalls and see him approach through the lingering fog. *Sorry*, he says, seeing my expression. *I just wanted to look around. You won't believe what I found farther around the mountain.*

What? I ask.

A mine entrance—an old one. It doesn't look like it's been used in a while.

There must have been people here then, I say, searching around as though I expect them too to appear through the mist.

At some point, he agrees. *I didn't go in, but the mine doesn't look nearly as big as ours. Do you want to look around before we go?*

I hesitate. We're down to one meal pack, and lingering puts us farther away from getting to more food. And yet the mystery of the mine is too alluring. Who would have worked in it? Certainly no one from our village. Did workers come up from the township? Or is there some settlement here on this forested plateau?

We need more water as well, so we agree to make finding it part of our exploration. We split the last meal, and as that food disappears, I find myself thinking of the village we left behind. A full day has gone by now, and our absence will have long been discovered. What will people think of us? What will Zhang Jing think? Will my note be enough to maintain her faith in me?

A sound I've learned to recognize by now soon alerts me to a water source. I steer Li Wei toward it, and we find a small trickling tributary that runs through the plateau. He looks impressed, and I can't help but feel a little pride as I fill our canteens.

I wouldn't have found that nearly so quickly, he admits.

I hand him his canteen and tuck my own away. *I guess I'm of some use after all.*

He smiles at that. *General, you've long since proved your use.*

Don't call me— My hands drop as my eye catches something in the trees beyond him. Seeing my change of expression, he turns, searching for what I noticed. Soon he sees it too: the large, looming shape of a building on the other side of the trees. Turning back to me, he meets my eyes, and I give a quick nod of agreement. We head in that direction . . .

. . . and find not one but many buildings.

We have stumbled onto a small village—much smaller than our own but clearly meant to have some permanency. The implications of this are staggering, and we both stare around wide-eyed. No one in our village has had any contact with the outside world, short of the line keeper's notes. Entering this settlement is akin to having fallen into one of the magical lands in the old stories.

No one's been here for a while, Li Wei says, pointing at some of the disrepair on the buildings. I see instantly what he's referring to. The wood is worn, even rotted in some places, and the elements have long won out. We split up and walk around, and I feel a mix of both excitement and apprehension. Once again, I find myself thinking in terms of the record, how I would report on this amazing discovery. For the most part, the little houses are built similarly to ours, but I spy minute architectural differences that fascinate me. I wish I'd brought ink and paper for notes. I'll have to rely on my own memory to share this when I get back home.

I find a house with a door hanging ajar, having rotted out of its holdings. I push it all the way open and again hear that sound doors make that I have no word for.

Inside, the house reminds me of the modest home Zhang Jing and I grew up in. It is built with three bays, and a deteriorating screen blocks the rest of the house from my view. There is a large clay stove that has been cold for some time and looks as though its most recent use was by nesting birds. A small shrine marks where the household gods sat with burned-out clumps of candle wax.

I pick up a statue nestled in the shrine. It's mostly made of ordinary clay, but the detail in the carving is exceptional. It is a pixiu, its leonine head held proudly up as its mouth opens in a roar. Rubbing off some of the dirt on it, I see that the horns and wings are tipped with gold. Li Wei will want to see this, if only to admire the craftsmanship. Taking it feels a little like stealing, but it is clear no one has been here for a while and the statue has been abandoned.

Holding it in one hand, I walk over to the screen that separates this living space from the sleeping area. The screen is worn and rotting, with no design or ornamentation. When I touch it to move it away, part of the screen crumbles, and the whole thing collapses, kicking up dust. I step back, coughing and covering my face. When the dust finally settles again, I blink a few times and at last get a glimpse beyond the screen—

—and find myself face-to-face with a family of human skeletons grinning at me with sightless faces.

CHAPTER 8

A SCREAM CATCHES IN MY THROAT, and I back up as quickly as I can. The little pixiu statue slips from my fingers and hits the floor with a thud. I barely notice. I want nothing to do with this place. I need to get out.

I run through the living area and out the door—and straight into Li Wei. For a moment, I'm so panicked that I don't even realize it's him. I start to struggle against him and finally still when a glimmer of familiarity—the feel of his strong arms around me—is able to penetrate my fear. For a moment, I allow myself to relax in his embrace and then step back, still trembling.

Are you okay? he demands. *What's wrong?*

I have no words. I simply shake my head and point at the door. Li Wei gives me a once-over and proceeds toward the house to investigate. By the time he returns, I have calmed down a little. I'm embarrassed to show such weakness, but the memory of those grinning skulls is haunting. Li Wei wears a tight expression, and I see he's carrying the statue I dropped.

What are you doing? I ask. *We shouldn't take anything. This place is cursed.*

Li Wei tucks the little pixiu into his pocket. *That house, perhaps, but not this statue. The carving is incredible. I've heard about statues like these. People used to keep them in their homes for prosperity and good fortune.*

It didn't help these people, I point out.

Li Wei's face turns grimmer. *I don't know what happened in there, but I think it has little to do with the supernatural and more to do with man. Let's check out the rest of these buildings and figure it out.*

Maybe he's right. This village is too similar to our own. We have to find out what happened here to ensure that our village doesn't share this one's fate. *How do you suggest we search?* I ask.

Wait here, he says. He hurries off into the largest building in the settlement, one that looks less like a house and more like some sort of administrative or educational facility. It's eerie being left alone in this ghostly village, but I refuse to let superstition get the best of me. When Li Wei comes back out, there is excitement on his face.

It's just as I was hoping. There are records in there, almost like what we keep. It looks like this was where their elders resided. Can you get started going through those writings? They might be able to tell us what happened here, and you're better at understanding that sort of thing than I am.

What are you going to do? I ask.

He gestures around. *Continue searching the rest of the*

houses. I think those records will have most of our answers, but we need to rule everything out.

Be careful, I say.

He nods, heading off toward one of the houses.

I watch him a few moments and then turn toward the administrative building. It's smaller than the art school at home or our magistrate's center, but then, this village is also much smaller. The building is in a similar state as the house I was just in, smelling of dust and decay. But thankfully there are no skeletons or other signs of the dead to keep me company.

The room Li Wei referred to is similar to our library at the Peacock Court, and it has kept out the worst of the moisture and other damaging elements. Wall racks hold a neat collection of scrolls, and the rest of the room is dedicated to storing what looks like this village's equivalent of daily records. They're smaller than ours and not nearly as elaborate as the murals we create, nor do they show the artistic flair and precision that we are encouraged to put into our work. But they are factual and orderly and contain the information I need to unravel what has happened in this village. I make myself comfortable and begin reading scrolls by the dusty light filtering in from a high window.

What I discover is shocking. Numbing, even. I lose track of time and am only startled out of my study when I hear Li Wei's steps in the adjacent hall. *Did you find anything?* I ask when he enters. I manage to appear calm, but inside, I'm reeling.

More than I wanted, he tells me. *Most of the homes are empty, but others have bones as well. I don't know what killed them.*

I do, I say, setting down one of the records. *Starvation and sickness.* My attempts at control begin to falter. My hands are shaking, and I clasp them in my lap. It's not fear that has unsettled me so much as shock.

Do you want to go outside to talk? Li Wei asks. *It's getting warmer.*

I nod. I feel chilled in this place full of memories and ghosts. I need to be back out in the sun, back among living and growing things. We travel toward last night's camp, but just as we are at the edge of the village, we encounter another gruesome sight: skeletons shackled to a stone block. My stomach turns at the thought of the terrible fate they must have endured there. Characters etched into the stone condemn them for their crime: *food thieves.*

With a shudder, I avert my gaze and see Li Wei scowling. I'm not surprised he's upset, considering the way he protected the thief in our village. *This is savage*, he states. *At least our people have never taken punishment to such an extreme.*

They might, I say, thinking of what I learned. *If our village ever has to face what this one did.*

What do you mean? he asks.

We reach our camp, now enjoying the full force of morning sunlight. It helps chase away the gloom of what I uncovered in the library—but only a little. Li Wei looks at me expectantly once we are there.

They were like us, I tell him finally. *Exactly like us. A mining town. They lost their hearing and became trapped up here, with no easy way to climb down, but they established a deal with the township. They had their own line and sent metals down the mountain in exchange for food. And just like us, they began to go blind.*

Those similarities are still too shocking, too unbelievable, and that's what makes it hard to keep going. This village's history was so much like our own: Had I just taken a walk in my own future? Is this what's in store for us in ten years? Five years? One year? Fear makes me lose track of my story—not for myself, but for those we left behind. What fate is waiting for Zhang Jing? For the masters and other students?

What happened? How did they die? Li Wei asks, his expression urgent. *Fei, you said starvation?*

I swallow and try to regain my composure. *With blindness, their mining output depleted, and just like with us, the township started limiting their food. They weren't exactly like us—they stopped feeding their beggars altogether. The blindness also resulted in more accidents, so some died that way too. Near the end, their water supply got contaminated. The record keepers believed some of the bodies weren't disposed of properly and fouled the water. People grew sick and died before they discovered the problem. It was a couple of years ago, so it eventually cleared,* I add, seeing him shoot a concerned look at our canteens. *By then, there was hardly anyone left. The township stopped food shipments completely, and chaos broke out. Those that didn't die of starvation attempted to climb down, but it's unknown how many made it. The elevation is lower, but from what I've* read, the stone on the cliffs below is softer—more prone to avalanches, less likely to hold ropes and body weight. Some may have escaped. Some didn't. Some may have thrown themselves over purposefully.

I sink to the ground, unable to shake the thought of this happening to our village. Li Wei paces in front of me, his expression dark. He bravely investigated the ghost village, with all its horrors, but now I can tell his resolve is wavering. Or maybe he's just losing hope.

Is this what it comes to then? he asks. *Is this what our village can expect? Food disappearing altogether? Despair and hopelessness?*

We can't know that, I say. *We can't know anything until we speak to the line keeper. And our village isn't like theirs . . . not yet.*

Isn't it? he asks angrily. *It's already happening! The blindness has started. The metals have decreased. The food has decreased. Just the other day, the township said they were sending less as "punishment." How much longer until they stop the food? How long until our own people turn on each other in desperation? Is this what my father died for? How many other villages has the township done this to?*

I don't know. We must talk to the line keeper.

We need to do something, he snaps. *But I don't know if talking is enough.*

Li Wei is understandably worked up, and I know it's from more than just the gruesome discoveries in this village. The pain of his father's death is still fresh, making everything that much worse . . . and desperate.

He sighs. *Perhaps there was some misunderstanding with this village. Perhaps they asked for too much.*

Perhaps, I agree.

I can tell we're both trying to put on good faces for each other. In reality, I know we are both filled with doubts. We want to believe the best, that the line keeper can help us, but we've seen and suffered too much. And if the line keeper can't help, then what? It's that uncertainty that casts the real pall over us.

I summon an image of Zhang Jing and muster my courage as I follow Li Wei to a spot he deems suitable for continuing our descent down the cliffs. The warnings of the writings stick with us, and he is extra cautious as he begins planting the ropes into the rock face. Some of the stone is softer in this area, and he won't let us descend until he's certain each stake and rope will hold.

Even though we have less distance to cover than we did the previous day, it's still a long way down to the base of the mountain. Every inch we travel is filled with fear that the rock is going to crumble and loosen our stakes, sending us plummeting. More avalanches tumble after us, and again, my hearing only just saves us on more than one occasion. Sometimes I'm not quick enough, and we both earn new bruises and cuts to go with yesterday's injuries. Adding to all this is the knowledge that we are out of food. Hunger gnaws at the edges of my stomach.

And yet a strange exhilaration is filling me as we get lower and lower and see the ground at the base of the mountain. A lush valley filled with trees spreads out before us, drawing nearer, and beyond it I can see a haze of green land that looks as though it has no trees at all. Is it possible that's farmland? The library has books about cultivation and growing, but after the avalanches cut off the passes to our village's fertile lands, farming has become as fantastic a concept as flying—or hearing. Dreams of what may be waiting for us spur me on in the last stretch of our climb.

Then, incredibly, we set foot on the ground. I look up and am stunned to see my own mountain and its neighbors towering off into the sky. I can't even see the tops, as early evening clouds have moved in. It's an entirely different perspective from the view I've seen my whole life: peaks surrounding us and mist-covered depths below. I realize I'm standing in the place where my ancestors first migrated from, and that's a heady thought too.

Ready to see what this place has to offer? Li Wei asks.

He walks over to me to undo the ropes that have bound us together. His hands work deftly on the knots around my waist, and I hope it's not obvious that I'm holding my breath. Again I am amazed at how delicate his touch is for someone so large. When he finishes, his hands linger on my waist a fraction longer than they need to, and then he steps back.

Do you know where to go? I ask.

He puts a hand up to his eyes and scans around, taking in the sun's position over our mountain. We spent a lot of time in the empty village, and it will be evening soon. After a little scrutiny, he points to the north.

That is where our zip line descends. We've gotten a bit off course climbing down. We'll need to go over there to find its end—to find the line keeper.

I glance down at my dirty clothes and scraped hands, then make note of the late hour. *Maybe we should rest and clean up tonight,* I say. *We aren't in any condition to parlay with a man like him.*

Li Wei nods in agreement and adds, *It might very well be dark by the time we make it to his station. Let's explore a little and see if there's a good place for a camp.* He gestures around the expanse of woods. *Any preference?*

I shake my head. *You choose.*

He hesitates and then pulls out the little pixiu statue. He flips it once in the air and then skillfully catches it one-handed. The pixiu is facing east. Li Wei puts it back in his pack and says, *East it is.*

We walk off into the eastern copse of woods, and I am particularly vigilant. I've learned that humans make a lot of noise in overgrown forest like this, so I'm mindful of sounds that might indicate we aren't alone. We run into nothing and no one troublesome, however, and soon find a small glen where a bubbling brook pools slightly before running off through the woods. It's a good spot to rest and clean, though we are nervous about lighting a fire when we might be close to civilized lands. Fortunately it's warmer at this lower elevation, and we decide we can endure the night without a blaze.

You brought extra clothes to meet the line keeper? Li Wei

asks when he sees me getting out the other set I took from the school.

I shrug. *It just seemed practical. I wasn't thinking about him at the time, but now I'm glad. I want to represent our village honorably.*

I guess I'll represent ours the only way I can, he says, giving a wry glance to his own shirt. It's one of the dingy miners' garments, now torn and dappled with blood from the journey down. He left the white mourning shirt back in the village. *But then, I'm a barbarian, so it's to be expected.*

Perhaps we can clean it, I say, though I'm not so certain. *Let me see it.*

He takes off his shirt without hesitation, and I try not to let my jaw drop. We engaged in all sorts of adventures and games as children, but none of them involved his shirt coming off. It's impossible not to be aware of his strength and build even when he's dressed. Without the shirt, he's like one of the invincible heroes from the stories my father used to tell us. I take the shirt from him and try not to think about what Elder Lian would say about this situation I've inadvertently put myself in.

There's a boulder overgrown with moss nearby with a cuplike depression in its center. I pour water into it and do my best to soak and scrub the shirt, making a little progress—but not much. I'm fighting against dirt gathered from much more than just this journey. The linen is probably permanently dyed the color of the mines.

I didn't think artists had to do their own laundry, he remarks as I work.

108

I lift my wet hands to make a retort but stop when inspiration hits. I go back to my pack and find my belt pouch, which I brought with me from the Peacock Court. It still contains the packets of pigment I used to bring with me on my observations. After a few moments, I select the one that makes green paint and dump its entire contents into the water. Li Wei comes up beside me, muscled arms crossed over his broad chest and a curious expression on his face. I take a deep breath, more than aware of how close he's standing.

If we can't get the dirt out, maybe we can cover it up, I explain. He looks dubious, and I add, *Well, it can't be any worse. Once it's set in the dye for a while, we'll hang it to dry in that tree—*

My hands freeze midsentence as my eye catches something. I forget all about dyes. I forget about shirts. I even briefly forget about Li Wei as I take in this new discovery. Most of the trees around here are evergreen, but a few are deciduous and just barely showing the signs of late summer giving way to autumn. The tree I'd nodded at is one, a kind I've never seen before. While I don't know what type it is, I do know what I see in its highest branches. I point, and Li Wei follows the motion, his eyes widening when he sees what I spotted.

Fruit.

No fruit trees grow in our village. We've tried planting seeds and pits on the rare occasions we receive fruit in the shipments, but they just don't take. I've always known fruit comes from trees, but seeing it here in the flesh is unbelievable. Maybe Li

Wei's little statue is helping us after all. With food at such a premium where we come from, it's downright magical to find it growing on a tree in front of us, just waiting for us to pick and eat.

If we can reach it.

Li Wei strides over to the tree, then hesitates as he scrutinizes it more closely. *I can get up there*, he tells me. *But I'm not sure if the branches can support my weight—especially the high ones.*

They can support my weight, I say confidently.

He looks me over, glances at the tree, and then looks back at me. *It can probably support ten of you. We just need to get you up there.* He beckons me over and holds out his arms to lift me.

My indecision over his half-naked state and Elder Lian's disapproval is short-lived. I let go of my fears, and suddenly it is like we are children again, off on some adventure in the woods. I step forward, and he grips my waist, his strong hands careful as he raises me. I stretch my arms up but can't quite reach the lowest branch. Li Wei shifts, sliding his hands down so that he can hold me up by my legs and raise me higher. For a moment, I lose my balance as he adjusts, and I slip down. He catches me before I can fall, and for the space of a heartbeat, he holds me in his arms, our bodies pressed together.

As I meet his eyes, noting how very close we are, I think, *No, we are not children.*

He seems to be thinking the same thing, and a flush fills his cheeks. Quickly, he boosts me up again, holding me by my ankles so that I can reach higher. Resolutely, I push aside thoughts of the way his arms felt or how the lingering scent of sandalwood still clings to him. My fingers make contact with a limb, and from there I'm at last able to swing myself up and begin scaling the rest of the tree's branches. They're small and thin, but I find enough that can support me until I reach the fruit at the very top.

Up close, I see it's almost at the end of its season and starting to wither. I pluck one and sniff, grinning when I recognize persimmon. It's a rare treat in our village, occasionally given to us chopped up with other food. I glance down at Li Wei, who is watching me anxiously.

Be careful, he signs. *We didn't just survive a lethal mountain climb only to have you fall from a fruit tree.*

By way of answer, I toss the persimmon down to him and then begin picking all the rest. There are about a dozen total, and when I've thrown them all down, I climb back, feeling a bit of pride that I'm able to swing off the last branch and land without his help.

It must be true, he says wonderingly. He has gathered all the persimmons together. *We've been in the lowlands for barely an hour and have already stumbled across food. They must have an abundance.*

Someone came through and picked over the rest of the tree earlier in the season, I point out. *There may be people nearby.*

He nods, growing serious. *We'll be careful tonight and take watches again.*

We make a dinner of the persimmons, prudently saving some for tomorrow's journey—though I know we're both secretly hoping to find more food along the way. When we finish eating, I take his shirt out of the dye. It isn't as dark a green as I'd hoped, but it's definitely an improvement. I change into my clean robe and give him my travel-stained one to wear overnight. He can't even fully cinch it, leaving a comical gap over his chest, but at least it will provide warmth.

We are in good spirits as we settle down for the night, playing another round of xiangqi before the sun goes down. I still can't beat him, and he gently tries to coach me. *The moves you make seem good, but you aren't thinking far enough into the future. Plan at least two moves ahead of your opponent.*

I sigh. *You'd think I'd be better at that, with all the planning and organizing I normally have to do in my work.*

A small hesitation is the only sign of Li Wei's unease as he asks, *Is marrying Sheng part of your plans?*

The question catches me completely off-guard. Sheng has never come up in conversation between us before. Honestly, Sheng hasn't even crossed my mind on this trip.

It's part of the elders' plans, I respond carefully.

I see.

You know how it is, I add when he says nothing more. *You can't be surprised at that. Artists always marry other artists.*

Yes . . . but does it have to be him? asks Li Wei, a wry look on his face. *It seems like there are better choices among the apprentices. Sheng is so . . .*

Arrogant? Obnoxious? I supply.

Now Li Wei looks surprised. *That doesn't bother you?*

I don't think much about it, I say. *He is the best apprentice among the boys. I'm the best girl. The elders think it is a wise match.*

But that is all? Li Wei pushes. *It's the elders who want the match? Not you?*

It doesn't matter, I remind him. *I will still abide by their wishes.*

Li Wei is indignant. *You shouldn't marry because of someone else's wishes—because it's a wise match. You should marry someone who loves you. Someone who loves you passionately and would change the world for you.*

The world would have to change indeed for that to happen, I point out. *Do you see it changing anytime soon?*

He gestures around us. *It already has, Fei.*

Not enough, I say after several long, weighted moments. I know what he is hinting at and need to discourage it. *And even if it did, what was between us is in the past.*

So you say. But you've done an awful lot to keep me alive. He gestures at the green shirt. *And well dressed.*

Only so you won't embarrass me, I say loftily.

Whatever you say, apprentice, he replies. He prepares for bed with a glint in his eye, and I know he doesn't believe me.

CHAPTER 9

MORE STRANGE DREAMS PLAGUE my sleep that night. I again feel as though something or someone is calling out to me, this time through a mist. I run through it, trying to find my way, but only grow more and more disoriented. Soon I lose sense of whether someone is trying to reach out to me—or capture me. I begin running, full of panic and unable to see my destination.

I wake up with a start, flailing and terrified. To my astonishment, Li Wei is kneeling by my makeshift bed, and before I know what I'm doing, I throw myself into his arms. The phantoms in my dream fade, and his presence grounds me, calming me down. He strokes my hair gently, and it takes me a moment to slip from his embrace.

Sorry about that, I say.

I was worried, he tells me. *You were so restless, tossing and turning. Kicking. And this isn't the first time I've seen it while you're sleeping.*

It isn't? I ask, feeling mortified.

What are you dreaming of that upsets you so much? he asks.

Although he knows about my hearing, I haven't told him the full details of how it started or my recurring dreams of being called to. I nearly tell him now, but something fearful and personal holds me back. *It's nothing,* I say, getting to my feet. *Sorry for worrying you.*

He touches my arm briefly, turning me so I must face him. *Fei, I'm here for you. No matter what else has happened between us, I hope you know that. Don't be afraid to tell me anything.*

I nod but don't elaborate. How can I explain what I myself don't understand?

He doesn't press me for answers as we get ready for the day. We eat all but two persimmons and finish cleaning ourselves up. Li Wei's "new" shirt, now fully dry, has ended up as a kind of sickly green, but it's still better than before. I stand before him, helping smooth some of the fabric as I survey him with a critical eye.

I guess you'll do, I say, certainly not about to admit that even in rags, he is magnificent.

I feel confident in my own clean set of artist's clothes, though I wish I'd thought to pack a girl's set. It isn't completely unheard of for women to wear pants in our village, but the more I think about meeting a venerable figure like the line keeper, the more I wish I could put on a strong, formal appearance.

I remember when I first interviewed to help out with the artists, I tell Li Wei as we are breaking camp. *Before I officially became an apprentice. I had to undergo extensive tests and interviews. My mother scrubbed me until I hurt and traded three days' worth of her own rations for some new cloth to make me a robe.* "When you're meeting someone in power, someone with the ability to change your life for better or worse, it's important you show them you're worth it," she told me. I pause, feeling a bittersweet tug at the memory. My mother had died before learning the results. *I wonder what she would think of me now: going to see the line keeper, dressed like a boy.*

Li Wei grins, revealing a phantom dimple I've always liked. *You might be dressed like a boy, but no one's going to think you're one.*

Despite his teasing, there is a heated undercurrent in his words, and I can't help but think of our conversation last night: *You should marry someone who loves you. Someone who loves you passionately and would change the world for you.*

Has it changed? I wonder. And will I be able to change with it?

Those thoughts weigh on me, but as the sun rises higher, concern for Zhang Jing is more pressing. When I've finished pinning up my hair, I ask, *Is there anything else we need to do? Should we work out what we're going to say to the line keeper?*

We'll tell him our problems and ask for help, Li Wei says simply.

The answer doesn't surprise me. Li Wei is more straightforward about some things than I am. Coming from the Peacock Court, where we work with more structure and formalities, I'm hesitant just to rush forward without a concrete plan. *You're still assuming that what happened to the other village was part of some misunderstanding,* I say. *What if it wasn't? What if he knows and did nothing?*

Then we will have nothing to do with him, Li Wei says. *We'll take matters into our own hands.*

I don't know how I feel about that—or how we'd even go about it—but I decide not to argue the matter until we know for sure the line keeper was complicit. For now, we must go to him and find out what we can.

The usual morning mist covers the mountains, but the day is warming quickly, promising us that summer hasn't quite left yet. Li Wei has a better sense of how and where we descended the mountain, and he leads us back in the direction of the zip line. We walk through more forest, seeing little sign of human civilization but keeping our eyes open for more persimmons or other edibles. We also pass a few small woodland animals, causing us both to pause in contemplation. Game is as rare as agriculture up in our village, and sadly, animals usually don't last long due to the lack of sustenance in our rocky soil. We make no attempts at hunting today—not when we're so near our goal.

Soon enough we see the line coming down the mountain, suspended high over the trees and treacherous cliffs. Seeing it this way is just as surreal to me as this new bottom view of the mountains. For all my life, I've seen shipments of precious food come up that line from a mysterious location. Never did I dream we'd arrive there—or that it would be so underwhelming.

I'm not sure what I was expecting, but it certainly wasn't a small, nondescript shed at the base of the zip line. Sitting beside it, getting what shade he can from the overhanging of the thatched roof, is a middle-aged man with thinning hair. Two things about him strike me immediately. The first is his clothing. It's made of cotton, just like my artist's attire, but there's a freshness to it that's rarely seen in our village, where cloth is at such a premium that new clothing is a luxury. The other thing about him that takes me aback is that he's . . . plump. Outside of babies and drawings from old stories, I've never really seen anyone with extra fat, and I find myself gaping.

Li Wei and I stand there, neither of us sure what to do. The man is slumped against the shack's walls, looking as though he might be dozing. Li Wei shifts slightly, making his pack rattle, and the man's eyes open in in surprise. He can hear, I realize. He jumps to his feet, putting a rumpled cotton hat on his head, and looks between our faces expectantly. Then something truly remarkable happens: Sound comes from his lips.

It's not a scream, not laughter. It's like nothing I've yet encountered in my brief experience with hearing, a series of rapid sounds of different lengths and shapes. I realize, with a start, that I must be hearing human speech for the first time. Only, I have no idea what it means. And I certainly have no idea how to make it in return.

Hesitantly, I lift my hands. Our records say that the language we use with our hands is based on a preexisting one used by our migratory ancestors, specifically those who lost hearing through diseases or other known causes. I have no idea if that means others in the lowlands still use this method of communication or if only those without hearing do. Regardless, I bow and then sign a greeting: *Hello, most exalted line keeper. My name is Fei, and this is Li Wei. We have traveled a great distance from the village on the top of the mountain to speak with you about grave matters.*

The man gapes, and his eyes bug out. It's clear that he doesn't understand what I've said . . . but it seems to me he recognizes that I was speaking with my hands, as though perhaps he's encountered others who do as well.

What do we do? Li Wei asks me when no immediate answer comes.

I make a motion of painting or writing with my hand and then look at the man expectantly. The line keeper occasionally sends notes to communicate with us, so surely he must keep supplies here. I think my meaning is clear, but it takes a few more repeated attempts before he understands. When he does, he shakes his head, which surprises me. How was he communicating with our lead supplier if he has no writing tools on hand?

Stumped, we resort to much more basic attempts. Li Wei touches my shoulder and his own chest, then points up to the top of the mountain, tracing along the zip line. He then signals that we have descended the mountain, coming to this spot. I watch the line keeper closely as Li Wei maneuvers, and I feel myself growing increasingly puzzled. This isn't at all the kind of man I expected. At the very least, I imagined someone a little more intelligent. Maybe we can't communicate in the same language, but Li Wei's gesturing is pretty basic. The man finally seems to grasp where we've come from, and that realization almost frightens him. He shifts from foot to foot, looking troubled and conflicted.

At last, he gestures that we should sit down. He points at himself, then at the small dirt road winding away from the shed, and indicates he will return. When Li Wei takes a couple of steps forward to suggest we accompany him, the man frantically shakes his head and reiterates that we should sit and wait.

Li Wei and I exchange looks. *What else can we do?* I ask. *Maybe he's going to get someone who knows our language. Or at least some paper and ink.*

Our deliberation slams to a halt when the man hurriedly goes inside the shed and returns with a crate. He sets it on the ground and opens it, beckoning us over. We come closer, and I can't help but gasp. The crate is filled with food. I've never seen so much at once. Small buns, radishes, onions, rice, dried fruit. It is staggering, and I know my awe is reflected in Li Wei's face. The man gestures grandly that it is for us, his motions sweeping and generous. He urges us to sit down and eat while he is gone, and it is an offer we have a very difficult time refusing. The persimmons were a joyous discovery, but the one I ate this morning didn't make much of a filling breakfast.

The man watches a few moments more as we look over the box, and then he begins making his way down the road that leads from the mountain, occasionally glancing back. He seems uneasy. Nervous, even. There were more crates in the shed, and I wonder if he thinks we'll take advantage of his hospitality by helping ourselves to more than was offered. I wish I had the words to reassure him and tell him how grateful we are for what he's given, but my bows only go so far.

When he is nearly out of sight around a curve in the road, Li Wei pauses in feasting to ask me, *Do you think that in eating this, we're taking away from our village's rations?*

I freeze midbite. It's a terrible thought, and I glance down at the crate guiltily. We've each already eaten more than a normal ration in our village. After some thought, I shake my head. *That would be poor hospitality on his part. I don't think the line keeper is a man like that. He's given us this as welcome, as a way of showing generosity. And clearly he has more.* For the first time, I'm daring to hope this plan might truly result in change for my village—despite a worrisome voice in my head that keeps pointing out how things didn't work out for that other village.

Li Wei chews some dried fruit, his brow furrowed in thought. *I don't think that's the line keeper.*

I raise an eyebrow. *Who else would it be?*

I don't know, he admits. *A servant? But don't you think he behaved strangely? He's so . . . unsure of himself. The line keeper always speaks with authority and seems so decisive. This man jumps at his own shadow.*

I did think it was weird that he didn't have paper or writing tools around, I concede. *Especially with all the notes he writes us.*

Li Wei nods. *Exactly. Something doesn't feel right.* He gazes off down the road winding through the trees. Our host is long out of sight. *I'm not sure if we should wait for him to come back. This might be a trap.*

What kind of trap? I ask in surprise. *And to what end?*

I don't know that either. It's just my gut. But the gift of food aside, he didn't seem very welcoming. I'm afraid of whom he's going to bring back.

I point at the crate. *But this is what we came for. It's right in front of us. Food and the potential to feed our people! If we leave after he gifted us with this and told us to stay, what kind of message will that send? Where is the honor in that?*

Li Wei is torn, and the irony of our situation isn't lost on me. Until now, he has been the one so brazen and certain great things would come of this trip, while I worried. Now I am the one who wants to trust it will be fine, while he has doubts. He looks back down the road and makes a decision.

From what we know, that road probably leads to the township. If he's seeking help or supplies, it makes sense that's where he'd go. I say we go there ourselves and try to get a better sense of what's going on—of what these people are like. If I'm wrong, we can apologize later, claim we didn't understand his directions. If I am right, and there is something sinister going on . . . He doesn't elaborate, and he doesn't need to, not with the memory of the ghost village fresh in our minds. Instead, he simply shrugs and adds, *Well, that's what I think, at least. But I'm only the advisor.*

I give a faint smile at the joke of referring to himself as xiangqi's second most powerful piece, but there's little humor in anything else. Between the line keeper's strange behavior and what we read in the other village, it's clear that caution is vital. *Okay,* I say. *Let's go. And let's take some of this food with us. He did offer us the crate.*

We follow the road away from the mountain, and I try not to think about how much farther I'm getting from the only home I've ever known. The road widens as we walk down it, the dirt smooth and hard-packed from many feet and wagons. I have read enough to know that our village is small in comparison to other settlements, that there are people in the world who live in much larger and more populated settlements and cities. The reality of that has never hit me until now, when I try to imagine the number of people who would require such a large road. Soon the road changes from dirt to flat stones, and that too is another surprise. We have nothing even remotely comparable in our small village.

I eventually detect sounds that indicate others are ahead of us, and I put out an arm to stop Li Wei. I motion that we should get off the road and walk where we will have the cover of the trees to keep us from immediate discovery. He agrees. We both want to believe the best of these new people, but we are also too tense from our dangerous journey here to assume anything or anyone is safe. We make the rest of our journey in the woods, keeping the road in sight. When we reach the township at last, however, it isn't fear that dominates my emotions.

It is awe.

Just as I knew there were larger settlements outside of our village, I've always known the township is one such place. The road was my first clue, but now, face-to-face with this place, I am truly stunned by just how much it dwarfs my home—and I'm only seeing it from the outside.

The township is walled and gated. Men with weapons watch

from atop wooden towers embedded in the walls, and they interrogate those who come to the gate. There is a backup on the road right now, some sort of delay with a group near the front, leaving about fifty people waiting impatiently to get inside. Fifty people! That's more than all of the Peacock Court's residents. Something tells me this is only a small part of what we'll find inside. *If* we can get inside.

The holdup seems to be over a wagon at the front of the line, and the sight of it—or rather, what's pulling it—leaves both Li Wei and me transfixed: horses. We've read about them in books, of course, but neither of us has ever dreamed of seeing them in real life. Back when the mountain passes were open, our ancestors brought a few domesticated animals with them. Those eventually died off, and when avalanches shut off the overland routes, bringing animals up the zip line was simply impossible. I've never seen a creature so big, and I'm struck by the horses' beauty. That itch to paint overcomes me, a burning need to capture the blue-black sheen of the animals' coats and the way they toss their heads as they wait for their masters to finish.

I drag my gaze from the horses and try to assess what else is happening. I hear more of those sounds—speech sounds—like I heard the line keeper using, and I'm both perplexed and intrigued. The noises are nonsensical, but some intrinsic part of me understands that they are a means of communication, the sort of vocalization referred to in our ancient records. I wonder how long it takes to learn speech like that. I'm already swimming in more sounds and stimuli than I can keep track of. In fact, the mixture of so many different noises coming from so many differ-ent people is starting to make my head hurt again.

But even if I can't understand the words, I recognize the signs of quarrel. The man sitting in the lead wagon is even fatter than the line keeper, and it's clear he's upset about something. The guards appear equally annoyed, and the sounds coming out of all their mouths grow increasingly louder as the discussion continues. The animosity radiating from all of them unnerves me.

At one point, the man in the wagon opens a crate and lifts out a bolt of yellow silk. Li Wei and I both gasp. Never have I seen such a thing. Any silk that made its way to our village was already in scraps, at best, used only as adornment for those of high rank. To see a swathe of it like this is mesmerizing. Equally astonishing is its color, a rich, vibrant gold that is far superior to any dye we've ever managed to manufacture.

Perhaps he is the king, suggests Li Wei. *How else would he have such luxury? It would also explain how he's able to eat so much.*

I don't think so, I reply, observing the argument. *I don't think the guards would be having this kind of dispute with a king.*

The guards eventually insist on checking every crate in the wagon, much to the annoyance of their owner and those in line on the road. Several people, apparently the man's servants, look weary and wander from the wagon as the guards conduct their search. I continue watching with wide eyes as more and more exquisite bolts of silk are revealed in an unending rainbow of colors. Only in my dreams have I envisioned such radiance.

How will we get in? asks Li Wei. *If they're this cautious about cloth, they're probably extra suspicious of outsiders— especially based on the line keeper's reaction.*

I agree, and an answer suddenly presents itself. The wagon search finishes, and the fat man makes a loud sound that brings the meandering servants scurrying back. I grab Li Wei's arm and hurry us forward into the crowd. With so many people waiting and mingling about, nobody pays attention to us. The search completed, the guards are eager to wave the silk owner and his retinue through. Li Wei and I fall in behind some of the servants and move quickly as the guards direct us to the gates.

Just as we are about to step through, a guard suddenly steps out in front of us, holding a long pointed spear to block our way. He utters a series of harsh sounds that leave me staring stupidly. A handful of servants have come to a stop with us, and the guard's eyes rake over all of us as he repeats those sounds. My heart beats rapidly in my chest, and I feel Li Wei tensing beside me as he braces for confrontation. Somehow, we've been spotted as outsiders.

The guard repeats himself a third time, and it's obvious he's getting upset. I wish desperately that I understood what he wants. The temptation to sign is overwhelming, but before I can, I hear a voice answer quietly near us. It is another servant. The guard fixes his eyes on her, and she shrinks back in fear, pointing up at the fat man on the wagon. The guard looks up and issues his challenge once more.

Standing this close to the fat man, I notice he holds a small flask that he continually drinks from. He sits unsteadily on his perch and regards the guard with a mix of bleariness and disdain. Alcohol is rare in our village, but I've seen it and recognize the signs of drunkenness. At the guard's question, the fat man glances at the crowd of servants around his cart and shrugs, which only seems to make the guard angrier. The guard looks around and begins pointing at each person with his finger. Counting, I realize. He says something to the fat man, and the man shakes his head adamantly. He then begins counting the heads of all the servants and looks mildly surprised when he finishes.

I hold my breath as I realize what must be happening. The guards are demanding a count of the servants, and Li Wei and I have thrown off the numbers. Taking his hand, I turn him so that we are angled slightly away from the fat man, keeping our faces from him. Drunk or not, surely he'll recognize we're not his if he gets a good look. He and the guards have another heated discourse, and I am prepared for the worst, expecting them to require all the servants to line up for inspection.

We are saved when another guard comes up to the first and whispers something while gesturing at the long line on the road. Apparently the difference in opinion about the number of servants is paling next to the inconvenience of the holdup on the road. After several more tense moments, the guards wave the wagon and servants through, much to the fat man's delight. He toasts the guards with his flask, earning a scowl from the first one.

And after a few short steps, Li Wei and I are inside the township.

My earlier quick thinking grinds to a halt, and my steps slow. Everything around us is so crowded and in motion, we're in danger of being swept away in it. Li Wei has enough of his senses to realize we can't just stand around, lest we be trampled, and grabs my hand, leading us forward. We trail in the wake of the silk wagon, gazing around at the sights before us. It's hard to know where to look. The number of people alone would be enough of a spectacle for me, but there's so much more than that. The buildings are bigger than anything I've ever seen, made of ornate materials as opposed to the simple thatch we use. Many of the structures are decorated and painted, and I wonder what Elder Chen would think of all of it. Our paint is strictly hoarded for communication.

The clash of sounds I heard outside the gates is nothing compared to the noise level inside, with so many people giving voice to their thoughts. I wonder how they make any sense of it. It's all meaningless chatter to me, grating in its excess. Even the horses—there are more here, inside the walls—make their own unique noises as their hooves strike the stone roads. Nonetheless, I find I am able to tune out the din somewhat because everywhere I look, I also see written signs using the same characters we use. That familiarity grounds me, giving me the tools to start to make sense of this place. We've followed the silk wagon into what I think might be a market, based on the multitude of signs advertising goods: fruit, meat, cloth, jewelry, pottery, and more. It seems you can acquire anything in the world here.

A horse-drawn wagon rumbles past us, kicking up mud in

its wake. Some of it splatters on the sleeve of my clean shirt, making me cry out in dismay. Li Wei and I, still holding hands, step off the main thoroughfare so that we won't be run over, and we pause to read what's around us. Both of us are at a loss. I thought it would be obvious how to find someone in charge who might offer insight on our village's situation, but as I look around at these busy people, I have the feeling our village means nothing to them.

Li Wei releases my hand to speak, his face alight with excitement. *Did you see that?* he signs. *Where they're selling bread? That woman just handed over a small piece of silver and carried off a basket full of rolls! We pull out many times that in silver each day in the mines! If we could trade that in the same way, we'd never be hungry. For the amount of metal we produce each day, we should have a bounty of food!*

It can't be that simple, I reply, frowning. *Otherwise why would the line keeper send us so little to eat? Perhaps there is something special about that woman.* But as I watch her carry off her rolls, I can't see that she's much different from anyone else around us. The more we watch, the more we see bits of metal exchanged for all kinds of goods, and I begin to share Li Wei's view. I know the amounts of metal our village produces. It's my duty to note it for the record every day. I've seen just a fraction of that metal change hands here and result in an abundance of supplies that would leave our village reeling. Why doesn't that kind of exchange apply to us?

I spy a group of children playing across the road. They are

holding hands, moving in a circle, and speaking. But it's a different kind of speech from what I've heard from others. For one thing, each child is saying the same thing at the same time. There's also a quality to it than I haven't encountered before. There's a beauty to the sounds the children are making, almost reminding me of when I first heard the thrush back in our village. With a start, I wonder if I am hearing human singing. Whatever it is, it makes me smile.

Before I can comment on this, a wizened woman standing at a table notices us. She's selling fruit and has a lull in her business. We make eye contact, and her face brightens. She holds up some fruit I've never seen, opening her mouth and making more unintelligible sounds. I shake my head, knowing she wants metal in exchange for it, and I have none. Misunderstanding me, she holds up a different fruit and speaks again. I shake my head and, out of habit, sign: *No, thank you.*

Instantly, the woman's demeanor changes. She recoils, her smile fading. She turns away from us, trying to solicit someone else—anyone else. When she dares a glance back, noticing we're still there, she makes a shooing gesture that's understandable to anyone. We back away, finding another out-of-the-way spot in the shadow of a large building that advertises medicine and herbs.

What was that all about? Li Wei asks.

I'm not sure, I say. *She reminded me a little of the line keeper: Both of them recognize signing, but neither seems comfortable with it.*

A man emerges from the building just then and catches sight of me finishing my sentence. He recoils and makes an abrupt turn, giving us a wide berth. I glance back at Li Wei to see whether he noticed. He did, and his face darkens.

I'm getting a bad feeling about this place and these people, he tells me. *Something isn't right. They know about us, or at least about people like us. And it scares them.*

Why would they be scared of us? I ask.

I don't think it's us so much as—

He drops his hands when a heavily cloaked figure appears beside us. Based on this person's height and hands, I'm guessing she's a woman. The hood makes it difficult to see her face, and she is careful to keep her gaze averted and avoid any further identification. She appears to have noticed us signing, and I expect her to behave as the others did. Instead, she makes a gesture of beckoning and leads us toward a narrow space between two buildings.

I think she wants us to follow her, I say to Li Wei.

Another passerby notices the signing and does a double take, sharing the same look of alarm as the fruit vendor. The mysterious woman stamps her foot impatiently and beckons again for us to follow. When we don't move, she gestures broadly to the other townspeople and then makes very deliberate motions with her hands. She is signing, but it's not exactly the same kind of signing I know. Some of the words and motions are foreign to me, but a few come through—especially when she points to the townspeople again and signs: *Dangerous.* She indicates once more that we should follow her, and I am able to understand: *Me . . . keep you safe.*

Li Wei and I exchange glances again. *We don't know any-thing about her,* he says.

We don't know anything about any of these people, I point out. *But she is the first to know our language. Kind of.*

The cloaked woman suddenly makes a sharp gesture. I follow where she points and see two guards from the front gate moving purposefully through the crowd, clearly in search of something. Their faces are hard, and they push people out of the way indiscriminately as their gazes dart around. A chill runs through me. I don't know for sure that they're looking for us, but we can't take the chance. Li Wei and I clasp hands and follow this stranger into the unknown.

CHAPTER 10

OUR GUIDE LEADS US around and in between buildings, taking a path so convoluted that I soon lose all sense of where the market is. We leave it far behind us along with a lot of the more populated areas—which makes me uneasy. This stranger spoke of saving us from danger, but is it possible we're simply walking into a trap?

At last, we reach what appears to be the opposite side of the township. I can see the towering wooden wall in the distance, but it isn't our final destination. Instead, our guide takes us to a squat two-story building with minimal decoration. Painted characters on the front read: *Red Myrtle Travelers' Inn*. With a quick gesture, we are beckoned around the back side of the building, to a nondescript door.

After glancing around to make sure we're alone, our guide pushes back her hood, and I am surprised to see she is our age and exceptionally pretty. She opens the door and starts to step through, pausing when she notices we don't follow. *It's okay*, she says.

No one will hurt you here.

Who are you? I ask.

And what is this place? Li Wei demands.

My name is Xiu Mei, the girl replies. *I work at this inn. I am its* . . . The word she signs isn't one I know. Seeing our confusion, intrigue lights her features. *Your language must be different. Come in, and we will get something to write with. Don't sign until we're secure.*

Li Wei and I exchange uncertain glances. I honestly don't know if we can trust anyone in this strange place, but at least Xiu Mei isn't openly shunning us like the vendors in the market. There is something open and disarming about her face, and the fact that she can use our language—or something like it—goes a long way toward providing a glimpse of order in what's otherwise a thoroughly chaotic situation. After a moment of hesitation, we follow her.

We step into a kitchen like no kitchen I've ever seen. Steam bellows from pots on a hot stove, making the small space hot and stuffy. I'm assaulted with smells I've never encountered before, probably from foods I've never encountered before. This isn't like our kitchen at home, with only a scarce handful of ingredients to carefully parse out. Here, two women and one boy scurry busily around, working with a vast array of vegetables and meats, sprinkling them with powders I've never seen. I feel my mouth begin to water and see a similar hunger in Li Wei's awestruck expression.

And, of course, there are sounds. So many sounds, most of which I don't have names for. Pots and pans are tossed heedlessly around, dishes set down without ceremony. Food dropped into hot skillets of oil makes a noise that leaves me staring, one never described by Feng Jie. Mixed with all this is the sound of human conversation, each of the workers chattering away as they go about their tasks. One of them sees us and gives us a polite nod, then says something directly to Xiu Mei. She smiles and answers back, surprising me. She can hear and is fluent in both spoken and hand communication.

I have little time to ponder that before she leads us out of the kitchen and into a much larger room. It is filled with tables, some of which sit out in the open and others of which are tucked away in corners, concealed by gauzy curtains. Scattered tapestries and scrolls adorn the walls, along with a few well-displayed pieces of pottery. Most of the people sitting at the tables are men, and their clothing covers a vast range of styles and colors. Some are dressed as humbly as Li Wei and I. Others rival the silk merchant we followed into the township. Aside from one older woman sitting with a large group in the open, the only other female besides Xiu Mei and me appears to work here. She is dressed in silk and has her back to us as she delivers food and drink.

I've read about inns in the archives, but Li Wei and I have no personal experience with any place like this. How could we? Who visits our village? Xiu Mei points us toward one of the private tables. We pass a grizzled man standing by the door with arms crossed over his chest. His face is scarred, and there is a tough, no-nonsense air about him. He watches Xiu Mei closely but makes no other movement toward us.

We sit down, and Xiu Mei draws the curtain around us. The smoky fabric is wondrous, sheer, and silky. I immediately find myself touching it. From the outside, it makes seeing the table difficult, but from this side, we can make out most of the goings on in the room. Although I am still nervous about what we've stumbled into, I nod politely and tell Xiu Mei our names.

It's nice to meet you. Wait here, she says. She darts away to a podium across the room, returning with paper and ink. When she addresses us again, her face is eager and curious.

We can talk in here, behind the curtain—but don't let anyone else see you sign unless I say so. Why are you different from the others? she asks. *Why is your language different?*

What others? I ask, wondering if I've missed something.

The others who can't hear. They also speak with their hands, but a few of your words aren't the same. They're like . . .

I don't follow her next sign, which kind of proves her point. Using her ink and paper, she writes out: *. . . variations of each other.*

I don't know the people you mean, I tell her. *As far as we know, we are the only ones from our village to have ever come here.*

Xiu Mei's eyebrows rise at that. *Where is your village?*

On top of the mountain. The largest mountain, I amend.

Her face tells me our sign for *mountain* isn't the same, and I draw it for her. It is a pattern we continue throughout our conversation. She is very quick to pick up on the differences, however, and soon needs little help.

I didn't know there were people up there, she says. *They're all like you? All deaf?*

Yes, I say, not bothering to enlighten her about my state.

The curtain rustles, and the grizzled man from the door appears. He says something to Xiu Mei, his voice deep and harsh. I find him intimidating, but Xiu Mei seems unfazed. She answers back cheerily, and after a brief exchange, the man returns to his post.

Who was that? asks Li Wei.

My father, she says. *He wanted to know who you were. He is nervous about me talking to you, but he doesn't agree with the . . .*

Again, she writes out the word when we don't understand it: *decree.* Seeing our confused expressions, she explains, *There is a decree against your people—or, well, people like you. Those who can't hear. A number of them live here in the township, but we are discouraged from communicating with them or doing business with them.*

Do you know where they came from? I ask eagerly. If there are others like us, those who have made a home in this strange place, I'm suddenly hopeful they might be able to help us.

No, she says. *The ones I've talked to have been reluctant to describe their past. Mostly I speak to them in order to learn the hand signs. I have an interest in languages. It was my specialty back when I was trying to get into one of the schools in the capital.*

If you aren't supposed to speak to us, why did you pull us aside back in the market? Li Wei asks suspiciously.

It was obvious you two were lost, she says. *Outsiders. I watched you using the signs and was intrigued that yours were a little different from the ones I know. When I overheard some soldiers talking about finding two people who matched your description, I knew you needed help. It's so strange that there are more of you—more without hearing. I wonder if all your ancestors started out with the same sign language and then it changed over time? That would explain why some signs are different.* She strikes me as someone whose academic curiosity consumes her so much that it frequently takes her off-topic.

You still didn't explain why *you helped,* Li Wei points out, steering her back.

She laughs. *I suppose not. Sorry. This is all just so fascinating. I helped because . . . well, part of it's just curiosity. But also, my father and I aren't supporters of the king's regime. Things weren't so bad with the old king, but when Jianjun came to power, much changed.*

Jianjun? I ask. *Is that the current king?* We've always known a king ruled in Beiguo, but our village long lost track of the successors.

Xiu Mei nods. *Yes. He treats the army badly, which is why my father resigned—making a lot of enemies when he did. And then Jianjun stopped letting women into the academies, so we left the capital and ended up here in this poor excuse for a city.*

Li Wei's eyes widen. *This place is huge!*

This makes her laugh again. *You really have come from the top of a mountain. This is nothing. There are bigger, grander* cities out there, ones where you can go far if you have the right skills and connections. But for a dishonored veteran and his scholar daughter? The options are limited. The man who owns this place needs a bodyguard and someone who can balance the books. He's not a friendly man, but at least he doesn't care that I'm a girl.

It must be interesting work, I observe politely.

Very much so, she agrees. We see people from all over Beiguo—even from outside of it. Every day some group is off to a new destination. Every day someone new comes through our doors. Today it's you. What brought you from the top of your mountain?

We hoped we could speak to the line keeper about getting more food to our village, I explain.

Her puzzled expression answers before she does. I don't know anything about that. I never even knew your village existed. And who is this line keeper?

The curtain shifts again, and the woman who was serving the tables appears before us. Tall and willowy, she is dressed in silk, but I'm unprepared for it up close. Skirts of purest white—a color rare in everyday dress in our village—are covered by a long robe of the richest green silk imaginable. It is like spring has been spun into fabric. Cranes embroidered in golden thread dance across her robe; their glitter reflects in the sparkling golden pins that hold her hair into two buns. Her hair is equally incredible, the color of sunlight, and her green eyes sparkle. I've never seen features like that, not in our village of dark hair and eyes.

Some sort of red paint makes her lips shine, and a dusting of powder gives her skin a fair, delicate hue. She is like someone from a story, and she makes me forget what we were talking about.

Beside her, I feel small, dirty, and plain. And that's *before* I see how Li Wei is looking at her. His eyes are wide, as though that is the only way he could possibly take in so much beauty. After several awed seconds, he clamps his mouth shut to stop himself from gaping. I'm pretty sure I looked exactly the same way when I saw him emerge covered in gold from the mines so long ago.

She smiles at both of us, lingering on Li Wei a beat longer than me, before turning to Xiu Mei. She speaks, and her voice is high and light, reminding me of the birds I've heard singing. Xiu Mei smiles in return, speaks briefly, and then turns toward us. *Lu Zhu is curious about you*, she signs. *Don't worry—she's used to me speaking with the others like you. She won't tell.*

Is that her real hair? Li Wei asks.

Xiu Mei says something to Lu Zhu, making both women laugh. Li Wei blushes, guessing the joke was at his expense. *Yes*, says Xiu Mei. *She comes from a land outside of Beiguo, and all her people are like that. She works here now, just as I do. She's come to see if you want dinner or rice wine, but I'm guessing neither of you has money.*

We shake our heads. Xiu Mei opens her mouth to speak, and then a loud noise draws their attention back toward the center of the room. Some of the men in the center have begun moving the heavy wooden tables. Lu Zhu shakes her head in dismay, and Xiu Mei looks annoyed as she gets to her feet.

What's going on? I ask.

They're playing that stupid game again, she says. *I need to go and make sure no one gets hurt by the* . . .

I don't understand the last word she says because it's another unknown sign. She hurries over to where a group of men is huddled around one of the tables. Li Wei and I exchange puzzled glances and then rise at the same time to see what is happening.

A man with a gray-streaked black beard holds a small box in front of him. He lifts the lid, and everyone leans forward. I need to get closer to see and am small enough to slip forward between two larger men. My breath catches when I discover what's in the box: a scorpion. It's a little smaller than my hand, its carapace gleaming black. The man says something and nods to a boy standing near him. The boy produces a small leather bag and spills its contents onto the table: a pile of gleaming gold coins.

Immediately, there is a flurry of action among the men. They begin speaking at once and offering forward coins of their own, as well as other items. One man hands over a ring. Another has an exquisitely painted fan. After some deliberation, the old man gestures toward a tall young man not much older than Li Wei and me. This causes even more excitement. The assistant begins collecting the various offerings and handing out small pieces of paper that he scrawls small characters on. Leaning forward, I'm able to read a few of them. The slips record what item was offered and then say either *for* or *against*.

When all the items have been gathered, the tall chosen man holds out his hand. Silence falls. To my horror, the bearded man lifts out the scorpion and sets it on the chosen one's outstretched hand. After several tense moments, the bearded man nods, and the silence shatters, making me jump. Everyone gathered starts making noise. Some of it consists of words, some consists of hums and cries and other sounds I don't know the word for. It grows to a frenzied, uncomfortable level, almost making me want to retreat. But I'm too curious about what's happening.

With sweat pouring down his forehead, the young man passes the scorpion between his hands, back and forth. The scorpion docilely obliges. His gaze focuses unblinkingly on the creature, and it's clear he's working hard to keep his arms steady. I imagine the noise from the throng isn't helping. Eight times he passes the scorpion. On the ninth time, the noise from the others rises sharply, and their excitement intensifies. The young man grows more nervous, his hands trembling. Just as he is about to make the tenth pass, the calm scorpion suddenly lashes out, its tail striking the man's arm. He jerks sharply, and the scorpion falls to the table. My own cry of surprise is lost in the uproar of the others. The old bearded man scoops up the scorpion into its box while his assistant pays out those whose slips read *against*.

When all the bets are settled, another man volunteers to hold the scorpion. The process repeats, with the crowd again creating a storm of noise in what I realize now is an attempt to distract the holder. This time, the competitor successfully completes ten passes and returns the scorpion to its box. There is more excitement, and the *for* bets are paid out. The victorious man is also paid, given both gold coins and some of the surrendered loot.

We watch a couple more rounds, and all those who volunteer end up getting stung. All the while, the bearded man's treasure accumulates. The stacks of coins grow and are joined by other items: a small corked bottle, a newly crafted knife, and a swathe of the reddest silk I've ever seen. I can't help but admire it, particularly after the damage done to my own shirt. Those men who've been defeated cradle hands that are swollen and purple, but otherwise they have suffered no ill effects—except maybe to their pride.

Li Wei and I retreat to our table, his eyes bright. *I've seen that type of scorpion in our village before. They're harmless unless disturbed. All you have to do is keep your hands steady—it shouldn't be that hard.*

The others are making noise, I explain. *Lots of it. It's distracting to me, and it would be even more distracting if I were holding a creature like that.* Another outburst occurs from the table, but I force my attention from the spectacle to focus on our current dilemma. *What should we do?* I ask Li Wei. *About our situation, I mean. Xiu Mei seems to genuinely want to help us, but I'm not sure that she can. She doesn't know anything about our village, and her father apparently doesn't have much influence.*

They have more than us, Li Wei notes dryly. *No one's even supposed to talk to us—or people like us.*

I think it's those other people we need to find, I say. *The others who can't hear. Perhaps they know something about our history or that of the other village. We need to get to them.*

That's where we'll find answers about what we should do to help our people.

I suppose so, says Li Wei. His eyes drift from me, and this time, rather than focusing on the scorpion game or Lu Zhu, he takes in the room as a whole. The diversity of people is over-whelming, and I think back to what Xiu Mei said, about how people are always coming and going through their doors. There is a sense of wonder on Li Wei's face, as though perhaps he imagines himself walking out the door with one of those traveling parties—not back to our village but to some exotic location far away.

A great cry from the table tells me another competitor has been stung. I shake my head in disgust. *It can't be worth it for that sort of injury!*

It isn't deadly, Li Wei says, face intrigued as he watches the spectacle again. *I've seen it happen to others. The swelling will go down in another day or so.*

It still doesn't seem like it's worth the risk, no matter the riches, and judging from Xiu Mei's exasperated expression as she supervises the matches, she agrees. After the last defeat, no other volunteers offer themselves up. The bearded man calmly nods to his assistant, who dumps more coins on the table. I see tempta-tion in the eyes of those gathered, but no one steps forward.

It is more difficult now, Li Wei tells me. *The scorpion is agitated, more likely to strike.*

The old man's assistant pours out still more coins. *It's not enough to entice anyone*, I remark. *No one is that foolish.*

Or so I think.

To my complete astonishment, Li Wei gets up and strides forward. Before I can even think to stop him, he has pushed through the crowd and holds out the pixiu statue to the assistant. The young man looks it over with a critical eye, particularly the gold trim, and then gives a sharp nod of acceptance. The crowd goes crazy, and I spur myself forward. I need to stop him, tell him he's being an idiot, but a warning look from Xiu Mei stills me. I can't sign to Li Wei—not in front of all these people.

Helpless, I watch as the bets are taken. Most of them are *against*. I don't need to understand what the others are saying to know their thoughts. From their expressions and nudges, it's clear they think Li Wei is some bumbling, naive boy who will almost certainly falter and fail. Untroubled by their comments, Li Wei's hard gaze is fixed squarely on the scorpion in its box. He never takes his eyes from it as the bets are collected, and his jaw is tightly clenched.

I'm nearly as tense and again have to fight the urge to drag him away from this madness. But there's no time. With the bets in, the bearded man has the scorpion out and on Li Wei's hand. I stop breathing. The crowd starts in with its cacophony, but that at least is one distraction Li Wei doesn't have to worry about. He is oblivious to the sounds, able to focus solely on keeping his hands and arms straight—which, even I have to admit, he does remarkably well. Back and forth he passes the scorpion, remaining calm and collected the entire time, while I grow increasingly anxious. What is he thinking? He can't risk that kind of injury to his hand, especially if we have to climb back soon! And what if he's wrong about how harmless the sting really is?

Six, seven, eight. On the ninth pass, the crowd goes wild, trying desperately to unnerve him as he nears his final pass. He doesn't twitch at all, but I am shaking so much that I wrap my arms around myself to stay steady. The tenth pass finishes, and triumphant, he returns the scorpion to its box. Pandemonium breaks out. Most of the spectators lost, but a few who bet on Li Wei will be paid handsomely. The assistant pushes an enormous stack of coins toward Li Wei, who shakes his head and points to the vivid red silk. After a quick conference with his master, the assistant collects a few of the coins and then hands the rest to Li Wei, along with the silk and pixiu statue.

Grinning, Li Wei gathers up his winnings and starts to step away when another man suddenly crosses his path. The man speaks, but Li Wei can't understand. He stares in confusion, which seems to agitate the man. Whatever he says next causes a few others to regard Li Wei speculatively, and I tense, wondering what is going wrong. Xiu Mei suddenly moves to his side and says something with an easy smile. This pacifies the others, though the original speaker looks suspicious. She steers Li Wei back to the seclusion of our table, and I quickly join them.

Are you out of your mind? I demand. *What would drive you to do something so dangerous? You were nearly stung!*

Nearly? Li Wei asks indignantly after setting down his goods. *I wasn't even close to that!*

I'll agree to that, Xiu Mei says wryly. *You were in more danger of being discovered as deaf, which many would see as an unfair advantage. That man thought you were too calm around the noise, and then you didn't answer him. I told him you come from far away and don't speak our language.*

Thank you, I tell her, needing to get us back on track from this madness. *Now, if you could help us find the others who—*

I stop as a new commotion draws my attention. Two men at the table have gotten into a physical confrontation over something. One man dives at another, knocking his chair backward. Xiu Mei sprints away, trying to intercede. Li Wei gets to his feet, ready to help her, but her father is already on the move. He darts across the room, clearly intent on breaking up the fight, but he isn't fast enough to stop what happens next.

The men keep grappling with each other, and one is slammed into the wall with an impact so great, I can feel the vibrations across the room. A small shelf high on the wall displaying an ornate bowl wavers and then sends the bowl crashing to the floor. Lu Zhu puts her hand to her mouth and lets out a small scream.

By the time the men stop their fighting, Xiu Mei's father has them both by the necks of their shirts and is hauling them out of the inn. Xiu Mei and Lu Zhu both kneel around the broken bowl, their faces stricken with worry and fear. Li Wei watches them with concern but finally settles back down beside me when he observes no immediate danger.

I wonder what has happened, I say. Even though it has nothing to do with us, I can't help but feel bad for Xiu Mei, who is clearly distraught. Once her father has thrown the other men out, he comes to speak with her and Lu Zhu. The rest of the inn's patrons go on with their normal business, but those three remain upset. At last, Xiu Mei's father shakes his head sadly as he says something. Xiu Mei gives a great sigh and stares bleakly ahead, doing a double take as she catches sight of our curtained table. I think she had forgotten about us. Quickly, she hurries over and joins us within the curtained seclusion.

I'm sorry, she says. *You're going to have to leave. We all are. Our lives are in danger.*

CHAPTER 11

WHAT ARE YOU TALKING ABOUT? asks Li Wei, getting to his feet again. He looks around, ready for danger to leap out of the walls. *Did the soldiers find us?*

No, no, Xiu Mei says. *It has nothing to do with you. It's the bowl.* She opens her hand, revealing a broken shard. It is white porcelain, with a brightly colored design painted on it. *Our master—the man who owns this inn—is very proud of his collection. The last time one of his employees let something get broken, our master had him hunted down and beaten. Later, the servant died of his injuries.* She sighs again. *Fortunately, the master isn't due back for a while. My father and I have time to flee. Lu Zhu will probably go with us so that she's not blamed in our absence.*

We were hoping you could take us to the others who are like us, says Li Wei.

She shakes her head. *I'm sorry. We must use every bit of time we have to leave.*

I pick up the shard she's set on the table and hold it to the light. The porcelain looks nearly identical to what I saw in the kitchen, with nothing particularly special about it. It's the design that makes it unique, I suppose. I can't be sure, but it looks like part of a phoenix.

Does your master inspect his art each day? I ask.

No, but he will instantly be able to tell something is missing from the wall, Xiu Mei says.

I look up to where the shelf is on the opposite side of the room. It is prominent enough to be noticed but too high for whatever's on it to be viewed too closely. Glancing down, I study the design again. *Do you have paints?* I ask. *If you got me a bowl from the kitchen, I could re-create this. Your master would never know.*

Xiu Mei looks at me like I'm a crazy person. *That's impossible.*

Not for her, says Li Wei proudly, catching on to my plan. *If you replace the bowl, you and your father won't have to run away.*

That would be great, she says grudgingly, *but even if you could do such a thing, we only have a few hours at most.*

Just get me the supplies I need, I say.

Disbelievingly, Xiu Mei gets up to speak to her father and Lu Zhu. Minutes later, they have gathered at our table, bringing me a clean bowl from the kitchen, the fragments of the broken one, and as many paints as they could muster. Some look like household paints, the kinds used for repairs. Others are of a more delicate quality, and Xiu Mei explains that those are used for paperwork and documents. The colors aren't an exact match, but I have enough of a variety to feel confident in what I can do. I arrange all the broken pieces together to get a sense of the original and then dive into my work.

All is silent for a while, and then Lu Zhu says something that makes Xiu Mei nod. She turns to Li Wei, and I see her sign in my periphery: *You weren't kidding. Where did she learn that?*

In our village, Li Wei says. *She is the most talented artist of all our people.*

I set down my brush long enough to say, *Hush. That's not true.*

Lu Zhu returns to serving tables. Xiu Mei and her father have a conversation, and then she tells us, *I'll go talk to my contact among the silent ones and see if she will meet with you.*

Silent ones? Li Wei asks.

It's what we call your kind, she explains. *As long as you stay concealed here, you should be fine. My father and Lu Zhu will keep watch. Get one of them if you have any issues. I will return shortly.*

She leaves the inn, and her father resumes his watch of the common room. I continue my work with mixed feelings. Part of me is anxious for Xiu Mei. Will my work be good enough? Will I only get them into more trouble? At the same time, I feel a secret thrill at being able to paint something that is simply beautiful. Until now, I've only ever dreamed of that, and it is a delight to imitate the intricate pattern of phoenixes and plum blossoms on the bowl.

I lose track of my surroundings and am startled by a soft

sound that I recognize as Li Wei laughing. I glance up and see him watching me intently. *What?* I ask, pausing to set down my brush.

I think you're tenser working on this than I was with the scorpion, he tells me.

I can't help it, I say. *There's a lot at stake.*

He nods, his smile fading. *But you're also into it—I can see it. There's a light in your face as you work.*

I can't help that either, I tell him. *I always see things—imagine them, I mean. Beautiful scenes. They burn in me, and I have to get them out.*

Keeping you from this life and forcing you to work in the mines would have been a tragedy, he says solemnly.

I'm unprepared for that. With the recent flurry of activity since coming to the township, I've had little time to ruminate on all the unresolved issues between us. Now, looking at him, I'm surprised to see a mix of admiration . . . and an almost reluctant acceptance.

There's more to it than that, I say. *It wasn't easy, that decision. Never think it was easy. I still—*

You still what? he prompts when I don't finish.

I shake my head and look away, unable to convey what's truly in my heart. How can I explain that I have thought about him every day since we parted? That in that first year of officially being an apprentice, I constantly questioned whether I'd made the right choice in walking away from him? My desire to make art and for Zhang Jing's security got me through many low moments.

My eyes come to rest on the bowl, and I suddenly stiffen.

Now that I'm looking at the larger picture and not the individual shards, I notice that although the main design depicts a phoenix, the border appears to be a mix of all sorts of animals, both real and imagined. I see tigers, qilins, cranes, elephants, dragons, and more. I pick up each piece one by one and feel that strange tugging in my chest.

What's wrong? Li Wei asks.

I set down a shard with a pixiu and a deer on it. This one in particular seems to resonate with me. *Nothing. Just something from a dream.*

The same dream that keeps disturbing your sleep? he asks sagely.

It's not important, I say. I start to avoid his gaze again, and he reaches out, tipping my chin up so that I must meet his eyes.

Fei, you know you can trust me. I'm here for you. I always have been and always will be. Tell me what's wrong.

You can't keep rescuing me, I say.

Of course not, he agrees. *You can rescue yourself—but perhaps I can give you a hand now and then.*

I smile faintly, but there is an ache in my chest as I think back to that long-ago day, trapped in the rubble when a beautiful, glittering boy held out his hand to pull me out. A moment later I find myself telling him everything about the night my hearing came to me and the dream I had of everyone in our village opening their mouths in a single cry.

You think this pull you've been feeling is tied to your hearing? To why it returned? he asks.

I don't know, I admit. *I don't understand why any of this happened to me.*

I want to say more, but over his shoulder, I see Lu Zhu going about her work. Her pretty face is drawn with worry, and I remind myself I must help these people first. I can give in to my own worries later. I paint with a renewed vigor, conscious that time is pressing upon us. When I finally finish and compare my copy to the broken one, I am more than pleased at what I've wrought.

You did it, Li Wei says. *It's a perfect match.*

Not a perfect match, I say. *My blue is darker than the original.*

Well, I'm no painter, but it looks amazing to me. His eyes lift to something behind me. *And not a moment too soon.*

I turn and see Xiu Mei hurrying through the door toward us. *Our master is returning!* she tells us once she reaches our table. *I saw him on the way back and was just able to get ahead of him and—* She stops when she sees my bowl, looking back and forth between it and the broken pieces I copied. *That's it? You did this?*

I nod, suddenly feeling flustered. I can't interpret her expression, and I fear the worst, that she'll tell me it's a ridiculous imitation and that I've just given her and her father a death sentence.

I don't know what's more incredible, she says, *that you did it at all or that you did it in so short a time. There are renowned masters in the capital who would fight to take you on as an apprentice.*

I already have a great master, I say proudly, thinking of Master Chen.

Xiu Mei gets rid of the broken pieces and then hands the copied bowl to her father. Careful of the wet paint, he cautiously places it on the shelf just minutes before the inn's master returns. When he walks in the door, I can immediately see how he might order someone beaten for an accident. His face is narrow and drawn, and he has the expression of someone who is perpetually displeased with everything he sees. He scrutinizes the room as he enters, taking in the number of guests and how his employees work. His pinched eyes scan the wall of art but find nothing amiss, and I exhale a breath I hadn't even realized I was holding. Continuing on his way, he snaps something loud and hostile-sounding at the kitchen boy, who scurries away in fear. The master then approaches Xiu Mei at the podium, and she greets him with a bow. A conversation ensues between them, and after another wary survey, the man stalks away.

When he has disappeared into a back room, Xiu Mei returns to us, grinning. *He suspects nothing. Thank you.*

It was my pleasure to help, I say honestly.

And now I can help you. Nuan is willing to speak with you later, closer to sunset. I have some duties to attend to and will take you to her in a couple of hours. Come. She beckons for us to stand up. *I'll get you some dinner.*

Li Wei starts to hand her some of his coins, but Xiu Mei shakes her head. *After what Fei did today, believe me, your dinner is paid for.*

Li Wei's eyes sparkle. *Fei is the hero now. My daring feat with the scorpion isn't so impressive anymore.*

We all laugh at that, relieved that the earlier tension has lightened. I see other patrons eating in the common room and am puzzled as to why we wouldn't just eat at our curtained table. We followed her out to another small staircase and go up one floor. The room she leads us into leaves me gaping.

I thought I had seen many beautiful and wondrous things since coming to the township, but this room puts them all to shame. Screens and tapestries fill it with color and whimsy, each scene lovelier than the last. I see goldfish swimming on a pattern of blue and white flowers, silver pheasants on a backdrop of black and blue. The scenes go on and on, and I feel like I could spend hours staring at each one. Jade vases of flowers sit in the corners, and the middle of the room holds a small low table of gleaming black wood. The far side of the room isn't screened but is a made of a fine wooden mesh. When I get closer, I see that it looks down on the common room below. Ornate lanterns bathe everything around me in a gentle glow.

What is this place? I ask.

We call it the Egret Pavilion—even though it's not really a pavilion. Xiu Mei rolls her eyes. *The master is trying to emulate some of the really high-class inns in the capital.*

This isn't high class? I ask in disbelief.

Not compared to some of the ones I've seen, she says. *But it's fine for some wealthy guests who come through to host parties or eat a private dinner. No one's renting it out today, and our master is busy. You won't be disturbed. Relax, and Lu Zhu will be up with some food. As soon as I finish some accounting, I'll take you to Nuan.*

I'm so overwhelmed by the beauty of this room that I can't help but bow to Xiu Mei. *Thank you. I think you've done far more for us than we have for you.*

Nonsense, she says. *Meeting you has given me a lot to think about.*

She leaves us alone in the exquisite room, and we pause to clean our hands and faces in bowls of crystal-clear water. Then we explore the space more closely, finding new and dazzling things to point out to each other. Before long, Lu Zhu slides back the door and enters with a kitchen boy. They set the black table with steaming bowls of noodles and vegetables, as well as cups and a small bottle of rice wine. The food is overwhelming in and of itself, but I find I am just as enthralled by the dishes it's served in. The bowls are beautifully painted, and the cups are exquisite, made of amber and agate.

Such a table is almost too gorgeous to eat at, and I glance down at my muddied robe in dismay. *I don't feel worthy of this,* I tell Li Wei.

How do you think I feel? he asks, gesturing to his semi-green shirt. *There's nothing a barbarian like me can do. But you . . .* He walks over to where he set his pack down and astonishes me when he lifts out the vermillion silk he won in the scorpion match. I'd completely forgotten about it after everything else that happened. It moves like water between his fingers, and as he straightens it out, I see that it isn't actually a bolt of cloth like I'd thought. It is a dress, high-waisted with a long, flowing skirt. He hands it to me. *Here; it is for you.*

Never have I been able to imagine such a texture. It is smooth and cool between my fingers and extraordinarily light. Up close, I see a pattern of golden plum blossoms worked into it. Putting it over one arm, I sign, *For me?*

Well, I'm not going to wear it, he says. *Go ahead. Try it on.*

I hesitate. With everything else going on, it seems so foolish . . . and yet I can't help but be transfixed. All my time in the Peacock Court, I've admired those bits of silken trim on the elders' robes. To be holding an entire garment of that wondrous material is almost unbelievable. I slip behind a screen of red bats and change out of my artist's clothes. The dress is a little long for me, which isn't surprising, given my size. A sash at the waist helps keep it in place, and on impulse, I redo the bun that holds my hair. When I step out from behind the screen, I see Li Wei over at the mesh wall, looking down on the common room. He glances up at my approach and freezes.

What? I ask in alarm, thinking I must look ridiculous.

It takes him several moments to answer. *This*, he replies. *Remember when you asked me why I'd be so foolish as to risk being injured by the scorpion?* He gestures at me in the dress. *It's because of this. And it would have been worth getting stung for.*

Don't say that. I feel a deep flush spreading over my cheeks. *Let's eat before the food gets cold. We've wasted enough time on my vanity.*

Li Wei admires me for several more breathless moments. I don't know whether to feel relieved or disappointed when he finally nods and sits down at the table. I sit opposite him, nervously arranging the full skirt around me.

The crate we received at the zip line was amazing, but this meal is on an entirely different level. Noodles are a rarity in the food baskets received in our village. We've certainly never had them cooked this way, simmering in a spiced broth of meat with the freshest vegetables I've ever tasted. The ones we receive are always a little wilted. The aroma is intoxicating, enough to make me take a break to eat. The taste is exquisite, and before long, I find myself licking the bottom of the bowl. Food has always been such a practical necessity in my world. I never dreamed of finding pleasure in it.

The rice wine I'm less enchanted by. One sip makes me gag. Li Wei laughs at my reaction, and I push my cup toward him. *You can have mine.*

He shakes his head, amused. *We need to keep clear heads.* He gazes around the room, that earlier look of wonder returning. *Can you imagine living like this? Eating food like this? Having access to so much? Meeting people from all over the world?*

I haven't thought much about it, I say honestly. *Maybe after we help our village, there will be time to learn more.*

He frowns and looks as though he will argue, but Lu Zhu enters just then. She takes in my dress with a knowing look and sweeps away the empty dishes. Noticing our untouched wine, she returns with a kettle of tea and tiny porcelain cups. Non-medicinal tea is another luxury item in our village, usually only reserved for the elders. I feel decadent sipping it, and as I relax in my dress and the beautiful room, I wonder if Li Wei is right to dream of living in a world like this.

A new noise draws me up short. I go very still, listening to sounds I've never encountered before. They hang in the air like colors on a canvas, reminding me of when the blue thrush sang.

What is it? Li Wei asks.

I don't know, I tell him, getting to my feet. *But it's amazing.*

I go to the mesh wall and look down. Lu Zhu has returned to the common room and sits there with what I recognize from scrolls as a musical instrument. A pipa, I believe. She plucks the strings delicately, and I see that I am not the only one entranced. Several other patrons have gone silent, watching with rapt looks. Some place coins at her feet.

It is music, I tell Li Wei. He knows the term, but its nature is meaningless to him. *It is wonderful . . . like a dream.*

I've gained new insight as to how sounds can be helpful for communication and survival, but until this moment, it never occurred to me that sounds could be enjoyable too. The birdsong I've heard on our journey made me smile, but this reaches into my heart. Lu Zhu's playing is a type of art. Listening to the pipa, I find myself relaxing as a tranquil joy spreads through me. The tension leaves my body, and I briefly forget about the woes of my village. Li Wei can't experience the music like I can, but something in my mood must come through to him. He stands very close behind me, putting his arm around my waist to draw me near. At first, I stiffen as a new kind of tension and fear fills me. Moments later I find myself relaxing, leaning into him. There's an overwhelming *rightness* to the moment that is difficult for me to articulate.

Forgetting the music, I turn to regard him, lifting my face toward his. He rests his hands on my waist, and his gaze is electric, running over every part of me. I never knew it was possible to be both elated and terrified at the same time. It takes me a moment to recover myself and find the words I need.

You . . . you can't look at me like that, I tell him.

He lifts his hands to answer, his fingertips brushing my waist. *Like what?*

You know what, I scold.

Why? he asks, taking a tantalizing step closer. *Because you're an artist and I'm a miner?*

I swallow, mesmerized by how close his lips are to mine. *Yes*, I say. *And because . . .*

He leans toward me, knowing I'm out of excuses. *Because?*

My heart thunders in my chest as I close my eyes and lift my face toward his. I feel drunk, not from wine but from being with him in this way. I realize it's not even about the setting or the clothes or the food. What marks this moment is that for the first time in our acquaintance, there really is no rank here. No artist, no miner. It's just us.

And Xiu Mei. The sound of the door and her entry into the room end the spell, and I jerk back with a start. Li Wei backs away too, and I know we must look guilty. If she noticed anything between us, she doesn't comment on it.

How was dinner? she asks.

Incredible, I say honestly, still a little dazed. *We've never had anything like it.*

It was an exquisite experience, Li Wei adds.

I'm glad to hear it, Xiu Mei says. *And I'm done with my work, so I can take you to Nuan now.*

Li Wei and I exchange brief glances, both of us understanding the same thing. We must wake up from this dream. The interlude is over. It's time to get back to the business of helping our village.

Your dress is lovely, Xiu Mei tells me. *But you'll probably want to change.*

True, I say, wistfully touching the red silk. *I wouldn't want to get it dirty.*

It's less about that than where we're going. Xiu Mei's face darkens. *Believe me, it isn't a part of town where you'll want to stand out. In fact, it's not a place anyone really wants to go.*

CHAPTER 12

PUZZLED BY HER OMINOUS WORDS, I don my artist's clothes again and help Li Wei gather up our few belongings. *Remember, don't sign or draw attention to yourselves out in public*, Xiu Mei warns.

Downstairs, the inn's master is in the common room, but he pays little attention to us. He is speaking to some patron, his chest puffed with pride as he gestures to the art collection on the wall.

Lu Zhu gives us a wink and a friendly smile as we pass by her. Xiu Mei's father simply nods, and something tells me he is glad to see us go. He might not agree with the king's decree, but he fears for his daughter's safety in speaking with us. Thinking of Zhang Jing, I can respect his protectiveness. I bow by way of thanks as we pass him.

Outside, the sun has sunk in the western sky, though the air is still warm and pleasant. Xiu Mei covers herself up again and leads us back through the twisting streets of the township. I might not be overly familiar with cities and towns, but it soon becomes obvious to me that she is taking us to a less than desirable place. The market we were in earlier didn't smell great, but the odor is much worse here, making me frequently want to cover my nose. The streets are dirtier too, and the buildings no longer have much in the way of decoration. Soon we don't see any real buildings at all. We've come upon a cluster of tents and a handful of dilapidated shacks. The people moving around this area don't wear the colors or fabrics we observed in the marketplace, and they are all thin, just like us.

They're also all signing.

Flashes of signed conversation that I observe appear to be the same type of language Xiu Mei uses. I think about the stories of how the language my village uses came from one used by our migratory ancestors. Xiu Mei's guess, that our two peoples changed the language over time, makes sense. We've each added and dropped words until parts are unrecognizable.

Some of those milling among the tents recognize us as outsiders and stop to stare. Xiu Mei leads us to a threadbare tent, and we must duck to enter its low door. There, inside, an old woman sits cross-legged. Lines and wrinkles mark her face, and she is dressed in rags. Back at the inn, I felt poorly dressed, but here, my artist's uniform, even with the splattered mud, appears luxurious. Xiu Mei bows and tells the woman, *These are the ones I told you about.* To us, she says, *I must get back. I'm glad we met and hope you find what you're looking for. Thank you for your help.*

Li Wei and I bow. *Thank you for yours,* I say. When she is gone, I bow to the old woman. *Thank you for speaking with us.*

She indicates that we should join her on the floor, and we do. *My name is Nuan,* she tells us. *Who are you? Where are you from?*

We give her our names, and when I tell her we come from the mountain, she looks puzzled. I remember that this word was different for Xiu Mei too, and I wish we'd brought our paper and ink. Li Wei rummages through his sack and finds the stick I used to draw a game board. He draws the character for *mountain,* and she nods in understanding.

We use a different sign, she explains. She shows us how her people sign *mountain.* It's different from ours, but I can see how both signs had a common origin. *You can't be from the mountain,* she adds. *I know everyone who came with us from the . . .*

I don't know the words she uses, and we must again pause to draw it out: *plateau.* Realization and shock hit me.

You're from the plateau! I say. *From the dead village! You're one of the ones who escaped!*

She watches my hands avidly, and I can tell she's having the same issues I have, not always immediately grasping some words. She's less able to follow along than Xiu Mei, but she understands enough to get what I'm saying and nods. *Yes. But you aren't from there.*

We are from the top of the mountain, Li Wei explains.

Nuan looks so confused that for a moment I think she must not have understood his words. At last, she says, *There are people at the top?*

Our village, I say. *We are miners, just like your village is. Was. There is another mine?* she asks, but she doesn't wait for me to answer. *Yes, of course.* She pauses, gazing into space a few moments as she lets this new understanding settle in. That's *where the new metals are coming from. We've wondered for a long time how the supply lines were still running long after our village was shut down. Are you all like us? Deaf?*

Yes, I say. *And some people are going blind too.* I draw the character for *blind* to make sure she understands, but she has already guessed. Looking saddened, she launches into a story, pausing when necessary to draw out words we don't know.

It happened to us too. It's the metals. There's a contaminant that makes mining dangerous there. It gets into the air, in the water. Once removed from the earth, melting and other manipulation purifies the metal. But if you live and work around it? It's deadly. It deprives us of our senses. Hearing is the first sense lost. Then, over many generations, blindness follows. It would not be worth the risk, except that the mountain is rich in precious metals—far richer than any other known source in the kingdom. And this king is even more ruthless about getting those riches out.

King Jianjun? I clarify.

Yes, she says. *He and his predecessors have trapped people on the mountain for generations, forcing them to mine for their survival, masking it as kindness by sending up barely enough food to survive. And all the while, those closest to the metals suffer greatly.*

Understanding hits me like a slap to the face. The shock is so strong, it's a wonder I don't go reeling. *Zhang Jing,* I say.

Nuan looks confused, and I clarify. *My sister. She isn't a miner, but she has been losing her sight. But now it makes sense: Her observation post is in the mine. She is exposed to all the same toxins—just like you,* I add, glancing at Li Wei.

I've worked in there for years and still have my sight, he tells Nuan.

She shrugs. *It affects people differently. Some can fight it longer. And the direst effects take generations to build up. But it will only be a matter of time now. That's how it was with our people. Once the first cases of blindness came, the ailment ran rampant within a year.*

Li Wei and I look at each other again, both thinking about how the blindness in our village first became noticeable a few months ago. *We need to get them out of there,* I say. *If you and I climbed down, so can the others. It will take time, but it will be worth it if it saves them.*

Perhaps . . . but I think we'll have a hard time convincing them, Li Wei says grimly. *You've seen how they are. They resist change. And that's if they even believe us!*

We must make them believe, I say adamantly, thinking of Zhang Jing and Master Chen. *Lives depend on it. We must get them out.*

He shakes his head. *Fei, it was hard enough getting the two of us down! How will you move three hundred? Especially with children and the elderly?*

How can you talk like this? I demand. *When we started this quest, you spoke about helping our whole village! You acted as though we could do the impossible. Do you only talk about courage when the task is easy?*

A spark of anger flashes in his eyes. *You know I'm up for difficult tasks—but that doesn't mean I'm foolish either. Assuming we can miraculously get all those people down the mountain, where will they go? To tents like this? What kind of livelihood can they possibly have beyond the mines?*

There must be other places to go in Beiguo, I insist. *You saw all the travelers at the inn.*

Nuan watches our conversation thoughtfully, carefully keeping out of our dispute. *Is your mine still active? It's not empty?*

I look to Li Wei for confirmation, and he responds, *Believe me, if we were running out, there'd be a panic.*

Nuan sighs, and I'm fascinated at how a simple exhalation of breath can convey such sadness. *It would be better for you if it were empty,* she says unexpectedly. *If you truly want your village to escape and find a new life. Once, in our history, a number of villagers attempted it, and the king's men stopped them. They needed slaves to keep working our mine. It was only a year and a half ago, when the mine went empty just as the blindness came, that they didn't bother stopping us anymore. There was no need. They had what they wanted from us and didn't care where we went. So here we are.* She lifts her hands, indicating the threadbare tent. *Gone from one prison to another. Here we live in this squalor, second-class citizens who are scorned by the others. Sometimes we get work. Sometimes we simply live on scraps.*

Li Wei looks at me expectantly as Nuan's words confirm

how difficult it will be to find a new existence for our people. I ignore him as I answer back. *But there is food here. At least it's available. And you're away from the toxins in the metals. It would still be a better life for our people.*

Nuan shakes her head. *I'm telling you, they won't let you go. They need your village to keep working the mine. The king covets those metals too much. It keeps him rich and in power.*

But if our village goes blind, no one will be able to mine anything! I protest.

They don't care, says Nuan. *My villagers' lives, yours . . . they are nothing compared to riches in the eyes of those more powerful than us.*

We sit there and let those words sink in. Finally I turn to Li Wei. *We must take this news back to our village. We must let them decide and weigh the options.*

I can tell from his expression that he wants to protest, to tell me again that the task is impossible. But as he gazes into my eyes, he finally gives a reluctant nod. *I will help you take this news back to the elders,* he says. *Perhaps they will have an idea we haven't thought of.* I can tell he doubts it.

Be careful, says Nuan. *If any official realizes you're here, they aren't going to like it. They won't want your village knowing the truth.*

Someone does know we're here, I reply. *The line keeper. And Xiu Mei thought she saw soldiers looking for us as well.*

We tell Nuan about our initial encounter, how the man told us to wait but how we ended up sneaking away. When we finish, Nuan remarks, *All of them are appointed by the regime. He probably ran straight to the king's men. You were right to leave.*

All of them? I ask, thinking I misunderstood. *What do you mean?*

The men who run the line, she explains. *There are a number who rotate through that job.*

Li Wei and I are dumbfounded, and he says, *We always thought there was one person in charge there, one person making decisions and sending notes.*

Nuan laughs, a thin sound that feels dry. *No, they don't make decisions. Whoever was sending you messages was someone much more powerful.*

I think back to the nervous man and suppose I shouldn't be surprised to learn this.

They will all know you're in the township by now, Nuan continues. *The gate will be watched. There is a secret entrance out of the walls, not far from this encampment, that I can show you. If you stick to the trees and keep your wits about you, you should be able to make it back to your people undetected.*

Li Wei and I both stand to bow to her. Maybe we are far from home, but we aren't bereft of our manners. *Thank you,* I tell her with as much reverence as I would one of our elders. *You may have saved our lives and those of our people. Please allow us to give you a gift.*

I look to Li Wei, who understands immediately. Perhaps Nuan's situation isn't as dire as our village's, but it's clear from her gaunt appearance that food is a luxury for her as well. Our packs are full of the food we took from the line keeper's crate, and Li Wei digs into his bag, producing some fruit, dried meat, and a bun. Nuan's wide eyes show us that this is a bounty for her, and I feel gladdened but also sad. Clearly, for the right people around here, there is plenty of food to be had. It infuriates me that her people and my own are so deprived.

As Li Wei cinches his pack back together, one of the xiangqi pieces falls out, a general. It rolls near Nuan, and she picks it up, studying the detail.

This is fine work, she says as she hands it back. *I've seen far less detailed game sets fetching a nice price at the market. This kind of skill would be prized anywhere in Beiguo.*

Li Wei made it, I say with pride.

It is nothing, he says, embarrassed. *Fei is the real artist.*

He busies himself with his pack, pretending it needs more rearranging than it does. Nuan watches him with a smile and then says to me, when he's not looking: *He's very handsome. He's your betrothed?*

Now I'm the one who's embarrassed. I feel heat flood my cheeks. *No! We are just . . . friends.*

There is a knowing look in Nuan's eyes. *If you want to save yourselves a lot of trouble, you could leave now. Forget trying to warn your village—the officials will stop you from getting back, you know. And they'll certainly stop your whole village from leaving the mountain. But just the two of you? Well, there are other cities, other places in Beiguo. The boy clearly has skill, and you say you are trained as well. You can find work, real work. Go off together and leave this cursed place.*

What she has suggested is so shocking, so unbelievable, that I'm momentarily frozen. Then new sounds make me jerk my head around. One thing I can say, at least, for this dirty collection of tents is that it is quieter than the rest of the township, since none of the residents use their voices. But now that quiet is interrupted as I recognize the sounds of many loud voices as well as a new noise I just learned: the sound of horses' hooves on the road.

Someone is coming. Men and horses, I say.

We hurry to peek out the entrance of the tent, where I heard the noise. There, on the far side of where we entered the deaf settlement, riders on horseback are approaching. I am just barely tall enough to make them out and see that they wear red-and-yellow armor.

Those are the king's men! Nuan says. *They know you're here. Someone probably reported you when you came to see me—they are my people, but they are desperate. You must go. Quickly. Over there, by that gray building? Go there, turn left, and then go straight until you reach the wall. Make another left and follow it until you see the opening.*

Thank you. I bow to her again and start to leave, but she catches my sleeve.

You heard them coming? she asks. *You can hear?*

Only as of a few days ago, I say. *I don't know why or how.*

The next sign she makes is incomprehensible to me, something involving wings.

What? I ask.

She makes it again, but I still can't understand. The sign isn't one from our language. Li Wei starts to reach for the stick we used to draw characters, but the sound of men and horses is getting closer. I shake my head and tell him, *No time. We must go.*

Nuan looks distraught, like she has more to tell us, but I can only shake my head at her and offer hurried thanks. Without a glance back at her, Li Wei and I dash off through the tents, heading toward the building Nuan indicated. The sound of men and horses is getting closer, but they aren't able to see us as well as we can see them, giving us a head start. Her directions are easy enough to follow, and we soon find the gap she means. There's a part in the wall where it joins to a watchtower. The two are made of different kinds of wood, and with time and weather, the seam has warped and split. A small space has been created, one that looks man-made, just big enough for one person to get through. It is an easy fit for me but takes some maneuvering for Li Wei, and he tears his shirt in the process.

Once we are both out, I hear shouts from above and look up. We may have escaped the guards in Nuan's camp, but the ones on this watchtower have seen us. Our only saving grace is that it will take them time to get down and out. That buys us faint, precious time, and we cannot linger, especially when a few arrows come shooting down after us.

Without another backward glance, Li Wei and I run for our lives into the woods.

CHAPTER 13

ONCE, WHEN I WAS A CHILD, some older kids in our village got it into their heads to steal lunches from the younger children. It only lasted a few days before some adults got wind of the bullies and put an end to it. But one of those days, I bravely sneaked into the part of the woods where the thieves were lording over their hoard, snatched a bunch of the lunches back, and took off running. It was one of the most terrifying chases of my life. My heart felt like it was going to explode out of my chest. I didn't have a chance to think about where I was going; I only knew I had to get away, to run as far and as fast as I could.

Outrunning the soldiers reminds me a lot of that day, with one exception: That childhood race was silent. This isn't.

My hearing is both a blessing and a curse as Li Wei and I desperately run for our lives. On the one hand, I can tell how close our pursuers are, whether they are gaining ground. But sound also adds to the terror of the chase. Having an extra set of stimuli increases my panic, making an already stressful situation that much worse. It's hard to focus and think coherently.

Li Wei stops after some time, breathing heavily and rubbing his ankle. I wonder if it still hurts from his fall, but I know he'll deny it if I ask. *Perhaps we've lost them*, he says.

I shake my head, still able to hear men and horses. Scanning, I point in what I think is the opposite direction of our pursuers. *There. We must go there.*

To Li Wei, all this forested area looks the same, but he trusts me enough to go without question. We take off again, running until my muscles burn and I am forced to stop and take in big gulps of air. Peering around, I realize the only sounds I hear are those I've come to associate with any forest: rustling leaves and birds calling. I look to Li Wei, who is bent over, hands resting on his knees as he too catches his breath.

I don't hear them, I say, watching him again nurse his ankle. *I think we've lost them. Are you okay?*

He waves me off. *Fine, fine. I just need a minute.*

We should hurry and begin climbing back, I tell him. *We have to reach our people.*

His smile fades, and he shakes his head. *Fei, that's impossible. We've lost them for now, but they're almost certainly going to go scout around the cliffs, expecting us to climb back. We won't be able to get far enough before they find us. They'll shoot us down with arrows. You thought the climb down was slow and painstaking? Going up is doubly so.*

I frown. *What are you saying then? How are we going to help them?*

We aren't, he states. *We can't get back up, and even if we could . . . Fei, I know you think—you hope—the elders will spur our village into action and make them leave for some new future. But do you really believe that? Think logically, not with an artist's imagination. Our people are fearful and know nothing of the world. They won't leave. They won't believe us.*

Then what are we supposed to do? I demand, stunned at this turn.

Go. He pauses and spreads his arms wide. *Anywhere. Anywhere we want to in Beiguo. Or outside of it. I saw what Nuan said about my carving. We are skilled. We can get out of here, join a group of travelers at the inn, and go some place far away, somewhere we can eat well every day and earn enough to wear silk. Someplace you can listen to music and do the art you truly want to do. Someplace where love is not dictated by our jobs— jobs that have been forced on us by others.*

His words send me reeling, but one in particular catches me. *Love?* I ask.

In a moment, he has closed the distance between us. An intensity burns in his eyes like I've never seen before. *Yes, Fei. Love. I loved you the moment you looked up at me so defiantly from the ruins of that broken shed. I loved you all the years we spent growing up together. I loved you when you told me you were leaving to join the artists. Throughout it all, my heart has only ever had one person's name on it—yours. And you can talk all you want about rank and how we can't be together, but I know you love me too.*

I raise my hands and actually think I might be able to

convincingly deny it. But my hands tremble, and something in my face tells him the truth—that I love him too, have loved him since that beautiful, glittering boy came to my rescue. A boy who's now become a man of passionate conviction, a pillar of strength at my side.

Then, before I realize what is happening, Li Wei pulls me to him and kisses me. Back when he nearly kissed me at the inn, he was timid and cautious. No more. There is a power and certainty in what he does as our bodies meld together and I lose myself in that kiss. Once I felt like I had too many senses, now I suddenly feel as though they've all disappeared. I hear nothing. I see nothing. All I'm aware of in the world at that moment is the feel of his lips on mine. It is dizzying and exhilarating, somehow leaving me both hot and cold all over and filling me up from my head to my toes with emotions that are as foreign to me as new sounds.

When we briefly break apart, I am breathless. I feel as though I am seeing the world with new eyes now that I'm no longer trying to convince myself I don't care about him. Opening myself to my feelings and the truth has freed me. Li Wei kisses me again. I'm a little more prepared—but only a little. That kiss floods me with heat and longing as well as a renewed sense of hope and purpose.

I've waited a long time for that, he tells me. *And I should have done it sooner. This is fate. You and me. Come on—let's go. Let's circle around and follow the road leading out of the township. We'll go wherever it takes us. There is nothing left for us in the village.*

I have spent much of my life dreaming, imagining things that aren't but could be. It is how I create my art. But this possibility facing me now is something I never dared hope for, that I could go off with this boy I've long loved, that we could live a dazzling life in which I could use my art to capture beauty instead of despair. It is heady and wonderful, and I want it so badly. I want to leave behind the darkness of our past and move forward to a future filled with beauty and sound and joy. . . .

Li Wei, I can't, I say.

Fei . . . you can't tell me you don't love me.

You're right, I can't tell you that, I agree. *Because I do love you. But it's not that simple.*

Nothing could be simpler, he insists.

You said there is nothing left for us in the village, but you're wrong. My sister is there. I can't leave her. I stop to take a deep breath and steel myself. How is it possible to have gone from such joy to such sorrow in the blink of an eye? For a moment, I felt like I had the world. Now I feel as though I'm losing it. *If you don't want to go back, I understand. You can go off and find that new life. But I have to go back for Zhang Jing, no matter how difficult.*

He shakes his head vehemently. *No, we can't be separated again. We must talk—we must figure this out—*

A noise from the forest forces me to quickly turn around. I peer into the depths of the trees, back in the direction we came from. I see nothing yet, but there's no mistaking it: the sounds of the soldiers. They're getting louder—closer.

They've tracked us, I tell Li Wei. A new panic seizes me, and as impossible as it seems, I'm forced to momentarily push aside all these conflicting feelings for him as survival mode takes precedence.

We probably left a trail as we ran, he says, face hard and serious once more. *Which way are they?* I point toward the sound, and he studies me for several long moments, deliberation all over his features. At last, he seems to come to a difficult decision. *Okay, let's go back to the mountain.*

He takes my hand, and we run once again. The forest thins, and the terrain begins to rise as we reach the mountain's base. We stop, and he points at something off to our right. The light is fading as dusk sets in, but I can still clearly see what he indicates: the supply line.

You want to get back to the village? That line is the only way, Li Wei says.

That's impossible, I state.

He smiles ruefully. *Look what we've done so far. We're pretty good at the impossible.*

The line can't hold us, I protest. *Plus, someone's going to have to turn the crank to move the line. I don't think the line keeper's going to help us.*

No, Li Wei concurs, his expression troubled as he gazes toward the line's summit. After a few more seconds, he takes a deep breath. *You'll go*, he states. *Alone.*

How does that change anything? I demand. *It still can't hold me. I weigh more than thirty kilos!*

It'll be close, he says. *But I've lifted the shipments sent down the line. I've lifted you. The difference is nothing. . . . The line would never hold me, but it could hold you. I'll turn the crank. You want to get back, and I'm going to make sure you get there.*

No! I'm not leaving without you, I tell him.

Fei, there's no other way.

What will happen to you then? I ask.

Once you're up, I'll evade the soldiers, he says simply, as though that isn't exactly what we've been trying to do for the last hour! *It'll be easier with just one of us.*

We both know that's not true. *You won't be able to hear them,* I argue. *You should be the one who goes back. I'll hide out here.*

It seems impossible that he can be so calm when my emotions are all in an upheaval. *You need to get back to your sister— to our people,* he says. *You're the best one to talk to them. Once you're safely up there, I'll lie low and then find a way either to get back up to you or make my fortune somewhere else.*

Although he seems confident about his own chances, I can tell he isn't. If he takes the time to send me up the zip line, he might not be able to elude the soldiers. And even if he does escape, there's no guarantee they won't post watches at the mountain's base in the hopes of catching him climbing back. With a start, I realize following this course of action means I may never see him again. Going now, following that dream of us running off together in a new life, might be the only chance we both have of surviving this. It is tempting—excruciatingly so. His kiss is still warm on my lips, and the thought of not having him in my life makes a hole open up inside me.

But he is not the only one I love. Zhang Jing is back in our village, along with Elder Chen and all the other people I've known my entire life. They are innocents in this. I cannot leave them blind—figuratively or literally—to this terrible fate. They need to know what is happening, what the township is doing to them. The wise ones must be alerted so that they can help find a way for our people to endure.

Li Wei . . . His name is all I can manage to get out. Inside me, my heart is breaking. A shout from the woods causes me to turn in that direction, and a new panic surges within me. I still see no one, but that cry was much louder than before. The soldiers are getting closer. I look at Li Wei, who has deduced I heard something. His face is filled with sadness and resignation.

There is no other way, Fei, he reiterates. *We're running out of time.*

Okay, I say. *What are we going to do about the line keeper?* Normally our village never receives messages at nightfall, leading us to assume that the line keeper—or who we thought was the line keeper—went home at sunset. But now we can just barely make out someone standing at the line. I wonder if he has stayed longer because of today's series of strange events.

I have an idea, Li Wei says. We begin walking in the line's direction. *He looks like he's alone. You go talk to him.*

About what? I ask incredulously.

Anything. Distract him with your charm.

My charm?

Li Wei nods and gives me one more urging gesture before disappearing from sight. Mystified, I continue toward the line keeper, ever conscious of the noises farther back in the woods. I wonder if the soldiers have any idea of our plan, if they'll come in this direction or spread around the mountain in search of a climbing spot. I just don't know.

I also don't know exactly what it is I'm supposed to say to the line keeper, especially since he can't understand me. Presumably I'm to be some kind of diversion while Li Wei enacts the next part of the plan. I don't know if I can be that captivating, but as I approach the line keeper, I can tell I already have his attention. It's a different man from the last one, confirming what Nuan said about this simply being a common laborer's job and not the exalted position we'd imagined. Although he hasn't seen me before, there's enough recognition in this man's face to make me think he's been given my description. I come to a halt before him, giving a great bow of respect.

Greetings, I say. *I know you probably can't understand a word I'm saying, but that's not important. What's important is that you pay enough attention for me to do whatever it is Li Wei needs.*

This line keeper looks almost as uneasy as the last one. He utters some of those unintelligible noises and then makes a motion suggesting I follow him down the road. Apparently he learned a lesson from his predecessor about leaving us alone while going for backup.

I smile and shake my head politely, noticing then that Li Wei has crept out of the shadows carrying a large limb. I begin signing with renewed vigor, hoping to keep the line keeper's interest. *I thank you for your gracious offer to escort me to the township, but I think both of us know that's not the place for me to be right now. And while we're on the topic of thanks, please express my gratitude to your colleague for his generous gift of food earlier—*

Li Wei is almost in position to swing the limb at the back of the line keeper's head—until he steps on a smaller twig that's fallen on the road. I hear it. So does the line keeper. He spins around, but Li Wei has already swung the limb. It strikes the side of the line keeper's head—a blow great enough to render him unconscious. I kneel down, checking the man's breathing. It is even and steady.

Li Wei and I hurry over to the zip line's terminus, and it's all I can do not to demand we give up on this crazy plan right now. How can Li Wei hope to hold out against these people? How can he hide from them when they have the advantage of hearing? Even just now, his plan was nearly foiled when he made a noise and didn't even realize it. But despite my fears, I stay silent. He has made his choice and is ready to face the danger of staying here so that I can warn our people. My doubts will only hinder him, and I vow to remain calm and strong.

We do a quick rearranging of our packs, giving him the bulk of the food for weight purposes. I would give it all to him, but he insists I bring some as proof to our people about where we've been. I curl up in the basket that normally holds metals and food, and he loosely binds me to the line with an extra length of rope, just as a precaution. I hold on to the line as well, of course, my grip tight through the gloves. I look up toward the mountain, which is falling deeper and deeper into shadows, giving it an ominous feel. It seems like an eternity away, endlessly high and impossible to reach.

It won't take that long, Li Wei tells me. *You've seen them send stuff down before. You'll be up a lot faster than it took us to get down—though I'm sure this line has never held such valuable cargo before.*

He leans in and kisses me again, a kiss that manages to be both tender yet still full of that earlier intensity and passion. It completely undoes me, and I wish I could wrap my arms around him and never let him go. I think about his earlier words, about how he should have kissed me sooner. The time we've wasted leaves an ache in my heart, especially knowing I may never see him again.

Goodbye, Fei, he says when he straightens back up again. *Save our people . . . and don't forget about me.*

Tears threaten me. I release the line long enough to sign, *There will never be another name on my heart.*

His eyes shining, he gives me one last kiss and then begins turning the crank. With a jerk, I lurch forward up the line, rocking back and forth with each turn of the crank. The basket and ropes holding me suddenly seem terribly fragile, and whatever skill and bravery I thought I'd earned from our descent blow away in the wind wailing around me. Coming down the mountain, I at least held my fate in my own hands. I wasn't facing these dizzying, lethal heights in a basket at the mercy of someone else's resolve.

No, I realize. Not just someone. Li Wei. As I twist around to look back, my eyes lock with his. His gaze is dark and steady, never leaving my face as he turns the zip line's crank with every bit of strength he has. Moving me up the line at such a fast speed is no small feat, especially after all the work we did climbing down. But there is a relentless air about Li Wei as he turns, a determination that tells me I have nothing to fear so long as my fate is in his hands. He will guide me up to the top of the mountain, no matter the cost to him. His resolve wraps around me, securing me more than any rope could.

I hold on to his gaze as long as I can, taking strength from it, even as the ache in my chest grows with the distance between us. Evening's shadows wrap around him, making him a small, dark figure, his form blurry as tears sting my eyes. Soon he is out of sight altogether, and I feel terribly alone. But as I rise higher and higher, I know he is still with me and helping me. At first, the height isn't that troublesome. I tell myself it's not unlike climbing a tree. When I surpass even the tree heights, I remember that I survived the climb down from a much higher distance. Surely this should be no different.

Except that during the climb down, I at least felt some measure of control. I chose where I placed each hand and foot. Also, I had the partial security of knowing the rope I was using could hold my weight. Here, as I tremulously move up the line, I am acutely aware that I am testing the limits of what this zip line was built for. At any moment, the line could decide I am too much and snap, sending me to the depths below. I can't see every detail of the ground anymore, not with night setting in, but I am well aware of how far the drop is. That black gulf looms ominously below me.

No, I tell myself sternly. *You have nothing to fear with Li Wei at your back. As long as Li Wei is controlling the line, you will make it safely home. You just have to hang on.*

Suddenly, without warning, I come to a teeth-rattling halt. The line stops moving, and I sway where I'm at in the wind. I twist my head to look back and gasp at what I see: small pinpricks of flickering light at the line keeper's station. Torches. I can't make out all the details from the distance, but there's no mistaking the horde of men swarming around one single thing— or rather, person.

Li Wei is no longer in control of the line.

The soldiers have found and intercepted him. I watch in horror as that circle of torchlight moves, ushering away their prisoner. My heart cries out for Li Wei, and my lips want to cry out as well, but I keep my mouth firmly shut, lest I reveal myself.

Whatever is happening back there, they don't realize I'm out on the line. It's too dark for them to see me at this distance, and Li Wei's purpose at the line's terminus apparently hasn't hit them yet. The torches flutter around a little bit, and I imagine they are probably carrying away the unconscious line worker as well. Soon the whole cluster begins getting smaller, moving away from me as the guards head down the road back toward the township—with Li Wei as their prisoner.

Panic fills me—panic and guilt. If we'd left together, we could have escaped. What will they do with him now? Leave him in the camp with Nuan? Send him somewhere worse? Torture him? Kill him? I'm desperate to know his fate . . . but it occurs to me that I have another fate of much more pressing concern to worry about.

My own.

I'm hanging here, in the darkness, suspended between heaven and earth with nothing propelling me forward anymore. Li Wei managed to send me a fair distance before his capture, moving me at a much faster rate than our painstaking climb down. But there is still a long way to go—and an even longer way behind me.

Acting against Li Wei's earlier warnings, I dare a glance down to better assess my situation.

My eyes have adjusted enough to the darkness that I can make out faint details by moonlight. Mist has rolled in for the night in the land beneath me, but as it swirls and shifts, I can catch occasional glimpses of the terrain below. It is rocky and jagged, dotted with occasional evergreens that shoot up from the earth like spikes, ready to impale. They look tiny from this distance, like an illustration from a book, which only serves to remind me how precarious my situation is. I swallow and look away.

A blast of wind suddenly rocks my basket, and I sway from side to side. I grip the rope more tightly, gritting my teeth until the gust passes. As I rock, I notice the handles of the basket seem to be straining. They don't appear to be in any danger of snapping—yet—but how long will that remain true? The basket wasn't meant to hold someone of my weight. Right now, it gives me an extra level of protection, but I can't count on it to last.

A wave of fear rolls over me, nearly as powerful as the wind. I can picture the basket snapping at any moment, and then how long will my hands—already wet with sweat—hold me?

How did I get out here anyway? Why didn't I just stay in the safety of the art studio? If I hadn't questioned things, if I'd just continued with the status quo, none of this would have happened. I'd be back at home with Zhang Jing. Li Wei would never have had to risk himself to get me back to our village. We'd be safe.

And deceived.

I would've continued being part of the township's agenda. My loved ones are still unknowingly part of that agenda, risking their lives for it, and I am the only one capable of warning them now. That knowledge steadies me, allowing me to shift my gaze from the treacherous fall. Above me, the stars glitter with a cold beauty, and as I focus on them instead, I find a similar clarity settling over me. I think of Zhang Jing, waiting in the village above with no clue of the dangers she and the others are facing. I think of Li Wei, bravely risking his freedom below so that I could be up here. The distance I have to cover seems insurmountable . . . but there is no choice. A part of me longs to climb down and go after Li Wei, but I know what he would tell me to do: go forward and finish my task.

So, with a deep breath, I begin to climb.

Hand over hand, I inch my way up the zip line, wriggling out of the basket and the protection it offered. It's hard, agonizing work, far more difficult than coming down. I still have the ropes loosely binding me to the line as an added safeguard, but the strength and stamina required to work my way up must all come from me. And much like the basket, I'm not sure if the ropes will indefinitely bear my weight. Every part of me aches, but I push through my exhaustion, climbing higher and higher. I take small breaks when I can, pausing to unkink my fingers and wipe my sweaty palms, but my rest is short-lived. I am driven by the sacrifice that Li Wei has made, compelled by the knowledge that it's imperative I get back to my village.

More gusts of wind blow, forcing me to a stop as I sway back and forth on the line. Once, I'm so startled that my hands lose their grip. I have the brief sensation of falling before the safety ropes catch me. I can tell they're being pushed to their limits, and I frantically grope for the line again to take some of the pressure off. The wind's interference slows me, but at last I manage to grasp the line again. I breathe a deep sigh of relief, even as I accept a frightening truth: If I lose my grip again, there's no telling if the ropes will hold me.

The moon shifts through the sky as I climb, and my heart leaps as I see the top of the mountain coming into view. I've nearly made it. A new surge of adrenaline spurs me on, and I increase my speed, fighting the pain and stiffness in my body. Within an hour, I'll be at the end of the zip line.

As that triumphant thought fills me, a jolt on the line suddenly makes me lose my grip. The ropes catch me again, and I quickly manage to regain my hold—just in time for another jolt. It takes me a moment to figure out what is going on: I'm slowly being pulled backward.

Someone at the base of the mountain is winding the line back down.

CHAPTER 14

FOR A FEW TERRIFYING SECONDS, I don't know what to do. Then, seeing all the precious ground I've made slipping away from me, I frantically begin climbing up the line again, desperate to outpace whoever is pulling down below. It's too late at night for the line keeper to be back at his post. I wonder whether the soldiers finally deduced what happened to me. Or is it possible that they forced Li Wei to talk and interpreted with the help of one of Nuan's people?

That last thought—of what they might have had to do to get Li Wei to reveal my location—is too horrible to endure. I push it out of my mind as I fight to regain my position and move faster than the line is being lowered. I barely manage it, but I know I can't sustain it. It was already excruciating going up when I didn't have someone working against me. Now I can already feel myself losing the battle. My hands—bloody and raw through the now-tattered gloves—slip a number of times, delaying me as the strained ropes catch me and force me to get a new and increasingly painful hold. My distance gained shrinks, and soon I'm almost at a standstill. In moments, I will be descending again.

I glance down, desperate for a way out. In the moonlight, I see a wide, rocky ledge jutting out from the cliff's side below me. It won't be a comfortable drop, but I can make it and survive. What I'll do from there remains to be seen, but it's either that or let all my progress vanish as my unseen opponent pulls me back down.

In a second, my decision is made.

I wiggle my way out of the loose safety ropes, an action that costs me some elevation as I'm jerked back down the line. I suppose now I don't have to worry about whether the ropes will hold my weight anymore. Once free, I grit my teeth and summon more of that desperate strength to climb forward against the pull, enough to get myself in a safe position over the ledge. It is grueling work, made more terrifying by the knowledge that I have no security and will plummet to the depths below if my hands fail me.

I manage, barely getting situated above the outcropping before my strength gives out and I let go of the zip line, dropping down to the ledge, making sure to pull the security rope along with me. It and I land in an ungraceful, jarring heap, and it's a relief not to be fighting anymore. That relief is short-lived, however, as the force of swinging into the cliff triggers a cascade of rocks from above. I cringe against the mountain's side until the avalanche passes, praying the ledge I'm standing on won't crumble beneath me as well.

When the avalanche finally ceases, I'm almost too afraid to move for fear of what might happen next. The muscles in my arms and legs are weak and shaking from their exertion, and as I gaze down across the vast blackness of the mountain slope, I'm a bit in awe of the distance I've managed to cover. I can only just make out a tiny point of light at what I think is the zip line's terminus; presumably it's held by whoever pulled me back. I shudder to think of what would have happened if I hadn't been able to jump to safety.

Of course, now I have a whole new set of problems.

In the phantom lighting, I can see the face of the mountain leading up to my village. It is jagged and irregular, filled with places to get a hand- or foothold or even use the rope for support. The distance is also a fraction of what I've already covered, but it's still going to be painstaking work. I can't do it just yet, no matter the press of time. I sit down to catch my breath, rummaging through the pack for some water and a bite to eat. As I search, I find one of the game pieces—the general—and I smile. Just before we parted, Li Wei had considered giving me the pixiu for luck. It ended up staying with him because of weight issues, but apparently he still wanted me to have some token of fortune. I squeeze the wooden disc tight in my hand, willing myself to be worthy of his regard. Then I say a prayer to all the gods I know, hoping that we all come out of this safely.

When I feel as rested as I think I'm going to get, given the conditions, I steel myself for the next part of this journey: getting back to my village. Li Wei told me a little about how we'd ascend the mountain again, and I know some of the basic principles. My destination is within my sight; it's just a matter of getting to it.

I have the rope I salvaged from the zip line, and I use it to begin the first part of the climb. I am able to throw it high and hook it around a jagged rock outcropping, locking it securely so that I can scale the cliff face.

But when I reach the rope's end, there is no other place to secure a rope. The zip line's start is still far out of reach. I must climb with my hands now, praying I make the right choices and that my holds won't crumble to dust in my fingers and send me plummeting back below. Amazingly, everything holds, but just as I'm almost finally near the end, I hear the rumblings of a small rock fall from above. Unlike before, there is nowhere to seek shelter, no rope to swing out of danger on. All I can do is cling to the mountain and hide my face, hoping this avalanche will miss me.

Several sharp rocks strike my arms and face, causing me to flinch, and I must summon all my resolve simply to hold on and maintain my hand- and footholds. When silence returns again, I slowly lift my head, listening for further signs of trouble. None come, and I make my move, scrambling up as quickly as I dare, needing to reach the top. When I see the zip line station, I nearly cry in relief. With trembling arms, I pull myself up and grip an outcropping of rock that will let me pull myself over onto solid ground. Almost immediately, I feel the rock crumble in my hands. There's nothing else to grasp, and I scream as I fall backward, back down the cliff into the blackness below.

I land back-first on the ledge I was on earlier, hitting with an impact so great that it momentarily knocks the wind out of me. I lay there, gasping, staring up at all the distance I just lost. Tears spring to my eyes, and the urge to give up threatens to engulf me. I feel despair not only for myself but for Li Wei. Out on the line, I couldn't allow myself to worry too much about him, not with my survival in the balance. Now all those fears come tumbling back. What has happened to him? Is he even alive? Worse still is the guilt of knowing that if I'd simply run away with him, I could have saved him from his fate. That would have meant abandoning Zhang Jing . . . but what does it matter? I've failed everyone now.

Stop that, Fei, I tell myself sternly. *All is not lost. Make Li Wei proud. You climbed down the mountain. You want to go back up it. You can see your goal—don't give up now.*

Sniffling, hurting everywhere, I manage to make my way to my feet. I have bruises and aches in parts of my body I didn't even know existed, but I refuse to let them master me. Gritting my teeth, I retrace this last, painstaking climb up to the top. My hands are bloodied by the time I make it up, and without the outcropping from earlier, pulling myself up at the end is much more difficult. I must rely on the strength of the rest of my body—a body pushed past its limits. For a brief moment, as I try to haul myself up and onto the mountain's top, my muscles can't quite do it. I am stuck there, clinging to the cliff, knowing it will take only the briefest of slips to send me plummeting back to the ledge below—or worse.

Do it for Zhang Jing. Do it for Li Wei.

The feel of their names in my mind gives me courage. I cry out, pulling myself over the edge, touching the rocky—but solid—

ground with gratitude. It's now the middle of the night, but against all odds, I have made it to the zip line station. I have made it home.

I rise to my feet, my legs still weak and shaking, knowing I have no time to rest—despite how much my body is screaming to. I need to alert the others to what is happening. I press forward and nearly trip over several dark bundles on the ground near the zip line station. I can't tell what they are in the darkness, so I kneel down to unwrap one and am astonished to find it full of glittering gold ore. Another bag reveals silver. These are mined metals, a day's work, waiting to go down. Why are they still here, just sitting out? These would provide the day's food.

I know I won't find out by sticking around. I make my way back to the heart of the village, more relieved than I can say to be in my homeland after the adventures of these last couple of days. I'm not entirely sure how I'm going to fix things or alert people, but my feet take me, almost of their own volition, back to the one place I feel safest: the Peacock Court.

Getting inside presents a new challenge. I'm not yet ready to announce my return to the others, so I don't want to use any of the doors that might alert one of the servants on watch. Instead, I go to an out-of-the-way window in the back of the building, one that opens near a storage room where we keep art supplies. A latticework of narrow wooden slats covers the paper window-pane, and with a grimace, I begin breaking and prying out the wooden guards. It makes a terrible amount of noise—as does the paper windowpane, when I'm finally able to rip it out—but I at least have the reassurance of knowing I'm the only one who can hear it.

When I've created a big enough opening, I climb through and land just outside the supply room, as expected. From there, it's just a matter of making my way through the school to the servants' wing. Along the way, I dodge more servants on patrol than I recall seeing last time, which seems odd. Fortunately, their sounds alert me, and no one is on guard in the servants' actual sleeping wing. I sneak into the women's room, and there, just as I last saw her, is Zhang Jing sleeping in her bed.

Although it's only been a matter of days, I feel like years have passed since I saw my sister. My whole world has opened up on my journey. I don't even feel like the same person. Zhang Jing is the same, though. Still sweet and beautiful, her face peaceful in sleep. I watch her for several moments, overwhelmed by my love for her, and then wipe tears back from my eyes. Trying to be as gentle but as firm as I can, I shake her awake. She stirs, blinking in confusion, and then manages to focus on me in the dimness. She gasps, her eyes widening.

I throw my arms around her, and she buries her face in my shoulder. I have tears in my eyes again and can feel them on her face as well. When she finally pulls back to look at me, her pretty face is a mixture of emotions: confusion, relief, suspicion.

Fei, she signs, *where have you been? What's happened? I've been so worried about you.*

It's a long story, I say. *But I'm okay—for now. The truth is that we're all in danger. That's why I've come back.*

What did you do? she asks. *What did you do to make them stop the food?*

Now I am the confused one. *What do you mean?*

Yesterday morning, she explains. *The suppliers sent their first shipment of metals down the zip line. No food came up. Instead, a note came from the line keeper about betrayal and spies. No one really understood what it meant, but they kept sending metals, hoping food would come. It didn't. The line keeper started sending the metals back.*

I think back to the glittering bundles sitting out on the ground. *I saw them,* I say.

People are saying it's your fault—yours and Li Wei's. That you did something to anger the line keeper and—

There is no line keeper, I interrupt. *Only a group of workers who take turns pulling the line. We've been lied to, Zhang Jing. The notes and food come from a larger regime that's keeping us up here to mine metals for them—metals that are toxic. That's why we lost the ability to hear, why you and some of the others are going blind. We need to change something—to get away from this place.*

That's impossible, she says. It's not clear to me which of the many things I've just told her is causing her the most disbelief. All of them are a shock to the world she has always known.

It's not, I say simply. *You know me. Would I lie to you?*

She meets my gaze for a very long time. *No,* she says at last. *But maybe you're confused. People say Li Wei is a rebel, that his grief has deluded him and that he's corrupted you into doing*

*something that's angered the line keeper. If you just go to Elder
Chen, I'm sure you can explain things and get your place back.
Maybe we can fix things before people get too hungry.*

I don't even bother correcting her about the line keeper.
*Zhang Jing, if we don't take action, there won't be a place for
me. There won't be anything for any of us except death and
despair. We have to explain this to the others.*

But inside my heart is sinking a little as Li Wei's warning
rings true. If my own sister won't believe what I've learned, how
will the others? And how am I going to convey the full scope
of what I've seen? Will anyone even listen to me? The township
overlords have already done a neat job of turning my people
against me, attacking in the most powerful way they can: by
withholding food. Zhang Jing's words about people getting too
hungry aren't lost on me. They are already hungry. In our village,
we have at most one extra day's supply of food at any given
time. If no food came up today, the villagers would have had
to use that tiny reserve and would have rationed it out pretty
strictly. That's why there were extra servants on watch tonight.
No wonder people have been quick to believe the worst of Li Wei
and me. They are starving and desperate, just as the township
wants. Who will believe our story now? How will I even get them
to pay attention?

An idea suddenly hits me. It isn't ideal, but it's the best one
I've got. It's the *only* one I've got. I think back to when I was
standing outside the school, breaking the window. Based on the
moon's descent in the sky, I probably have about three more

hours until the first people in the village start waking up. It's not a lot of time, and I'm so exhausted from the feat of climbing, but what choice do I have? Everything is riding on what I do next.

I rise from where I'm sitting on Zhang Jing's bed, beckoning her forward. *Come on*, I say. *I'm going to need your help.*

With what? she asks, startled.

It's time to make the record.

CHAPTER 15

ZHANG JING FOLLOWS ME as we head to the school's work studio. Along the way, we encounter two servants patrolling the halls. I hear them before they see us and am able to dodge them each time, keeping us concealed. Zhang Jing observes all of this without comment until we're safely behind the closed door of the workroom. I begin lighting lanterns for us to work by.

Fei, she says at last. *How are you able to do that? What's happened to you? Did you receive some kind of enchantment while you were down the mountain?*

I smile, imagining how what I've been able to do would seem like magic. And really, for all I know, maybe there is some sort of magic involved, since I have yet to understand why this is happening to me. *I've regained my hearing,* I tell her. It surprises me how easily I am able to say those words. I guess after everything I've gone through and learned, my hearing is just one more incredible thing. And seeing as how Zhang Jing is having enough trouble believing the rest, I figure I have nothing to lose by sharing this too.

That's impossible, she says. It's becoming her standard line. *Believe me, I know,* I say. *I'll tell you more about it later, when there's time. Right now, we need to get to work.*

And so, as usual, Zhang Jing follows my lead. The room is set up the way it always is, with the previous day's record still in progress on assorted pieces of canvas. A glance at what my fellow apprentices have been working on confirms Zhang Jing's earlier story. It is an accounting of yesterday, covering the rejection of the metals and refusal of food. Even Li Wei and I are mentioned—probably the first time we've been included in the record since our birth announcements. There are also recaps of emergency meetings and arguments that have already broken out since the food shortage began. Elder Chen's other apprentice, Jin Luan, has done a commendable job of painting a scene of some disgruntled miners gathering for a meeting in the village's center. She's probably the only person glad for my disappearance.

I direct Zhang Jing to help set up new canvases for me to paint. I visualize the layout of the various pieces of the record and how I want to create my message. It is going to be a daunting task, and there is no time for any of the skill and fine detail I've been so painstakingly trained to use. I must get my message out, and the only thing that really matters is its truth.

I start with the words, drawing characters in big, bold calligraphy to tell my story. Zhang Jing stays nearby, watching as I work, ready to mix fresh ink when she sees I am running low. First, I tell how Li Wei and I climbed down the mountain. I gloss over the details, for time's sake, emphasizing that it was dangerous but possible. If there's a chance our village may be leaving this place, I want them to know it can be done without scaring them too badly—at least not about this. There are plenty of other things for them to be scared of.

When I reach the part about Nuan's village, I include more detail, about the dead bodies and the records of a village in chaos—a village just like ours. It is a grim memory, one I don't like repeating, but it too must be told. When I get to the point where Li Wei and I make it to the bottom and see the township for the first time, I pause. The artist in me, the one who sees the world and wants to capture it, wishes I could spare the time to truly describe the township. For all its evils, it is still a remarkable place, the closest thing to a real city any of us will ever get to. I want to paint pictures of those embellished buildings, list all the things for sale, convey the singing children . . . but there is no time. I simply describe it as a busy, vivid place—emphasizing that it has plenty of food—and then go on to Nuan's tale.

This is the part I elaborate on in the greatest detail, pointing out the similarities between our peoples and how the mines destroyed them—and how the township gave up on them. I tell of their encampment and treatment by the others, how many have given up hope and are just as hungry as they were when they still lived on the plateau. Finally, I close my account with a brief recap of how the soldiers chased us, and how Li Wei and I split up. Although it is certainly a thrilling part of the tale, I again use brevity. My own hardships don't matter at this point. It is Li Wei's sacrifice and the township's ruthlessness I want my village to know about.

When I step back, I am amazed at the amount of calligraphy I've painted. This much text normally would be the work of at least half a dozen apprentices. It would also have been painted with much more precision, each brushstroke placed with care and beauty. My work, though not entirely neat, is thorough and legible. I used big, broad strokes, ensuring it can be read from a distance.

Zhang Jing now supplies me with colored paints as I start the illustrations. My pictures are even more hurried than my text, but I'm a strong enough artist that my skills still shine through. For one picture, I depict the house in Nuan's village, showing the room in disrepair and the bodies of the family that starved to death. It is a gruesome creation, but the shock in Zhang Jing's face tells me it's effective. For my second image, I paint where Nuan's people live now: the dilapidated village of tents, its people thin and dirty. It is something else my people need to see.

I don't know where I find the energy to do all this painting. The earlier harrowing climb has left me in a state far past exhaustion. It is Zhang Jing's future—hers and others like her, I decide—that gives me the added rush of adrenaline and inspiration to complete this frantic, ominous masterpiece. And Li Wei, of course. Always, always he is in the back of my mind, urging me on. My sister keeps me supplied with paint, so I have no delays, save for pausing and dipping my brush or switching colors.

It is almost a shock when, at long last, I realize I've accomplished all I can possibly do in this time. Standing still after such frenetic work feels almost unnatural, but I force myself to take in all the pieces of canvas, my greatest and most terrible work.

We must take this to the village's center, I tell Zhang Jing.

Her eyes are wide as she takes in the extent of my work. She has been watching the entire time, making no comment until now. *It really is true, isn't it?* she asks at last. *All of this. What happened to those people. What will happen to us.*

Yes, I say.

You say nothing about your hearing, she points out. *Isn't that important?*

I hesitate before answering. *Not to our village's fate. There will be time later to figure out what's happening to me. For now, we must help the others.*

Zhang Jing nods in acceptance. *Tell me what you need me to do.*

For a moment, the love and faith in her eyes overwhelms me so much that I fear I'll break down and start crying. I hide my discomfort with a hug so that she is unable to see me blinking back tears. When I step away, I hope I look more confident than I feel about what is to come. *Okay,* I tell her. *Now we need to carry these out to the center of the village.*

The task is a bit more complicated than it might appear. Although most of the patrolling servants are staying near the kitchen to guard the food, there is still the chance one might wander into the wing where the workroom is. That requires extra caution as we smuggle the canvases outside. Equally challenging is handling the canvases themselves. Even when the apprentices do touch-ups to the record in the morning, most of the work has had time to dry overnight. Now Zhang Jing and I must manage still-wet paint, taking care not to ruin the words and images I have just labored over.

It also requires many trips. I never thought of that daily morning trek as particularly long or difficult, but now, doing it multiple times in my current state, my mind starts to think it's almost as taxing as the climb down the mountain. Many beggars sleep in the town's center, their bodies huddled together in piles for warmth. We are careful to step around and not disturb them, but the sight of them makes my insides twist when I think how it's a very real possibility that others—including Zhang Jing— may share their fate if we don't take action.

Zhang Jing and I finish assembling my record just as the eastern sky turns purple. Soon the villagers will be waking. Soon they will see what I've created.

You must go back before anyone realizes you've been a part of this, I tell her. *Go wake with the others, have breakfast as normal. Then we will see what happens.*

My sister gives me a sweet, sad smile. *I would rather stand with you. Besides, there is no food for breakfast.*

The words hit me hard. I kneel down on the dais and open up my pack, pulling out some of the rations I brought back with me to show the others. Zhang Jing gasps at the sight of it, her hunger obvious in her eyes. I give her some fruit and the last bun.

Take these and go back, I insist. *I know you support me, but I'll feel better if you're back at the school. I don't know how people are going to react to this—to me. Especially if they think I've cost them their food.*

Zhang Jing places her hand over mine as I begin repacking my bag, giving me a brief squeeze. *If you need me, tell me.*

I will. The best way you can help at this point is to stay safe.

What is that? she asks, pointing at a flash of red in my bag.

I clench some of the red silk dress in my hand, my heart swelling as I think of Li Wei. *It's a gamble that paid off. Pray ours does as well. Now go.*

After another fierce, quick hug, Zhang Jing obeys and hurries off down the main village track, back to the school. I know I should probably eat as well, but for once I have no appetite. I'm too keyed up, my nerves frayed and on edge. I settle for water and then sit cross-legged, watching as the sky grows lighter and lighter, waiting for my village to waken.

The first person I see, aside from the sleeping beggars, is the lamplighter. He trudges down the main track with his torch, stifling a yawn. He's usually the first person up in our village, lighting the various lamps that will illuminate our paths until the sun is up. When he reaches the village's center, he comes to a complete standstill, frozen as he recognizes me and undoubtedly thinks of all that I've been accused of. Then, slowly, his eyes shift to the record beside me. Although it is still early, the stark black-on-white calligraphy is easy to discern. He reads, his jaw dropping as he goes further and further.

When he finishes, he says nothing to me, but his astonishment is obvious. The torch slips from his hand, burning harmlessly in the packed dirt. He turns around and goes running as fast as he can, back toward the residential part of town.

It isn't long before others begin filing in to the center. Some appear to be people out on their normal morning errands. Others arrive in haste, and I suspect they have heard the lamplighter's story. Word is spreading quickly, and when I see the elders and artist apprentices hurrying in ahead of their normal time, I know that my presence and unexpected creation have completely thrown the village off its schedule. Zhang Jing stands with the other servants behind the apprentices, and much to my relief, no one seems to be paying her any special attention.

The crowd swells, and soon I'm fairly certain the entire village is here. This isn't the first time I've stood on the dais, facing them all beside a completed record. But this is the first time that I'm as much of the draw as what's on the canvas. I meet their gazes as impassively as I can, proud of what I've done—both in ink and in my recent journey. I stand by my actions and what I must do to help these people.

For a long time, the gathering crowd simply takes me and my story in. A few brief signed conversations flutter, but for the most part, everyone seems to be coming to terms with what I'm telling them. This emboldens me enough to step forward and address the crowd. I'd originally thought I would let my work speak for me. But now I realize I must add my own plea to it. Facing all these people is terrifying, but I remind myself I can be no less brave than Li Wei, trapped somewhere in the township. I don't know what happened after the soldiers seized him, but I refuse to believe he's in some horrible prison—or dead. It strengthens me to think he's just waiting in one of those tents with Nuan, waiting for me to come join them with our people. Or maybe he's escaped, run far away, already planning a new life free of all this. It is the memory of his face, of the strength in his eyes, that pushes me as I speak.

Everything you see here is true, I sign to the crowd. *This is what Li Wei and I have learned over the last few days, what we have risked our lives for. The township is deceiving you. We need to come together and think of a way to save ourselves and our future. I know it is difficult to hear. I know how overwhelming it must seem. We can't let fear—or the township—rule us any longer. It may seem impossible, but it's not—not if we unite and work together.*

My hands slowly return to my side, and my heart aches as I recall Li Wei's brave, handsome face telling me: *We're pretty good at the impossible.* I have to force myself to remain calm and serious as I regard my people.

No one responds right away. Mostly they seem to again be processing what I've told them. Hope rises in me, and I dare to believe that my people are taking heed and will believe me so that we can all find a reasonable course to save ourselves.

As it turns out, I am wrong.

CHAPTER 16

A MAN I DISTANTLY KNOW, an older miner, is the first to act. He storms up onto the dais and tears down a section of my painting, hurling it to the ground. Tension has been building and swelling in the crowd as I speak, and it's as though that one defiant action spurs everyone to action. Chaos breaks out.

People storm the stage, attacking the rest of my record. Some simply want it down, others furiously work to destroy it, tearing it into unrecognizable pieces. And some people aren't interested in the painting at all—they come for me. Suddenly, getting my message across is no longer my primary goal. Staying alive is.

Angry faces loom in my vision as hands reach for me, clawing and groping. I never would have expected to fear attack from my own people, but the world as I've known it has drastically changed in a matter of days. Someone tears the sleeve of my shirt, and I feel nails gauge my cheek. Fearing worse, I hastily back up until there's no more surface on the stage left. My attackers move with me, and I only just escape them by hopping down, though a few bold ones do the same. On the ground, I am plunged into the chaos of the mob and soon lose those who are pursuing me as the crowd in the village's center becomes even more frenzied.

Many, not realizing that most of my paintings are gone and that I've left the stage, are still trying to get to the dais. Others are turning on one another. Conversations are flying fast and furious, too difficult for me to follow all the signs. But I see certain things repeated over and over—*lies*, *death*, and *food*. It's clear the majority of the people around me don't believe what I've told them. They seem to think I concocted all this to save myself, and my heart sinks—not because they'd think so little of me but because they've become so enslaved by this system that they are terrified of breaking out of it.

There are a few, however, who seem to think there's some truth to what I've said—but their support is almost detrimental. Some are those who've spoken out against the township before and are already angry and looking for a fight. They begin arguing with those who think I'm lying, and I am aghast to see actual physical altercations break out. I try to tell myself it's all because my people are hungry and scared, that the uncertainty of the last day's events has left them panicked and unsettled. But it's still hard to see them degenerate into this madness, turning on one another when it's imperative we stand together against the township.

Through the chaos, I see Zhang Jing at the back of the crowd, mostly out of the way of any danger. She is standing there wide-eyed, rooted to the spot with fear. Her gaze meets mine, and I quickly tell her, *Wait, I'm coming.* I don't know if she understands, as two people in a shoving match stumble into me, knocking me to the ground. My body, already sore, hurts more than it should from the impact, but I manage to scramble to my feet before I get trampled. I've lost sight of Zhang Jing, but I nonetheless doggedly head in the direction I last spotted her.

Stop, stop! I sign frantically when I come across two apprentices I know from the school fighting with each other. They don't even notice me, and without thinking, I force myself in between them to break up the fight. *Don't do this! We must unite!*

They stare, astonished to find me there in their midst. I have no idea what they were fighting over, but suddenly they are united—in their hatred for me. Snarls fill their faces, and they both lunge for me, forcing me to jump back. I run into a tall man I don't know who at first dismisses me and then does a double take when he recognizes who I am. Anger fills his face, and then he reaches for me too—

—just as a sound of unimaginable magnitude rips through our village.

Instinctively, I put my hands to my ears. Up until this point, the loudest sound I'd ever heard was the priest's gong. No longer. This new noise reminds me of that *boom* a bit, but it is much, much more intense. In fact, the sound is so big, so powerful, that the very ground beneath us shakes, causing many people—including my current assailants—to pause and look around curiously. A few even glance up, and I don't blame them. That kind of trembling is sometimes felt with thunder, but today the early morning sky is clear and full of sun.

A few shrug it off and immediately return to their squabbling. For others, it is a much-needed slap in the face, and I am relieved to see them step back from their conflict. But my relief is short-lived when I hear a new sound—an impossible sound, at least in our village. But there can be no question as the sound grows louder and louder: It is the noise made by horse hooves striking the earth, the very noise Li Wei and I were running from down below.

It can't be, I think. *There can't be horses up here!*

As the noise grows louder, I search around, trying to discern its source. I still have some difficulties gauging the location and distance of certain sounds. But as I get my bearings, I'm almost certain the horses are coming from the same direction as the initial *boom*. It's a part of the mountain we rarely go, a place that was once used because of the narrow pass that led to a fertile valley and a path down the back of the mountain. Avalanches buried that narrow gap, creating an impenetrable, high wall that none have been able to get through . . .

. . . until now.

A feeling of dread builds within me, growing as the sound of the hooves gets closer and closer. Through the tumultuous crowd, I catch another glimpse of Zhang Jing, still waiting for me. But there is no time, not anymore. *Go*, I sign to her. *Go and hide! Something terrible is about to happen!*

To my relief, she turns and runs just as a new burst of noise surges behind me. I spin around in time to see a veritable army of soldiers on horseback galloping into the village's center. With weapons raised, they ride in, uncaring of what or who is in their way. What I thought was chaotic earlier is nothing compared to what now ensues. It's not just the soldiers and their weapons that cause the panic: The horses are equally terrifying. Like me, my people have never seen them outside of pictures. Equally rare and frightening is the sight of outsiders in our village. We've all seen the same faces our entire lives. New ones are a shock—especially when it's clear these aren't friendly.

On top of all this, I have new sounds to cope with: the sounds of war. The soldiers scream harsh battle cries as they descend upon us, the noise ugly and hateful to my ears. Around me, cries and moans from my people also rise, born instinctually from high emotion. They don't even realize they're making these eerie sounds, which raise the hair on the back of my neck. For a moment, as those cries fill the air, I have a strange flashback to that first dream when my hearing began. In it, my people all cried out at the same time—almost like this but less chaotic. Still, I feel something tug inside me, that same stirring I've felt in other dreams, like I'm being called to. It's the first time I've truly felt it while awake, but I have no time to ponder it, not with what's happening.

The people around me stampede in different directions, everyone trying to find a way to save themselves and their loved ones. There is no strategy, no unity. I try to see what the soldiers are doing, to get a sense if they're capturing or killing, but it's all I can do not to get trampled by my own people.

I manage to climb back up on the stage, giving me a limited

view of the scene as well as a brief respite from the stampede. No one wants to be here; everyone is trying to get away. The soldiers are riding around the center, trying to trap my people within it. If some flee, the soldiers herd them back in. One man—the tall, intimidating one I encountered earlier—stands up to a soldier, but his brawn is no match for the sword that runs him through. I've never seen anyone killed that way, and the horror of it leaves me frozen for a moment. Another villager doesn't challenge the army, but he also doesn't get out of the way when a soldier comes thundering down on him on a large black horse. The man wavers, too petrified to move, and the soldier simply runs him down, trampling the man under those powerful hooves. That thoughtless killing is almost more gruesome than if he'd used his sword. It spurs me back to action.

Even those who are simply captured are subject to brutality, struck and herded with dispassionate force. I don't know what it all means, but I know I can't be caught here. I hop down, relying on my smaller size to weave through the panicked crowd. I head in the opposite direction the soldiers have come, hoping I can escape from the village's heart there. As I glance back, gauging the soldiers' position, I am shocked to see a group of people entering behind them: a group of thin, ragged people in chains. Even more shocking is when I recognize one of them: Li Wei.

He can't be here. He can't. It's impossible.

We're pretty good at the impossible.

Incredibly, despite the pandemonium filling the gulf between us, he spots me as well. Our eyes meet, and in a moment

I have changed direction and am heading back into the heart of the village. I don't care that it's the most dangerous place to be right now, not if Li Wei is there. He's standing on the fringe of the chained prisoners, where there are fewer guards. There also aren't many villagers there, as most of them are running in the opposite direction. I have to do a fair amount of dodging as I make my way across the center. A number of times I am shoved and kicked in the frenzy of capture-and-flee going on. A soldier on horseback eyes me as I run past him but then decides a larger, muscled miner is a better prize to go after.

Breathless, I reach the chained prisoners and find Li Wei, my heart lifting at the sight of his beloved face. I throw my arms around him, unable to believe he's real and in front of me, particularly after all the terrible outcomes I'd been imagining for him. He looks worn and tired, and there are new bruises on him, but the fire in his eyes glitters as fiercely as ever when we finally break away to regard each other. He can't speak easily to me, not with his hands chained, but suddenly a cry escapes his lips as his eyes focus on something behind me. I don't need to understand any spoken language to get his message, and I spin around in time to see a foot soldier waving a sword at me. Li Wei hurls himself forward, swinging his manacled hands up to intercept the blade coming toward my head. The soldier isn't prepared for Li Wei's considerable strength, and as chain and blade hit, the soldier is thrown backward, stumbling. His sword slips from his hands in a flash, and I pick it up, aiming it for the soldier's neck.

I've never held a sword before. Until our trip to the township, I'd never seen a real one. And I've certainly never killed someone before. But as I keep the blade at the soldier's neck, there must be something convincing in my face. Even though he is a trained fighter, even though he is bigger than me, he looks uneasy about this new situation he finds himself in. He should. Maybe I've never used a sword or killed anyone, but I won't hesitate to use one now. I will do whatever it takes to save Li Wei.

I jerk my head toward Li Wei, and the soldier stares in confusion. Frustrated, I wish not for the first time that I had vocal powers of communication. Quick as lightning, I swing the sword tip to Li Wei's manacles and then back to the soldier's neck. I give him a meaningful look, and he finally understands. I put on a fierce expression, hoping I appear as though I'm seconds from puncturing his neck with the blade.

Tentatively, he reaches forward to unlock Li Wei's manacles. It's a trick, though, and he suddenly makes a play for me, diving for the sword. I hold my ground, catching the man on the cheek with a deep cut that immediately begins bleeding. In his moment of surprise, Li Wei swings his bound arms together, making the chains smack the man's head. The soldier stumbles and falls, one more blow from Li Wei keeping him down. With trembling hands, I unlock Li Wei's manacles and then look uncertainly at the other bound prisoners standing nearby. I can't help them all, but perhaps some will be able to help each other. I toss the key to the ground in front of them, and Li Wei and I take off, running out of the village's center toward a cluster of trees.

It is quiet here, giving us a brief respite, and I run into his arms again. He holds me tightly, burying his face in my neck as the safety of his strength engulfs me.

Looks like you rescued me this time, he says, once we are able to speak.

How are you here? I was so worried about you, I say. *I didn't know what they'd done to you. I didn't know if you'd be able to escape.*

Actually, I did escape, he says. *And then I found out they were marching back here . . . so I surrendered.*

I try not to gape. *But why?*

I couldn't leave our people to this fate, especially once I experienced the cruelty of the soldiers for myself. And . . . He gently traces the line of my cheek before continuing. *I couldn't leave you, Fei. I don't care how dangerous it is here or what wonders Beiguo could hold for me. My place is with you, wherever that is.*

I'm glad you came back. It's an understatement. Shouts nearby force me to turn from him. *We must go*, I say, thinking frantically. *We must get back to the Peacock Court.*

It isn't safe, he counters. *They will most certainly attack an important building like that.*

There are underground storage rooms beneath it, I tell him. *I know a way that won't be obvious to the soldiers.*

His expression shows surprise at this news, but he gives a quick nod. *Okay, show me.*

We take off again, and I secretly hope Zhang Jing has also remembered the existence of the underground facility. Although the way to the school is fairly direct from here, we find many obstacles blocking our way. The soldiers have reorganized and are moving in small groups, trying to intercept those who made it out of the town square. Li Wei and I find ourselves taking a roundabout way, and at one point we cut very close to the mine itself. There, from the cover of the trees, we see a group of soldiers standing outside the entrance, having a heated conversation in those words I can't understand. From their gestures—and the shocked look of a miner who runs up and halts when he sees them there—the mine has been used as a place of refuge by some of the villagers. Now the soldiers are squabbling over whether to go in or simply wait out those trapped inside. I wonder if the soldiers know about the poisonous metals and fear them.

How did all of you even get up here? I ask Li Wei. *There's no way you could have climbed in so short a time. There's no way the horses could.*

We took the mountain passes, he explains. *If you go to the other side of the mountain, they lead straight up here.*

I know about the passes, of course. Everyone does. *But they are blocked*, I point out. *The giant boulders that fell in that ancient avalanche can't be moved by human hands. Those who tried in the past were crushed by rockfall.*

Human hands didn't move them today, says Li Wei. *They used some kind of black powder. I've never seen it before, but when enough of it was ignited, it exploded and blew apart the rocks so that we could pass.*

I stare at him in wonder, thinking back to that terrible sound

I heard just before the soldiers arrived. The township and the king's men are already terrifying enough. The thought that they possess such weapons makes our chances seem bleaker than ever. Sensing my fear, Li Wei gives me a reassuring pat on the shoulder. *Come on, general. I will explain more later. We need to keep moving.*

Our circuitous journey also takes us near the zip line, where I see more soldiers loading and sending down the abandoned metals from last night. Li Wei and I give them a wide berth, finally reaching the school. We observe it from a distance, noting the soldiers in the area. Some are gathering up villagers who have fled, putting them in chains and leading them away. Other soldiers remain and have started setting fire to some of the smaller houses. They seem to be leaving the Peacock Court alone for now, perhaps because they recognize it as a center of leadership and source of information. I take Li Wei's arm and lead him into the trees, to a patch of forest far behind the school and the soldiers' insidious work. I then begin stomping on the ground in various spots, pausing and searching the leafy undergrowth with a critical eye.

What are you doing? he asks.

Trying to remember, I reply. My foot hits a piece of wood cleverly concealed in the underbrush, and triumph flares within me. I kneel down, feeling around for the trapdoor's handle. I pull it open and glance up at an awestruck Li Wei. *Come on,* I say. *We will be safe here.*

We have no light to take with us, but from the sun that shines down, we make out a ladder built into the earthen wall, leading down into a tunnel. I go first, and then Li Wei follows, making sure that the door closes securely behind us. For a moment, we are plunged into darkness, and then a torch flares to life in front of us. Beside it is the blade of a knife, and I recoil until I recognize the faces of two of my fellow apprentices: Jin Luan and Sheng. They look relieved that we're not soldiers, but they still regard us with understandable wariness, given our reputations.

Are the elders down here? I ask. *We must speak to them.*

Sheng sheathes the blade and glares. *You are in no position to make demands, not after what you've done.*

We've done nothing, says Li Wei. *This is the township's doing—and the king's. Now let us pass!*

Sheng moves into a position that clearly blocks our path. *I don't know what you've done to corrupt Fei and twist her thinking, but there's no way you're getting past me.*

Li Wei's face hardens. *There are plenty of ways I can get past you. Haven't we been through this already? You didn't fare so well before.*

We have no time for this! I snap, infuriated with both of them. I turn to Jin Luan, hoping she at least will be sensible. *Please, you must help. We have valuable information for the elders. Are they here?*

She props the torch so that she can sign. From her troubled expression, I can tell she's trying to decide which story about me to believe. *Some of them. They brought a bunch of us here—as many as they could—and then sealed the door leading here from the school.*

221

I can't hold back any longer. *Was my sister with them?*
No. Jin Luan's face falls a little. *Not everyone made it in.*

I feel a pang in my chest, and Li Wei gives my arm a quick, comforting squeeze that Sheng's sharp eyes don't fail to notice. *We must talk to the elders,* I reiterate. *Can you take us to them?*

Jin Luan glances at Sheng. *One of us will have to stay here and stand guard.*

He stares at her in disbelief. *Are you serious? After what they've done?*

Jin Luan meets his gaze unblinkingly. *I'm serious about helping our people. And no one really knows what they've done—least of all you. It is for the elders to judge them.*

Sheng scowls, and for a few seconds, the two of them are locked in a battle of wills. I confess, I have never had more respect for her than I do right now. She's always been my artistic rival; I never realized her true strength.

Fine, Sheng says at last. He hands her the blade. *I will take them.*

I nod at her in thanks as we pass by and follow Sheng down the tunnel. With the torch behind us, we are soon swallowed by darkness. Without even realizing I'm doing it, I find Li Wei's hand as we walk. Our fingers intertwine, keeping us connected as our free hands feel along the tunnel's sides. When we reach the turn, faint illumination from more torches ahead begins to guide us, and we soon find ourselves walking into a wide, open room underground supported by stone posts and wooden beams. I tense, not sure what we'll encounter—I know about this area only by reputation. The bare walls have been plastered, and the floor is made of hard-packed earth. And we are not alone.

Masters, Sheng declares. *Look who I've found.*

I clasp Li Wei's hand tighter as I face the elders for the first time since I left the village.

Most of them are here, including Elder Chen and Elder Lian. Several apprentices and a few school servants are gathered around them. My heart sinks when I don't see Zhang Jing. I'd hoped Jin Luan was wrong about her. They all stop what they're doing when we enter, turning to stare at us. Beneath their scrutiny, I feel almost more vulnerable than I did when I stood on the dais and faced the whole village. These are my peers and my mentors, the people I've worked with every day. They thought the best of me, but then, because of my actions, that viewpoint changed. The impact of that weighs heavily on me.

When no one acts right away, I release Li Wei's hand and approach Elder Chen deferentially. I bow three times, low, before speaking. *Greetings, master. I beg your pardon for leaving without permission. I have come now to tell you all the things I've observed in my time away.*

Elder Chen studies me for a long time, and I tense, fearful of what he will do. He might very well have Li Wei and me thrown back outside into the chaos, and it would be completely within his rights. Perhaps I didn't cause our village's initial difficulties, but my actions are certainly what have caused our current ones.

Is it true? Elder Chen asks at last. *What you told us in your painting?*

Every word, master, I reply.

He studies me a bit longer, and then, to the complete astonishment of everyone in the room, Elder Chen bows to me. *It appears we may owe you a great debt,* he says once he straightens up. His eyes fall on Li Wei. *Both of you. Now. Let us talk about what you know.*

CHAPTER 17

I'M HONORED AND FLUSTERED but also self-conscious, because by this point I've already told the village all I know. The current actions of the township and the army are as much a mystery to me as to everyone else.

Li Wei steps forward, bowing to the elders before speaking. *If you'll allow me, I can add to what Fei has told you. I spent the night as one of their prisoners, marching up the mountain pass. I couldn't understand the guards, but a few of them can sign. I also met a prisoner—one of the plateau villagers—who has learned to read lips. Between them, I know some of what is happening.*

By all means, Elder Chen says. *Continue.*

Once they realized Fei had made it back up here, they decided to do a forced march up the passes with the soldiers and some of the other village's prisoners. They've apparently had this explosive powder for a while and could have cleared the passes long ago.

This leaves all of us dumbfounded for a moment. By now, I shouldn't be surprised by the township's cruelty . . . but it still comes as a shock. We've been beholden to the zip line system for so long, given no future except to mine for our survival. If the passes had been clear, we would have had access to trade and travel, not to mention the fertile valleys our ancestors allegedly grew crops in. But then, if we'd had those freedoms, the king and the township would have lost their source of metals.

Why open it now? I ask. *It costs them their hold on us: If we can leave the mountain, we no longer have to mine for our food. They no longer get their metals.*

That's why they brought the soldiers and the other prisoners, Li Wei explains. *They plan on doing one big push in the mines, using our people and the other displaced miners to get as much metal as possible while the soldiers stand guard and enforce their rule. They want to deplete the mine as quickly as possible, even if it kills the rest of us in the process.*

All this because we found out the truth? I say in disbelief. *Because I came back and told everyone what was going on?*

Now Li Wei turns unexpectedly hesitant, glancing between our audience and me. *It's more than that.*

What more can there be? I ask incredulously.

The soldiers interrogated Nuan, he says. *They know your secret.*

He is speaking carefully, I realize, to protect me. At this point, however, the secret he's referring to is the least of our worries. *I can hear,* I tell the others, bracing myself for the disbelief to come. Most of them look as though they think they misunderstood, so I elaborate: *It's true. I have my hearing, just as our ancestors did.*

What kind of lies are you spreading now? Sheng asks.

I'm not lying, I reply. *I don't understand how it happened, and I know it sounds crazy. But I can do any test you like to prove it.*

It's true, Li Wei confirms. *I've seen her prove it.* He gives my hand a brief, encouraging squeeze.

The others' faces are a mix of reactions, both wonder and outright skepticism. Elder Chen looks thoughtful. *Did it happen the day you stayed back sick at the school?*

Yes, master. It had come to me the previous night in a dream. I was adjusting to it and had a headache. I pause to reconsider my words. *Actually, I'm still adjusting. It's a very . . . disconcerting experience.*

Many in the room still look skeptical, but Elder Chen appears to take me at my word, and that faith in me means more than I can say. *I would imagine so,* he replies. *And you think this has something to do with the township's reaction?*

Li Wei nods. *When Nuan told them Fei could hear, panic arose among some of their leaders. Apparently the king has been afraid of this happening, that one of us would regain hearing. It's supposed to be an omen of something, but I'm not sure what. I couldn't follow all the other prisoners' signs—they're different from ours. But the king fears what Fei's hearing could mean, and that's why he wanted the mine emptied as quickly as possible. Fei's hearing is a sign of some change, of something returning that could be a threat to him.*

I remember Nuan's reaction to my hearing and the sign she made. I mimic it and ask Li Wei, *Was this part of what they thought was coming? What they feared?*

He nods. *Yes, something with wings. But I don't know the sign.*

I hear a sharp intake of breath and turn toward Elder Lian. She has gone very pale and looks at Elder Chen, who seems equally shocked. *Do you think it could be true?* he asks her.

It could be, if what has happened to Fei is real, Elder Lian says.

An apprentice leans on a rack of scrolls in the back of the room, causing them to fall with a clatter. It is out of everyone else's eyesight, and I jump, startled by the noise.

Elder Chen smiles when he sees what made me flinch. *I'd say what's happened to her is real. And if the rest is as well . . . this could change much.*

My patience is rapidly disappearing, and I'm itching to know what he means. I'm grateful that he believes us, that the others here have accepted us for the time being, but now that we're out of immediate danger, I am growing restless. Zhang Jing is not here. Based on what Li Wei has said, the odds seem good she may have been rounded up with the others being forced to work in the mines. The thought of my sister captured and terrified nauseates me. I worry also about what will happen if they learn her sight is diminished. If they want to empty the mines as quickly as possible, they're only going to want to keep the healthiest workers. I can't abandon her and keep myself in this safety.

But the old habits of respecting my master are hard to shake off. And although I shift restlessly from foot to foot, wanting to go out and fight the soldiers, I force myself to wait patiently as Elder Chen gets up and walks to the other side of the room. Along with the scrolls, there are stacks and stacks of what look like old records. The amount of information stored in here rivals the library up in the school.

What is this place? Li Wei asks.

It is our emergency storage facility, to preserve our history, Elder Lian says, her eyes flicking to Elder Chen as he continues searching for something in the documents. *In case something happens to the school, we keep copies of important documents as well as one record from each week down here. Admittedly, I don't think any of its builders envisioned some catastrophe like this.*

Elder Chen makes his way over to us, one of the scrolls in hand. He gives it to another apprentice, who kneels on the floor and spreads it open flat so we can read it. The illustrations practically jump from the page. Whoever made them was a fine artist. It is a scroll about mythical animals, a copy of the one he showed me that day in the library. There are dragons, phoenixes, and more, but it is the creature on the top of the page that he points to.

The pixiu, he says.

And as he makes the sign, I suddenly see how it derived from the one Nuan used.

I study the illustration. At a glance, the creature looks like some variant of a lion—another animal I've never seen in real life—complete with a mane. But closer examination reveals the head to have some similarities to that of a dragon, and there is a broad, sturdy nature to the creature's back that reminds me of a horse's. Then, of course, there are the feathered wings, which make it completely unlike a lion.

Beside me, Li Wei has grown excited. *It's like the story my mother used to tell, isn't it? That the pixius made all hearing disappear when they went to sleep, so that they would have peace and quiet.*

We know that's not true, I say, thinking it would be a cruel thing for one creature to do to another. *It's the metals that deprive us of our senses.*

Yes, I believe that part, about why we lost our hearing, is simply myth. But the rest of this scroll . . . Elder Chen gestures to it. *There are certain details in it that make more sense now. It claims the pixius used to roam here, eating metal and protecting humans from "dangerous consequences." It doesn't specify what those are, but I think somehow the pixius' presence must have protected us from the metals' toxicity. It's only when the pixius left that hearing began to disappear.* He meets my gaze squarely. *Fei, tell me exactly what happened the night you regained your hearing.*

I do, recounting the dream and how I saw the village in despair. When all the villagers opened their mouths to cry out, sound returned to me—as well as that sense of connection that I haven't been able to fully comprehend. Elder Chen nods as I explain, and then he seeks out another scroll. When he returns, I see it is even older than the other one, the paper fragile and flaking. He will not allow anyone else to touch it, and he kneels down on his old, weary knees to open it himself.

Most of the documents here are copies, Elder Lian comments as we watch Elder Chen skim for the information he seeks. *Some are kept down here simply because they are so precious and rare.*

The scroll is all text, no illustrations, and after a few agonizing minutes, Elder Chen finally looks up. *It's just as I remember. This document is from someone who claims to have lived among pixius, long ago. It says the pixius can form connections of the mind with people who are open to it, those special individuals who are able to fully visualize the world and its possibilities. I think you are one such person, Fei. And I think a pixiu was trying to tell you something. Here it says that the pixius bring protection and fortune to the righteous—that they respond to the cries of those in need.*

Everyone stares at me again when he finishes, and I take a step back, overwhelmed. *Master, I can't be one of those people. There's nothing special about me.*

Isn't there, Fei? he asks with amusement. *You're the only one of us who can hear. Somehow a pixiu has reached out to you. Your hearing is a sign of its mark. The fact that it showed your people crying out, just as this text says the pixius respond to such cries, is a sign.*

It is the sign that the king fears, says Li Wei eagerly. *Perhaps we can make a stand against the king's soldiers if we can summon the pixius back.*

What does that mean? asks another elder, speaking up at last. His name is Elder Ho, and it has been obvious to me since I arrived that he does not share Elder Chen's faith in my story. *We don't even know why the pixius disappeared or if they're even real. These scrolls could just be myth.*

They're real, I say, thinking back to that tug I keep feeling within me. I think back also to the moment I heard all the people crying out in my dream. At the time I was so overwhelmed by the strangeness of my first experience with sound that I couldn't comprehend much else. But simultaneously, in the back of my mind, I felt that stirring—that *otherness* activated by the people's cries, even in just a dream. And when the army attacked today and my people cried out erratically, I felt the stirring again.

What are you thinking, general? Li Wei asks, seeing me lost in memories.

I give him a faint smile at the old nickname before turning to the others. *I can't explain it . . . only that I can* feel *it, but I think Elder Chen is right. I think the pixius will respond to the cries of our people.* I think back to the dream, trying to recapture it exactly. *It must be all of them raised at once. And it must be loud. Intense,* I clarify when it's clear no one in the room understands what I mean by *loud. That's how it was in the dream. That's what the pixius need.*

Elder Ho still looks skeptical, but everyone else is warming to the idea. I wonder if it's because they believe me or because they are so desperate after the terrible turn of events in our village that they'll sign on to any plan that offers hope, no matter how farfetched.

We must tell them, says Li Wei. *If the soldiers are going through with their plan, they will have rounded up most of the villagers to force them to mine. I will go back outside and let them capture me. Then I can tell the others.*

I'll go with you, I say promptly.

No, says Elder Lian. *It's too dangerous. If you're known to them as the specific threat that might bring back the pixius, then you shouldn't be out there.*

And yet that is exactly why she must be in the midst of it, counters Elder Chen serenely. *She is the connection. She cannot hide away if it is her very presence that will affect the transformation of what is to come.*

It will still be chaotic out there, I say. Although I am speaking to everyone gathered, I purposely make eye contact with Li Wei. Something tells me he is the one who will need the most convincing that I should be in the line of danger. *And although the soldiers may have my description, most haven't actually seen me. They won't think I'm different from any other villager.*

Elder Lian nods thoughtfully. *Perhaps we can help. Perhaps there is a way to make you harder to detect.*

After a bit of consultation, a boy among the servants is forced to exchange his outfit for mine. Although I am still wearing pilfered boy clothes, these new ones are dull in color and more likely to blend in with the other villagers rather than mark me in the telltale blue of the apprentices. Elder Ho, to my surprise, gives me his hat, a small, nondescript cloth one that nonetheless hides much of my hair and is something generally only seen on men. A healthy dose of dirt smudged on my face goes a long way to complete the illusion.

There, says Elder Lian. *At a glance, the soldiers will not think you are the girl they're looking for. Most of our own people probably won't notice you either. I imagine they have bigger concerns now anyway.*

We discuss a few more points of strategy, and I am startled when several among the apprentices and servants want to come with us. *We want to add our voices*, explains the boy whose clothes I wear. *Besides, you won't be spotted so quickly if you're in a group.*

The elders agree but want to hold some people back just in case. While they make their choices, I try to remain patient, but the need to act burns within me, making me restless. I have one last hope about where Zhang Jing is, and I want to investigate it.

Li Wei catches me swiping at the dirt on my face. I can feel it and have to stop myself from wiping it off.

I look ridiculous, I remark to him.

He turns to me, touching my chin softly, the ghost of a smile on his lips. *You're as beautiful as ever. When this is over, we'll find a reason for you to wear the red dress again.*

I shake my head, feeling a tangle of emotions in my chest. *I still can't believe you're here. You were captured because of me....*

Fei, I was captured because you were brave enough to

return here. To save our village. You think it's your artistic skill that's your greatest strength? It's not. It's your courage. There is something in his eyes as he says this, something powerful and heated that reaches to my heart.

The elders give their blessings for our journey, and with that, we are finally on our way. Li Wei and I, along with our small cohort, traipse back out through the darkened tunnel, down to where Jin Luan still stands guard. She looks understandably startled to see all of us, more so when she finds out we're leaving.

You're going back out there? she exclaims. *You're crazy!*

Possibly, I agree.

But her job is to stop people from getting in, not prevent them from leaving. She steps aside so that we can pass, and she surprises me with the first genuine smile I've ever received from her. *Good luck, Fei.*

Li Wei goes first, climbing up the ladder that leads into the woods and peering around to ascertain no guards are present. When he deems it safe, he beckons for the rest of us to follow. There are seven of us in total, and as we all gather there in the woods behind the school, I notice it is quieter. Earlier, when Li Wei and I had made our frantic trip here, I'd still been able to hear screams and destruction. I wonder if that means the soldiers have rounded up most of the village.

Now, begins Li Wei, *I think our best plan is—*

Not yet, I interrupt.

He looks at me in astonishment. *What? We have to join the other prisoners.*

We will, I say. *But first we're making a detour.*

I know Li Wei well enough to recognize his frustration, but he stays composed in front of these onlookers. *What detour is that, exactly?*

We're not doing anything until we find my sister, I say.

CHAPTER 18

LI WEI CONSIDERS THIS and shakes his head, his expression compassionate despite his obvious impatience. *I would like to find her too, but we don't have time to search the village. We need to enact this plan.*

I know where she is, I tell him. I'm only half lying. *It won't take us that far out of our way.*

After a little more coaxing, he agrees, and our small group sets out. We move covertly, keeping off the main roads of the village and concealing ourselves in the trees. Around us, we see signs of the army's destruction, and smoke fills the air from the fires they've set. Most of the villagers seem to have been rounded up, but we still occasionally spot roaming bands of soldiers, and my hearing is able to alert us each time before we're spotted.

Soon we make it to the opposite side of the village, to the path that runs near the cliffside. We approach the lone cypress tree where my parents' ashes were scattered, and at first I think I am wrong. Then a slight form shifts, and I see Zhang Jing sitting against the tree, dangerously close to the cliff. The path shows the signs of many booted feet having gone by recently, but they apparently didn't notice her concealed by the tree. I breathe a sigh of relief, glad to know my hunch was correct. That in a time of great danger, this is the place she would seek out for solace.

I touch her arm gently, and she flinches, at first not recognizing me with my strange clothes and dirty face. Then joy fills her tear-stained features. She leaps to her feet and throws her arms around me. *Fei!* she says when we have broken apart. *I didn't know what happened to you. Everything got so confusing. What is going on? Who are those people?*

They are the king's soldiers, I say. *Now that we know the truth, they have come to try to enslave us. We have a plan to save ourselves, but first I wanted to make sure you're safe.* I glance back at the assembled apprentices and servants who have come with Li Wei and me. *Someone will take you back to the Peacock Court's underground storage rooms, where you can wait safely.*

Zhang Jing shakes her head adamantly. *No. Wherever you're going, I'm coming with you.*

I hesitate. While I'm quick to run into danger on my own, I'm less willing to get her involved. She is still my sister, still the one I protect, and I'd rather see her safely hidden away with the elders. But there is a fire in her eyes, and something tells me she is not going to go so easily.

I mean it, Fei, she says. *Let me come with you. Whatever it is, I'm not afraid.*

We can use her help, Li Wei notes. I can tell he is anxious about the delay. *Plus, we won't diminish our numbers this way.*

I am part of this village, Zhang Jing adds fiercely. *This is my fight too.*

I can't stand against both of them, and reluctantly, I agree. There's at least a small comfort in having her within my sight.

We backtrack toward the village, still moving covertly. Li Wei scouts ahead, searching for roaming bands of soldiers. We want them to catch us, but walking right up to them is out of the question. Our capture has to look as "natural" as possible, raising little suspicion.

Li Wei comes hurrying back, his face a mix of nerves and excitement. *Up ahead,* he says. *There are three soldiers patrolling.*

We move in on the soldiers' position, walking clumsily through the trees so as to make a lot of noise. The ruse works, and moments later we find ourselves surrounded by the three soldiers, who unwittingly think they've captured a group of hapless villagers trying to flee. We act appropriately frightened as they raise their swords—really, there's not much acting required for that—and Li Wei makes it look as though he is about to run. This earns him a blow to the head that makes me wince, but it convinces the soldiers there is nothing special about our particular group. With swords still drawn, they surround us and march us back in the direction of the mines. I exchange a glance with Li Wei as we walk, and although he is careful to keep his expression appropriately cowed, I see a fierceness in his eyes as our plan begins to unfold.

Back at the mine, the number of captured villagers has swelled, and the chained prisoners who came up the mountain have joined the group. It looks as though there are still some people hiding within the mines, but the soldiers are busy keeping the gathered prisoners in line and seem to be engaged in some type of sorting. One of the soldiers in our group shouts something, attracting the attention of a man who seems to be in charge. He glances over at us, looking surprised. My guess is that they probably thought they'd captured everyone by now. A party our size is unexpected.

He strolls over and assesses us, making some quick decisions. With a few gestures, he splits us into two groups. One is me, Zhang Jing, the boy whose clothes I took, and another young girl. Li Wei is with the others in the second group. I realize immediately that we've been sorted by size and strength, and the soldier indicates that Li Wei's group should join another similarly sized group. Zhang Jing and I are sent to a cluster of prisoners consisting mostly of smaller-sized women and young children. I catch Li Wei's eye as we move in different directions, and the message is clear: *The plan must proceed.*

Beyond him, I see the soldier in charge speaking with one of the prisoners from the plateau. The soldier makes those unintelligible sounds, and the prisoner follows his face avidly. I realize this must be the man who can read lips. Moments later, he turns and speaks to Li Wei's group, using the same sign language Nuan did: *They are going to send you into the mines to work. They say if you are diligent and do as you're*

told, your lives will be spared. Although his signs say one thing, his expression conveys something entirely different. The other prisoners notice this.

Is that really true? Li Wei asks.

The man hesitates only a moment before answering: *Probably not. But what choice do we have?*

I turn to look at the group clustered near me. There are soldiers surrounding us, but we are not under as heavy a guard as Li Wei's group. We are not chained. Because we are smaller, they probably see us as less of a threat. Knowing that this is the moment we've been waiting for, I signal to a group of women on the other side of Zhang Jing. I keep my motions small, so as not to attract much attention from the guards. I think few of them can understand us, but I don't want to take the chance.

Pay attention, I say. *There is a way to save us all, but it requires everyone participating. When I give the signal, you must all cry out.*

One woman looks at me as if I am crazy. *Cry out?* she questions.

I can't blame her. Although we make involuntary cries and screams all the time—in fact, there is a great deal of sorrowful sound around me even now—it is not something my people deliberately do. After all, none of us can hear the sounds when others make them. Instead, it is a residual instinct, something we acknowledge we do in times of great emotion. There is nothing more to it—until now.

Yes, I say. *Cry out. Scream. Give voice to your pain.*

You must all do it at the same time, and you must do it . . . I pause, remembering to put it in terms they'll understand. *You must do it with great intensity. You know the vibrations you feel in your throat? You must make sure they are very intense. Make your throat . . . shake as much as you can. Do you understand?*

They stare at me in confusion, but one little girl bravely steps forward. *I understand.*

Her mother draws her back and asks, *To what end? What can this possibly do? We are lost.*

No, I say adamantly. *We are not. I can't explain what this will do, but you must trust me that it will work. It is our best shot at salvation—but it is imperative we all work together.*

I work my way through the group, passing on the message. Looking across the clearing, I see Li Wei doing the same thing, discreetly signing so as not to attract the guards' attention. It looks like he's met with the same reaction. Most of the people are scared and skeptical that this bizarre request can accomplish anything. Yet, at the same time, they are desperate and see no hope around them and so are willing to take any chance offered to them, no matter how farfetched.

Trust me, I say for what feels like the hundredth time. *This will work if we do it together. Put all your emotion into it—all your hope and fear, all your doubt and faith.*

That particular word choice seems to resonate with the woman I'm currently speaking to. She nods, blinking back tears. Probably all she has left at this point are her emotions; giving voice to them, even if she can't hear it, is all she can do. As I turn

from her to see if there's anyone I missed in this group, a flurry of hands draws attention in my periphery. An older woman wearing the clothes of a supplier is signing furiously.

It's her! Fei! The one who started all this, she says. A few people near her do double takes, looking me over and starting with recognition.

Did she? asks another woman flatly. *It seems to me it's the township that started all this long ago.*

Only if you believe her lies! exclaims the first woman. *Someone call the guards over here! No doubt they are looking for her. If we turn her over, they will let the rest of us go!*

Have you lost your wits along with everything else? I demand. *They aren't letting any of us go! They are going to work us all to death in order to deplete the mines. They're starting with the strongest over there. When they're wiped out, they'll make us labor in their place. This plan—crying out as one—is our only hope.*

But the woman who first recognized me is no longer paying attention. Unable to rally an immediate supporter, she has gone seeking a soldier herself. She finds one and tugs his sleeve, making signs he doesn't understand. Irritated, he pushes her away, but she is insistent and resorts to simplified gestures, pointing at me through the crowd. The soldier regards me with a puzzled look. He doesn't understand why she's singling me out, but I am no longer beneath the soldiers' notice. I wanted to stay incognito, but that moment has passed. The soldier enters the throng of women and begins working his way toward me.

Looking across the grounds outside the mines, I search for Li Wei over in his group. They are being herded toward the mine's entrance, and I see Li Wei looking for me as well. *It must be now*, he signs to me, holding his hands high.

I nod in agreement and turn to Zhang Jing. The soldier has almost reached us. *Now*, I say, making my signs big and high. *Now! Everyone cry out!*

At first, the only voice I hear is my own. I put all my emotion into it, everything I've been carrying around for so long. I include my love for Zhang Jing and Li Wei in it, my grief for my parents, my fear for my village. The sound vibrates not just in my throat but through my whole body, sending waves of emotion radiating through me. I feel it on every level, with all my senses, and then I hear another cry echoing my own. It is Zhang Jing, raising a voice she cannot hear and filling it with the same emotional intensity that is burning within me. Beside her, another woman joins in. Then another. And another.

The soldier comes to a halt, looking around in bewilderment. He loses his interest in me and instead tries to figure out what is happening. The other soldiers on the grounds are equally perplexed. The sound has spread from person to person, in both my group and Li Wei's. For those of us with hearing, it is both spectacular and heart-wrenching. My people have no idea how much grief they are conveying.

In my chest, I feel that faint fluttering of connection, and my excitement grows. It is working! We are being heard! I lift my hands and signal to those around me: *More! More! Make it more intense—more vibrations! Tell others!* They spread the message, and it ripples through the crowd. Looking over the heads of those near me, I can make out Li Wei urging on those around him as well. The voices grow louder, and I raise mine, calling out to the pixiu who has chosen me to help us. I feel another hard tug in my chest—but see no other immediate signs that this is working.

The guards, however, are starting to react. They don't understand what's happening, but they don't like it. They begin saying things to us, the same command repeated, and my guess is they are demanding silence. The prisoners defy them—at least at first—and continue the cry. This angers some of the soldiers, and they start to resort to violence. The soldier near me cuffs a woman so hard, she falls to her knees. That startles a few others nearby into silence.

I raise my voice louder to compensate, urging others to do so, and the connection within me burns more brightly. The intensity is so great that it almost seems impossible for me to contain. It grows and grows—and then, abruptly, it seems to vanish. It's almost like the sensation of a bubble growing bigger and bigger before bursting. I'm unsure what has happened, but I only let my voice falter a moment before continuing on more loudly than before.

Around me, others are losing faith, both because of a lack of any results and also because of the brutality of the soldiers. They are silencing prisoners by any means necessary, striking and felling indiscriminately. Not far from me, an old man cries out as a soldier knocks him to the ground and follows up with a sharp kick. It's enough to scare a few others into silence, but I ignore it all, refusing to be cowed. I have no fear for what they might do to me.

Zhang Jing stands beside me proudly, voice uplifted, but when a soldier comes and knocks her down, she momentarily falls silent. I drop to the ground beside her and stop my own cry, too concerned about her. *Are you okay?* I ask.

She shakes her head, shrugging me off and opening her mouth to continue the cry. The same soldier who struck her before now backhands the side of her head to quiet her. I leap to my feet, thrusting myself between the man and my sister, ready to take whatever he is dealing out. But before either of us can act, the woman who recognized me earlier comes hurrying forward, pointing and gesturing frantically at me. This soldier can't understand her, but another comes striding up, a hard look in his gaze as his eyes fix on me. He's no one I know, but it's clear he has realized who I am.

He says something harsh to the soldier who struck Zhang Jing and then grabs me by the arm, dragging me toward the man who seems to be in charge near the mine. The crowds shrink back from us, and as we move, I notice that the cries around us have died down. A few people are still halfheartedly trying to carry on, but most either have been forcibly silenced or are in fear of what might happen to them.

And nothing has happened.

Only a need to appear undaunted in front of the soldiers prevents tears of frustration from springing to my eyes. I wanted to believe Elder Chen's story about the pixius. I wanted there to be an explanation for all that has been going on. I wanted a magical creature to come save us all.

But as the united cry disintegrates into frightened whimpers, it's clear there is no one out here in this desolate place but us humans. The realization nearly breaks my heart, and I must summon all my courage when I'm shoved to my knees in front of the lead soldier. He looks down on me with a sneer and speaks, but I shake my head, showing I don't understand.

He doesn't seem to care, though. I am the girl who started all this by climbing down the mountain and stirring up the king's fears about the pixius. And it's clear this soldier plans on putting an end to my mischief—and to me.

He gives an order, and the soldier who brought me drags me away. My heart is so heavy, my grief so great at our failure that at first I don't even realize where we're going. I'm too devastated that this has all been for nothing and that the township is going to win after all. A cry from the crowd—Zhang Jing's voice— snaps me out of my despair. *I must be strong for her*, I tell myself. I look up and realize the soldier is taking me to the cliff's side. He halts there, pushing me to my knees again, so that I'm facing the edge. The world reels as I see that fathomless drop off the mountain in front of me, with only the soldier's hand on my shoulder standing between a push or a pull. Swallowing my fear, I am just barely able to twist around back to the gaping crowd. There are tears on Zhang Jing's face, and the soldiers have to restrain Li Wei to keep him from coming to me.

The army's leader says something to the prisoner who can

read lips, and cringing, the man holds up his hands so that all can see. *Watch now and see what happens when you defy the great king!* The soldier's hand tenses on my shoulder. I know he is only seconds away from pushing me off the edge to my death. All he's waiting for is his leader's command. The prisoner continues as directed: *Those who attempt to stir discord will be punished accordingly. Those who are obedient will—*

The prisoner trails off as a shadow passes over his face.

Then another.

And another.

Eyes wide, he looks up to the sky . . . and that's when we see the impossible.

CHAPTER 19

A DOZEN GLITTERING FORMS circle above us, dazzling in the late afternoon sunlight, powered by strong wings. The soldier lets go of me, backing up and abandoning me on my precarious perch. I'm caught off guard by the sudden movement and find myself wavering on the cliff's edge. Using both hands and feet, I scramble to move backward, far from the dangerous precipice and onto more solid ground. All the while, I keep my eyes fixed above.

Those glittering beings circle lower and lower, and I feel tears prick my eyes as I see the same wondrous forms from Elder Chen's scroll: the regal bearing, dragon-like head, lion's mane, and full-feathered wings. Dream has become reality. Myth has been made flesh.

The pixius are here.

They are so beautiful, even with the ferocity of their sharp teeth and claws, that it makes my heart ache. That instinct I so often feel, to capture the world in my art, rears up within me, a thousand times stronger than ever before. I want to draw that exquisite profile, the way the pixius command such incredible power yet seem so graceful as they glide on currents of air. I want to convey the sense of the breeze rustling their thick manes. I want to recreate the glimmering metallic color of their coats, varying from shades of deep bronze to brightest silver, even though I have no idea how to begin. The color ripples on their fur almost like water. Capturing the full majesty of these creatures would probably be an impossible task, but in this moment, I could happily spend a lifetime trying.

When I can finally drag my gaze from their beauty, I see that chaos has returned below. The horses are rearing, and the soldiers try to calm them, splitting their attention between the animals, the villagers, and the majestic creatures in the sky. The reactions of my own people are mixed. Some are simply stunned, unable to move. Others, terrified, attempt to flee. Still others make the connection between our cries and the appearance of the pixius. Many of these people are older, familiar with the myths, and see this as our salvation. They fall to their knees, holding their hands up and raising their voices, though this time there is a note of joy to the cries.

One such supplicant is an older woman not far from me. I know her as someone who has lost much of her sight, but it's clear she can still make out the glittering of the pixius as they continue to circle above us. She lifts her hands in thanksgiving, crying out in happiness. A young soldier stands nearby, nervously watching the sky. When he hears the old woman, he strikes her in the head with the hilt of his sword.

In the blink of an eye, one of the pixius—a golden one—breaks formation and dives down, straight for the soldier. With talons glittering as brightly as that metallic fur, the pixiu snatches the soldier up and tosses him over the cliff in one smooth motion. His screams as he goes over raise the hair on the back of my neck.

That action is like a spark to tinder. The soldiers mobilize, seeing a clear and immediate threat in the pixius. The soldiers' leader begins shouting orders. Swords are raised, and a handful of men with bows and arrows come hurrying forward. Even though I can't understand the leader's words, his actions and expression convey his orders clearly: *Bring down the pixius!*

Arrows fly into the sky. Most are dodged easily by the swiftly moving pixius. Those arrows that do make contact bounce harmlessly off the pixius' hides. Their fur looks luxuriously soft but apparently has the impenetrability of the hardest rock. These direct attacks drive the pixius to action. They break out of their circling formation now, diving and striking with incredible speed as they pick off their enemies one by one. From my vantage, I notice the pixius easily distinguish soldier from captive and spare both my people and the plateau miners. As for the soldiers . . . they meet a different fate. Some are thrown over the cliffs. Others are simply torn apart.

For those in the thick of the crowd, it is not obvious that the pixius are sparing the prisoners. Villagers panic and begin running, once more nearly stampeding over one another in their haste to get away. Soon they are joined by panicked soldiers who realize the futility of trying to kill these creatures. The soldiers seem to be heading back toward the village, and my guess is that they are running away to the recently opened passes that will lead down the other side of the mountain. Frightened villagers, not wanting to cross paths with their former captors, head in the opposite direction, toward the mines to join those hiding within. Still others cannot move at all. They stay where they are, eyes trained upward at the beautiful, deadly display happening in the air.

Chaos reigns.

I leave my spot and head toward where I last saw my sister. The crowd around her has dispersed, but she is still there, transfixed by the sights above. She squints, her face filled with wonder. Someone fleeing pushes me from behind, causing me to bump into her. She glances down, smiling when she sees me.

You did it, Fei! You were able to—

I don't see what else she says because my attention is caught by a sound—a voice. It is one I know by now: Li Wei's. I would recognize it anywhere, and I have a brief, surreal memory of the blue thrush and how it could find its mate with a single cry. I don't have to see Li Wei's face now to hear the warning in his voice. Even without words, the message is clear. I spin around and am just in time to see a soldier barreling through, uncaring of who or what is in his way as he wields his swords.

Thanks to Li Wei's warning, I'm just barely able to grab Zhang Jing and dodge out of his path, though it knocks her and me to the ground. The soldier swings his swords where we stood and then pauses in his escape to regard us menacingly. Before he can decide what to do next, a bronze pixiu swoops down and intercepts him, carrying him off, only his screams ringing behind him. I hurry to help Zhang Jing stand. It is unclear what place will be the safest, and then I remember Li Wei's voice. I search in the direction it came from and see him standing over by the mines, where the majority of our people have gathered. He waves at me through the pandemonium, and, taking Zhang Jing's hand, I begin making my way toward him.

It's complete disorder, almost a repeat of when I was trying to cross the village's center earlier today. At least now no one is targeting me specifically, but danger still abounds. Everyone is so concerned with saving themselves that they pay little heed to who's in their way. The soldiers don't hesitate to use weapons and force to clear their paths, fear making them even more desperate and brutal. The pixius are coming for them, and they know it. I hear their screams, and they are awful, heart-wrenching sounds—even though I regard these men as my enemies. It makes me wish for silence again, and I wonder how soldiers can stand to devote their lives to war. Who could live with such confusion and despair on a regular basis?

At last, Zhang Jing and I join the rest of our people standing by the mines, and Li Wei puts his arms around me. Because Zhang Jing is still clinging to me, he ends up hugging us both. We huddle together with others by the mine's entrance and watch the scene around us. Most of the soldiers are gone, either dead or having escaped. A couple became trapped here in the clearing, and when they are spotted by pixius, their end is quick and bloody.

One soldier, seeing a pixiu coming for him, chooses an alternate ending: throwing himself off the cliff.

Around me, the mood is conflicted, and I share in that mixed emotion. We are all glad to see the soldiers removed, but there is a deadly edge to the pixius' beauty. When there are no more soldiers in sight, the pixius make a few more circling flights before turning their attention on us. They land in the center of the clearing in one great, glittering herd and approach us on foot. Li Wei's arm is around me, and I feel him tense. Fear shines on the faces of my people and Nuan's, and a few terrified individuals seek the safety of the mine.

I share their anxiety, looking over the approaching pixius and wondering what is to stop them from turning on us. For all I know, they saw the soldiers as the immediate threat and eliminated it before turning to easier prey.

The pixius come to a stop only a few feet away from where I stand. I hold my breath. They are so close that I can see all the multifaceted strands of fur that make up those rippling, metallic coats. Their claws glitter too—some are wet with blood. All of them have blue eyes, something the stories never mentioned. It is a clear, azure blue, like the sky they descended from. It is fitting, I decide. Those beautiful eyes watch us all solemnly now, as though they too are waiting for something.

From their midst, there is a stirring, and one pixiu steps out toward the front of the group. She—somehow, instinctively, I know this one is female—is one of the largest and has a coat of mixed silver and white strands. She shimmers like moonlight as she moves, and her beauty makes me weak in the knees. At the same time, I also experience that sensation again—that tugging in my chest that makes me feel like someone is summoning me over a great distance. It grows stronger and stronger as she approaches, until that sense of connection practically burns within me. Her eyes hold mine, beckoning. Unable to resist, I slip out of Li Wei's arm and step forward. He signals to me in my periphery.

Fei, be careful. You've seen what they're capable of. They have a taste for blood.

I nod in acknowledgment and move closer to the herd until I'm just a few feet away from the silver female. Both humans and pixius seem to be holding a collective breath, waiting to see how this drama will unfold. The silver one shifts and comes right up to me, and I hear a few gasps, as my people expect her to attack. But she doesn't.

Instead, she kneels.

I reach out and rest my hand on the side of her face, letting out a gasp of my own as my mind is suddenly bombarded with pictures and scenes. It's like having another sense. Images—hers, not mine—play out in my head, and I suddenly find myself witnessing memories from a time long, long ago. Pixius and humans—my ancestors—lived in harmony in these mountains. It was before the passes were blocked, and the village had access to fertile valleys and trade routes. The pixius draw strength from precious metals, and our ancestors would mine small amounts of ore as tokens of friendship to the pixius. In return, the pixius protected my ancestors from outside threats and also imparted an aura of energy and healing that prevented the toxins in the mines from causing harm.

But those serving the king of that time developed weapons capable of harming the pixius. Their armies came into the mountains, hunting the pixius both for their coats and to gain access to the rich mines. This last pixiu pride, weak and depleted, managed to elude its hunters and seek refuge in a magical hibernation within the mountain. They needed that sleep to recover their strength, even though it meant abandoning the humans they'd bonded to—humans who then became trapped and enslaved when avalanches closed the passes.

This female, alone of her pride, has sought a human she could share her dreams with—a human whose mind was as visually stimulated as the pixius'. It was she who reached out to me in my sleep, bonding to me, and that connection imparted the pixius' healing upon me, restoring my hearing. She was the one who showed me what I must do—raise the voices of my people— in order to wake the rest of her pride and remind them of the bonds they once had to our ancestors.

She tells me all this in pictures—her mind to mine—as I stare into her eyes. I read the images as easily as I do characters on paper. It is part of the reason she chose me. Not all humans are capable of communicating the way the pixius do, but I understand her perfectly. Her story is an epic one, with consequences I suspect I'm only beginning to grasp. Much will have to be worked out, but for now, I have only one question.

What is your name?

She doesn't speak in words as we do, but my query comes through to her. More images flash in my mind by way of answer. A glitter of brilliant silver, dazzling to behold. A gust of wind, stirring branches or providing an easy current for a pixiu to ride on.

Yin Feng, I think. *That is your name. Silver Wind.*

The pixiu bows again, and I remove my hand from her face, finding I am smiling. Li Wei and Zhang Jing are beside me, looking understandably puzzled by this silent exchange, not realizing the vast information I have just learned about our past—and, I suspect, our future.

What is happening? asks Li Wei.

A new beginning, I reply. *A new beginning for all of us.*

EPILOGUE

I AM AWAKE BEFORE my roommates, as usual, because I hear the servant in the hall. She sets down a pitcher of water and turns the crank that shakes our beds. One by one, the other girls awaken, yawning and stretching as they try to throw off the heaviness of sleep. Many are reluctant to leave their covers, for autumn is upon us and the room is cold.

Zhang Jing pulls the blankets around her like a hood, pouting when she sees my grin. *Time to wake up*, I tell her. *Don't worry—the sun will warm things soon. It's not winter yet.*

Since the pixius returned to our village two months ago, things have changed considerably. Before, I led a good life as a star apprentice among the artists. Now my life isn't just good— it's full of meaning. Until recently, I hadn't realized there was a difference.

I don my blue robes, and Zhang Jing puts on her green ones. The fabric of hers is new, acquired from recent trade, and I confess I am a little bit jealous. We finish our hair and check each

other over as usual and then head off to join the others for breakfast. The dining room is much more crowded these days, but we
manage to find two spots together at one of the low tables. The
Peacock Court has become not just a residence for artists but for
students of agriculture as well, and at last those empty rooms are
being put to use.

Breakfast is still fast and efficient. Everyone knows the last
nice days of autumn will be ending soon, and the gardeners are
anxious to go about their work for the day. They leave before
the artists do, Zhang Jing going with them in a flurry of green. I
wave, signing that I will see her later.

We artists finish our meals soon thereafter and then go to
the workroom to touch up the record we started last night. That
part of our lives hasn't changed, though the content of what we
paint certainly has. We no longer diligently record the amounts
of metals we mine and send to the township—because we no
longer give them anything. Metals are still pulled out as offerings
to the pixius and for help in our fledgling trade with those few
merchants who've been brave enough to come up the mountain
passes. After the defeat of the township's army, King Jianjun de-
clared our village anathema, but the lure of our buried riches was
enough to draw some daring souls out against his orders.

The record reflects news of that trade as well as of our prepa-
rations for the winter to come. Food is still a concern, especially
now that we no longer can rely on regular shipments from the
township. Our early attempts at trade have certainly been useful in
alleviating the problem, but we still have much to do. Along with

a small supply of livestock, we've also acquired seeds for some root vegetables that are hearty enough to grow in the autumn. When the passes were blown open, we were again given access to the pockets of fertile valleys that our ancestors cultivated. Wild berry bushes and fruit trees have grown there all these years and were in full fruit when we found them, giving us a jump start on our winter supplies. Our hope is that if we can yield a crop of vegetables and grow our livestock in those valleys, we can make it through until spring offers more possibilities.

Today's record also documents the activities of the pixius. They live openly on the mountain now, sometimes interacting with us and sometimes keeping to themselves. Those of us who still mine give the pixius offerings of metals, and in return we have enjoyed some of the healing that being in the creatures' presence offers. There have been no new cases of blindness, and those who were starting to lose their vision have progressed no further. To regain the senses fully, however, requires a pixiu's bonding. So far, only two humans in our village have been chosen for this. I am one of them.

My task in the record today is the kind of work I've always dreamed of: I am painting Yin Feng. I was up late last night working on her, and I still feel as though the work is incomplete. I've even been given access to special metallic paints, but no matter how many times I go over that rippling, glimmering coat, it just doesn't seem good enough.

You will drive yourself crazy, Elder Chen tells me, coming to stand by my canvas. *It is time for them to take this to the village's center. You've done excellent work.*

I sigh and look at my portrait. *It's not perfect.*

He smiles kindly. *Perfection is an admirable thing to strive for. But so is knowing when to stop.*

I take the hint and set my brush down. *Thank you, master.*

He nods toward the other apprentices as they gather up the canvases. *They will take care of this now. You should go on to your posts, both of you.*

This last bit is directed to me and Jin Luan, who is painting nearby. She is the other human who was chosen by a pixiu, the only other human—so far—to have her hearing restored. It is something I'm still coming to terms with. Despite our past rivalry, I am happy that such a great thing has happened to her. And it isn't lost on me that Elder Chen's two apprentices are, as far as the pixius are concerned, the most visually minded of us all. It reflects well on him, and I know he is proud, maybe even a little wistful.

But there is a selfish part of me that hopes those I am close to—specifically Zhang Jing and Li Wei—will be chosen by pixius too. I want them to share this journey of hearing with me, to understand what it's like to have all our senses restored. So far, the rest of the pixius are taking their time in choosing humans—if they ever will. I try not to be impatient, knowing it is a special and honored relationship that not everyone is ready for. And for pixius, who live much longer than humans, there especially seems to be no rush.

Jin Luan and I bow to Elder Chen and then leave the rest of our peers to transport the canvas. She and I step outside into the crisp autumn day, which is still cold but bright with the promise of sunshine. As we walk through the village, we see others out beginning their days as well. Some are gathering and waiting to see the record before going to work. Others, like the gardeners, have already set out on their tasks to make the most of daylight.

One such group we pass makes me frown. It is a small group of villagers working with Xiu Mei's father. Disgruntled with the king's rule, Xiu Mei and her father left the Red Myrtle Inn and came here when word spread of our village reconnecting with the world. His limp from the army is no deterrent, and his skills and knowledge are all still sharp. He has found work here training some of our young people how to be warriors, something else I feel conflicted about. After the attack from the township's army, I can understand the need for self-defense . . . but it saddens me to see my people turning down this path.

Jin Luan and I soon leave them behind as we move on from the village limits and out into one of the fertile valleys opened by the army's explosives. Gardeners are already at work, moving among the trees and plants in their green robes. I easily spot Zhang Jing kneeling in one of the vegetable gardens. Thanks to the pixius, her vision has not worsened, and she has discovered that her other senses—smell and touch—are strong and make her particularly well suited for this job. Even from this distance I can see her smile as she works, giving her more enjoyment here than she had as an artist.

Xiu Mei is late, Jin Luan remarks, glancing around. *Again.*

She is probably sleeping in, I say with a smile. With her

knowledge of both silent and vocal language, Xiu Mei became an obvious choice to teach Jin Luan and me how to speak. We are not very good at it, and I often dread these lessons. Elder Chen knows of my distaste but reminds me there may come a time when those in our village are going to have to communicate with the outside world. As one of the pixius' chosen, that responsibility falls on me.

If you're lucky, maybe she'll sleep a little longer, says Jin Luan slyly. At first, I think she's acknowledging my dislike of the lessons, but then she nods off toward the side of the valley. *I think someone would like to talk to you.*

I follow where she gestures and feel myself blush. Li Wei is there, an axe in hand, working on one of the garden fences. As though he can feel our gazes, he pauses to wipe sweat from his brow and turns in our direction. Jin Luan nudges me.

Go! she says. *Xiu Mei may sleep all morning.*

He watches me as I make my way over. *Language lessons?* he asks when I get close.

I nod. *But the teacher is late. What are you doing out here so early?*

He points to the wooden fence he is working on. *The gardeners got some peas and green beans from a merchant and want to try planting them. If the true cold holds off just a little longer, they think we might get a small crop before winter, so I'm building these for the vines to grow on.*

I thought you were going to work on your carving? I ask.

I will. And I do sometimes at night. He shrugs. *But the*

carving can wait. There are so many things to do . . . still so much rebuilding.

He's right. There's much uncertainty in our world right now, and our bruised village must use all its resources to survive this coming winter, particularly with King Jianjun's eye still upon us. This is a hopeful time for my people—but also a fearful one. Li Wei's brawn is of more value to our people right now than the burgeoning talent within him. I respect that but hope that someday the creativity within him will shine through and attract a pixiu. It is a secret wish I haven't dared express to him or anyone else.

In his usual way, Li Wei tries to distract me with a cheery thought. *Come over here*, he says. *I want your artistic opinion on something.* He beckons me toward a recently built supply shed used to house gardening tools. We walk to the far side of it, putting us out of sight of Jin Luan and the other gardeners. I peer at the shed's side, trying to figure out what he wants me to look at.

What is it? I ask.

This, he says, sweeping me into a powerful kiss. His lips touch mine, and an intoxicating heat spreads through me as he leans me against the shed. I put my arms around him and melt into him, amazed at how perfectly we seem to go together, despite our many differences. *Harmony*, I think. I'm still figuring out what exactly this thing between Li Wei and me is, but one thing I know is that it makes me feel stronger. There is a lot about the future we still don't know, but somehow, if he is by my side, I feel I can take on whatever is waiting for us.

You tricked me, I sign when we briefly break apart.

I did, he admits. *And that's why you'll never beat me in xiangqi.*

Because you cheat? I tease.

Yes. And don't forget that I'm a barbarian.

That's true, I agree. *It's a wonder I even let myself be seen with you.*

I'm glad you do, he says. *Because I've spoken with the elders . . . and they've given permission for us to marry.*

I stare, wondering if I misunderstood. *They have?*

He gestures around him. *The world has changed, Fei. There's no rank anymore, no artists lording above miners.*

It's true what he says. Most of our people have taken on new vocations as we work to rebuild our village. Those who still labor in the mines, generating metals for the pixius and outside trade, are regarded with as much esteem as everyone else. The old ways have fallen. We are all equal now.

Us . . . married, I say, still unable to believe it.

I knew we'd find a way to be together. I knew we'd always walk by each other's sides in this world. His smile grows. *And I did tell you we'd find another reason for you to wear the silk, didn't I?* The knowing look in his eyes suddenly turns uncertain. *That is, if you want to get married—*

By way of answer, I throw myself back into his arms and kiss him again, finally having the satisfaction of surprising him for a change. A new joy floods through me, and my imagination is filled not with things I might paint but with all the dazzling opportunities our future together holds. *Yes,* I say when I can finally bring myself to pull away from him and speak. *Yes and yes. As many yeses as it takes to—*

A loud sound on the other side of the shed makes me flinch and break off my ecstatic babbling. I jump back from Li Wei, who is startled in turn by my reaction. Walking around the building, I see Yin Feng has landed in the grass. The wind rustles her glittering fur, making me wish I could've spent more time on her portrait today.

You are ruining our moment, I tell her. She doesn't understand signs, but I think she perceives my meaning. I feel a flash of amusement from her, and then she busies herself preening. Beyond her, I see other glittering forms landing in the valley. Even when the pixius aren't directly interacting with us, they seem to take comfort just from being in our presence. The feeling is mutual, and Li Wei's arms encircle my waist as we observe the others land and stretch out in the sun. Happiness burns through me, and I lean my head against him. Across the valley, I see others, including Zhang Jing, also pausing to watch the pixius.

Below this mountain, the world is dangerous and uncertain. But here, for now, we have beauty and hope again, not to mention the strength of our loved ones beside us. It is enough to weather any storm, I decide. It is more than enough.

Acknowledgments

There's always a village behind any book I write. First and foremost among them are my family, and I'm so grateful for the way they patiently support me as I endure the many ups and downs that a creative person seems to go through each day! My "publishing family" has been just as amazing. Many thanks to literary agent Jim McCarthy for handling a million things behind the scenes and to the incredible team at Razorbill—particularly editor Jessica Almon, whose insight and skill helped make this book happen.

On the research side, I'm indebted to linguistics professor Katharine Hunt for letting me contact her out of the blue for help in better understanding language acquisition and hearing loss. Thank you also to Judy Liu for assistance with both the Mandarin language and the cultures of Taiwan and China.

Lastly, I owe an endless debt to my amazing readers. Thank you for inspiring me and loving what I do.